FOUR OF A KIND

Other Dani Ross Mysteries
One by One
And Then There Were Two
The End of Act Three

A Dani Ross Mystery

FOUR OF A KIND

GILBERT MORRIS

CROSSWAY BOOKS • WHEATON, ILLINOIS
A DIVISION OF GOOD NEWS PUBLISHERS

Four of a Kind

Copyright © 2001 by Gilbert Morris

Published by Crossway Books
            A division of Good News Publishers
            1300 Crescent Street
            Wheaton, Illinois 60187

Cover design: Cindy Kiple

Unless otherwise noted, Scripture quotations are taken from the *King James Version*.

First printing, 2001

Printed in the United States of America

Library of Congress Cataloging-in-Publication Data
Morris, Gilbert.
   Four of a kind / Gilbert Morris.
      p. cm. — (A Dani Ross mystery ; bk. 4)
   ISBN 1-58134-244-6
   1. Ross, Danielle (Fictitious character)—Fiction. 2. Women private investigators—Louisiana—New Orleans—Fiction. 3. New Orleans (La.)—Fiction. I. Title.
PS3563.O8742 F68   2001
813'.54—dc21

00-011664
CIP

15	14	13	12	11	10	09	08	07	06	05	04	03	02	01
15	14	13	12	11	10	9	8	7	6	5	4	3	2	1

To Rev. James Golden and his
lovely companion Murlene—
faithful witnesses to the people of Belize.

Your lives have spoken to me
for such a long time and in such a powerful way.
I have such fine memories of my time with you there.
We have laughed for years over the
Battle of the Hot Water Tank and
Salad Dressing Thief and had such sweet fellowship.
Johnnie and I love you very much and
pray that God will give you a bountiful harvest of souls.

CONTENTS

One

AN UNUSUAL CLIENT

Her eyes fixed on the still figure of the man who had turned his back to her, Dani Ross took a deep breath, then threw herself forward in a violent motion. She whipped her right arm over the man's shoulder and grasped her wrist with her other hand. She pulled back, forcing her forearm against the man's throat, and heaved with all of her strength.

According to what she had been taught, her victim should have begun gagging and reaching for her head. As Dani ducked down and placed her head between the man's shoulder blades, she was aware of the muscular frame of her opponent. Pulling with all her strength, she tried to cut off his air while avoiding his hands. She knew that a trained martial arts expert would attempt to grab her and throw her over his shoulder, and she was determined to keep control. She felt the man's muscles suddenly swell and gasped as she exerted all her strength to pull his head back and keep the pressure on his throat.

But her opponent didn't act according to the rules. Dani suddenly felt agonizing pain in her right foot, and involuntarily she released her grip. At that instant she felt steely hands grasp her shoulders, and suddenly the room seemed to revolve. She felt herself fly into the air, then did a complete flip and landed with a resounding thump on the mat. The blow drove the breath out of her, and she lay there helplessly.

"You okay, boss?"

Dani fought for breath, then felt Ben Savage's hands pulling her upright. She looked into his hazel eyes, ignoring the fact that she was getting little oxygen, and knocked his hands away. "Take your grimy hands off me!" she said angrily.

Savage just grinned at her. "You're doing better," he said cheerfully. "Let's try it again—and this time don't let me stomp your foot."

Dani cast an exasperated glare at Savage, then struggled to her feet. She was wearing a martial arts costume—loose white trousers and an even looser white jacket with a belt around the waist. As she stared at him, her anger reddened her cheeks. She had a square face, a wide mouth, and almond-shaped, gray-green eyes. A mass of rich auburn hair was tied up with a green ribbon, and her five-foot-eight-inch frame seemed to quiver as she said, "You stomped my foot! That wasn't fair!"

"Anything's fair in love or war." Savage again grinned at her. His Slavic features were set off by a squarish face, and his deep-set eyes were protected by a shelf of bone. He had rather coarse black hair and eyebrows fully as black, and even the looseness of the costume could not hide the powerful shoulders and sturdy body. "Always expect to get hurt," Savage said nodding at her. "When you jump somebody, if he's any good at all, he'll find a way to injure you. He'll jab his thumb in your eyes, ram the top of his head into your face, stomp your foot, maybe even bite your ear if he can get to it."

The two were standing in the middle of a room covered with a thick canvas mat. They came here as often as Ben Savage could convince Dani that she needed to learn how to take care of herself. The walls were padded six feet up, and Dani had learned why, for she had been thrown against them often enough. Pale sunlight streamed through high windows, and the room smelled of canvas, sweat, and varnish.

"I've had enough of this!" Dani snapped.

"Okay. You want to run some laps?"

"No, I don't want to run laps!" Dani's voice was sharp, for she always felt inferior when she worked out with Savage. She was a smart young woman and understood that no matter how hard she tried, her chief operative would always have an advantage; but that didn't mean she had to like it.

Ben was an expert at martial arts, a black belt, and kept in tip-top shape. He had once been an aerialist for a circus, and his reflexes were unusually quick. But Dani constantly told herself, "You have to be as good as Savage. You have to show him that though you're a woman you can keep up with him."

The two had been competing ever since Savage had walked into her office and offered his services to Ross Investigation Agency. Dani had taken him on reluctantly, and there had been antagonism between them from the very beginning. It seemed to her that Savage was convinced that a woman's place was in the home—having children, making herself pretty, and waiting for her man to come home. Dani believed these things were important, but as long as she was in charge of the agency she felt it necessary to prove that she could match the accomplishments of any man.

"I'm going to shower," she said briskly.

"Don't forget to wash behind your ears."

Ignoring Savage's comment, she started toward the door, but he was immediately at her side. "Are you sure you wouldn't rather get married and have a bunch of kids than go through all this?"

Giving Savage a furious look, Dani said, "Okay, what did I do wrong this time?"

"You loosened your grip, just a bit. Never relax. Why don't we try just one more time. This time let me sneak up on you."

A perverse thought came to Dani. "All right. One more time."

"Good. Go over there and turn your back to me. I'm going to throw my arm around you. Now remember, in a real situation you wouldn't be expecting this, so right now you have an advantage."

Dani took a deep breath, marched to the center of the room, and stood there with her arms at her side. *I have to do something different this time*, she thought grimly. *I have to show Ben that he can't always win.*

As those thoughts went through her mind, a hard arm grabbed

her by the throat. Dani knew he was expecting her to try to stomp his foot and hurt him just like he had done to her, or perhaps to grab his hair the way she usually did. Knowing he would be on guard for such actions, she suddenly twisted in his arms and managed to turn halfway around. His right arm was still around her, and she bit on his biceps as hard as she could. She felt intense satisfaction as she heard him let out a loud yell, and his grasp suddenly relaxed. Keeping her teeth clamped on him, she threw her arms around him, and the two waltzed around the floor as Savage yelled, "What do you think you're doing? Let go!"

Dani felt the rough cloth between her teeth, and a thrill ran through her. For once she had Ben Savage right where she wanted him!

But then his hand closed in on her neck with such force that she gasped and let him go. She turned to him and drove her elbow into his stomach and was rewarded by an "Oof!" as she stepped back.

"Biting's no fair!" Savage said furiously.

"All's fair in love and war." Dani grinned triumphantly. "Now go take a shower, and don't forget to wash behind your ears. Maybe you ought to get married," she added, "and stop getting hurt."

Savage's face showed explosive anger as he rubbed his biceps, but then he managed to grin. "You're getting better, boss. You really are."

◆ ◆ ◆

As Dani weaved through the traffic, headed toward downtown New Orleans, a sense of satisfaction filled her. She had bested Ben at his own game, something that happened very rarely. The two of them made a good team. They had worked together on several cases since Dani had arrived to take over the agency after her father's heart attack. At times they quarreled so badly that Angie Park, the secretary, thought they were going to actually come to physical blows. But at other times something passed between them that Dani could not understand completely, a growing mutual attraction and yet . . . She certainly had no intention of ever marrying a man like Ben Savage! If for no other reason, she would never marry him as long as he wasn't a Christian. Dani had thought this all out and knew well what the Bible said about marrying unbelievers. Now as she swung the Cougar around a white and red semi and heard an angry motorist blow his horn in a full-throated blast as she dodged in front of him, she wondered why the two of them fought so hard at times. Her father had said to her once, "You only quarrel with those you love. Those you don't love, well, it's just not worth the effort."

The traffic grew heavier as she reached the turnoff, and soon she felt the way she always did when she drove into the French Quarter of New Orleans. No matter how often she came here, she felt a strange sensation. Not for the first time, she regretted that the agency wasn't located somewhere else. But that had been her father's choice, and she would simply make the best of it.

To her, New Orleans had an air about it that no other city had. She had lived in Boston and even in Chicago for a while but had never felt the sense of evil that came to her when she entered the French Quarter. Some cities such as Chattanooga had a good feeling about them, at least for her. New York overwhelmed her, and she was somewhat frightened of it for a reason she could never explain. But New Orleans had its own aura of evil, almost as if fear caused by sin had become part of the stone buildings and the streets themselves.

Pulling the car into a parking place, she locked it carefully, then began walking down the street. A tall man with black, curly hair and flashing black eyes fell into step beside her. "Hey, *mon cherie*, what say we have a good time tonight?"

"You never give up, do you, Tony?"

"On a good-lookin' chick like you. Me? Not never. I'm going to win your heart one of these days. You wait and see."

"No offense, Tony, but it won't happen," she said with a smile.

Turning into a two-story building with the familiar black ironwork across the balcony that had come to be the symbol of the Quarter, Dani moved quickly up the stairs and opened the door that bore the legend of the Ross Investigation Agency. The outer office was not large, containing little else besides Angie Park's desk and six chairs upholstered in brown leather. Three paintings were on the wall, all impressionistic, from the Cubist school. Dani liked them for some reason, although Ben had argued violently, "A picture ought to look like something. Anybody can paint squares and rectangles." It was the colors Dani liked, although she felt Ben had a point.

"Hello, Angie."

Angie Park greeted her employer with a smile. She was an attractive blonde woman, twenty-seven years old, and her large blue eyes contained a hint of vulnerability. She had been divorced twice, both times to men who had not been kind. She had the knack of falling for such men, but nothing Dani could say seemed to convince her of that fact.

"Anything new?" Dani asked.

Angie ran over a list of items that she thought Dani might be interested in and then casually added, "I'm thinking of getting some cosmetic surgery."

Dani had been running her eyes down a sheet of paper, but Angie's words surprised her. She looked up quickly and studied her secretary. "Whatever for? You look fine."

"Oh, I don't know . . ." Angie said nervously.

"Are you thinking of this because of that new boyfriend of yours?"

"No, that's not it!"

"I'll bet it is. You think you have to change yourself for him. He's no good for you, Angie. He's good-looking enough, but I think beneath the surface he's a guy who uses women for his own purposes."

"You don't know him, Dani," Angie said quickly. "You don't know him at all. He's really nice." Angie's new love was a policeman named Hal Borman. She had been dating him for nearly a month now, and Dani had been grieved to see that Angie was getting serious about the man. She thought of Angie more as a friend than an employee, and the two had had long talks together. Now she listened sadly as Angie said, "I can get a face-lift for 5,000 dollars, a breast augmentation for 3,000, and a tummy tuck for 5,000."

"Angie, that's 13,000 dollars!"

"I know, but I can get a loan and make monthly payments. I've already talked to the surgeon. He says it's a piece of cake."

"He's wrong about that. You remember Marie Watkins?"

"Yes. What about her?"

"She had that kind of surgery, and she said the pain was worse than having a cesarean. When they did the face-lift she couldn't even turn her head to look around."

"I don't mind a little pain, as long as it works. Could I have some time off?"

"Angie, don't rush into anything like this. There's nothing wrong with the way you look now."

"But I want to do something different. I don't like the way I look."

"You know, I've known several beauty queens. A Miss Tennessee was my best friend. She was a beautiful girl, but she was never satisfied with her looks. Many women who are in beauty contests feel that way. They think they need to look different."

"So what's wrong with that?"

"I went to a seminar once, and the man who led it asked us all a question. He said, 'How many of you look in the mirror and would like to change something you see?' Well, of course almost everyone admitted to that. Then he said, 'If that's what you're saying, you're finding fault with God. He made you the way you are. If you start being unhappy with what God's done, you're headed for trouble.'"

"That doesn't make any sense. All of us try to look better. We wear makeup, we get our hair fixed, we look for nice clothes," Angie protested.

With a sigh Dani shook her head. "I can't explain the difference, but there is one. Getting your hair fixed a different way just isn't the same thing as getting a tummy tuck. If all a man's interested in is what you look like, he's not the man for you."

A bitter line formed at each side of Angie's well-shaped lips. "What planet are you from, Dani? Men look at women. Men care about how we look."

"I know they do—most of them anyway—but if you hang on for a while, and if you just trust the Lord, He'll bring a man into your life who will love you not for what you look like but for who you are, inside. You're a fine person, Angie." Dani reached over and put her hand on Angie's shoulder, and her voice grew warm. "You have so many good qualities and so much to offer a man, but you keep connecting with guys who just use you. Find someone who would love you if you had an accident and got scarred, someone who knows what's really important, who really cares about *you*."

Angie Park stared at Dani silently, wishing she could break free from the sadness that always seemed to control her. More than anything else she longed to have a home, a husband and children, but these had not come her way. Now she was reaching out to grab for the brass ring, and her eyes were fixed on the wrong man, at least according to Dani.

"Angie, promise me you won't do anything too quickly."

"Well . . . all right, I promise."

"Good girl. Now you and I are going out to lunch together today. We're going to go to the fanciest restaurant we can find and spend way too much money for food that doesn't taste nearly as good as it does at a fast-food place."

"Sounds like a winner to me."

Dani moved into her inner office and shut the door behind her. Walking across the room she was conscious of a pleasure that came from the room itself. She had redecorated it recently and now glanced up at the picture of her ancestor, Colonel Daniel Monroe Ross. The colonel was dressed in the ash-gray uniform of the Confederacy, and the red scarf around his waist made a vivid splash of color. The aquiline nose, the direct eyes exactly the same color as Dani's own, and the clean-cut structure in the facial bones matched Dani's own as well.

"Good morning, Colonel Ross," Dani said. She had formed a habit of speaking to the portrait. Though that felt foolish at times, somehow she felt a kinship with this lean ancestor of hers who had fought for a lost cause with an honor that she admired. Once, arguing with a friend of hers from the north, Dani had summed up her ideas about the Civil War. "The South was romantic and wrong," she had said. "And the North was repulsive and right."

Now she folded her arms across her chest and studied the face of the Confederate officer. "I wonder what you'd make of things today. You wouldn't like them, I imagine."

Dani suddenly smiled at her own foolishness in talking to a painting, but her father, who had studied the life of Colonel Daniel Monroe Ross and had written several articles for prominent magazines about this ancestor, had informed her, "You're a lot like him, Dani. If you were living in those days, I expect you would have dressed up like a man and become a Confederate soldier."

Dani moved over to the rosewood desk, a gift from a grateful client, and ran her hand over the smooth top. The large desk gave her plenty of room for favorite objects she liked to have near her. She picked up a hand-carved pelican she had bought in Belize and rubbed her hands over the smooth surface. It was made of some kind of dark wood she couldn't name, but the artist had caught the very essence of the bird. Dani had always liked pelicans, and her favorite time on the Gulf was spent watching them fold their wings and throw themselves into a crash dive, striking the water with a blow that should have stunned them and yet coming up with silvery fish in their bills.

Replacing the carving, Dani began going over the facts of current cases. She had several operatives working for her now and insisted on proper reports handed in on time. The intercom buzzed. "Yes, Angie?"

"A gentleman's here to see you, Miss Ross. A preacher. Reverend Alvin Flatt."

The name was not familiar to Dani, but clients often came into her office without an appointment. "Send him right in, Angie."

"Yes, Miss Ross."

Dani rose from her desk to meet her caller. "Reverend Flatt, I'm Dani Ross."

"Pleased to meet you, Miss Ross."

Alvin Flatt, Dani judged, was somewhere around seventy. He had silver hair, badly cut, and the type of old-style cavalry mustache not seen very often anymore. It covered his upper lip but not the two creases beside his mouth. The sun had dried him out and given him creases and wrinkles around his eyes, which were pale blue and very direct. He was a thin man, no more than five-nine or so. As he said, "Thanks for seein' me," she caught the southern twang and labeled it as Mississippi or Arkansas. He was wearing a faded pair of gray pants, a dark blue coat, and a white shirt covered partly with a vest that had a gold chain disappearing into a pocket. The tie he wore was very broad and unusual—it had a picture of a bottle of Tabasco sauce on it. His shoes were black and well worn but well polished.

"Won't you sit down, reverend?"

"Thank you, ma'am." Flatt nodded. "Sorry to come bustin' in here without an appointment."

"That's quite all right. I have some free time."

The visitor put his hat down, a brown fedora, the kind most men don't wear anymore; it looked as though it had been around for more than a few years. He held it on his lap, moving it around with his hands, which Dani saw were lean and callused. His fingernails were clean and trimmed, and there was an air of authority about him despite his appearance.

"Are you a pastor, Reverend Flatt?"

"Yes, ma'am. At The Greater Fire Baptized Church of Jesus Christ." The old man grinned suddenly, and his eyes twinkled with a merry light. "I reckon you never heard of that one."

"I'm afraid I haven't. Is it in the city?"

"Yep. Over on the east side, on Maribone Street."

Maribone Street, Dani knew for a fact, was one of the least appe-
tizing in all of New Orleans. Because it was located close to the
projects, drug traffic was heavy there. "I don't remember ever seeing
your church."

"Well, we just got a little bitty sign out, but it was a freight house
at one time. Right across the street from the old firehouse."

Dani did remember the firehouse but couldn't picture the
church.

"Have you been there long?"

"Oh, about two years," he said. Flatt suddenly bent his head forward and stared at her with bright eyes. "I come from Texas, ma'am.
I was a bad sinner most of my life, but the Lord reached down and
got ahold of me and turned me wrong side out."

"Is that your way of telling me you got converted?"

"Yes, ma'am, I sure did. It was a miracle. I run from God for
more than fifty years, but when the Lord Jesus got me, He gave me
a new life and a new walk." He paused, then said, "I heard how
you were a believer."

"Yes, I am." Dani nodded proudly. "I've been a Christian since
I was a young girl."

"I'm glad to hear it, ma'am."

Dani studied the eyes of the preacher, somehow faded and yet
lively at the same time. "How can I help you?"

"Well, it's like this—after I finally got saved by the blood I took
to readin' the Scripture. I read and I read and I let it soak into me.
Somehow I felt all the time that God was going to ask me to do
somethin', but I wasn't sure what it was. Then right during
Christmas week, if I recollect rightly, I woke up, and there was an
angel sittin' on the foot of my bed."

Dani had a sinking feeling. She suddenly wished Alvin Flatt had
visited some other agency, but she knew better than to let her feelings show.

"How did you know it was an angel?"

"I just knowed. Well, anyhow, he told me that I was a chosen
vessel."

Again Dani tried not to let what was going on in her mind reveal itself. *This man is a fanatic.* But then she thought, *But Paul was a fanatic, and so were Luther and John Wesley.* She leaned forward and asked, "Chosen for what?"

"Well, I fasted, and I prayed, and I read the Word for six months, Miss Ross. And God told me to sell our little piece of land and go to New Orleans and preach the Gospel. I'll tell you, that shook me up quite a bit, but we done 'er. We sold out, took all our savings, and come here. I'd just as soon go to Sodom or Gomorrah as here, but when God says go, you got to go where He says."

Dani's discomfort eased, for there was an innocence and yet a strong determination about this man. His appearance was not impressive, but there was a spirit in him that she sensed was very strong. "I admire you for obeying God. So you started a church, did you?"

"Yep. We came here, me and the missus, and we prayed, and we prayed, and finally we took what money we had and bought that old freight buildin'. Took almost all we had. Didn't even have money for the first month's rent."

"I see. And how did you pay the rent?"

"God just sent some folks by to help us. We started preachin', and at first it was only half a dozen. People didn't trust us; but God told me to preach the Word, and that's what I done."

"That's a rough neighborhood."

"Well, I'm a rough man, Miss Dani, and God sent me to minister to rough people."

Dani sat there quietly listening as Reverend Flatt told her of the struggles he'd had. At first only a few people had come, some only to mock. The church had no music except an old piano that Flatt's wife Myrtle played. "I don't like to go into it too much," Flatt said, "but Myrtle played in a honky-tonk for a long time before she got saved. Sometimes she's playin' 'Amazing Grace' and it still sounds like a honky-tonk tune. But God blesses it. It's the only way she knows."

"Well, I think that's fine, reverend. How is the church doing?"

"Well, ma'am, it was doin' fine until recently. We was havin' 200, sometimes more, and we was able to feed a bunch of folks too. One of the church members set up a hot meal program, and it worked out real well. Seen lots of young folks on drugs saved, and some of 'em not so young neither. Even some fallen ladies came to know the Lord. The woman that plays our lead guitar now . . . why, she was a soiled dove, but she's on fire for Jesus now."

Dani began to grow more interested as she listened to the silver-haired man. He grew excited when he told her about the work and the conversions, but then a cloud passed across his face. "A man come by about two months ago. Said he wanted to buy the building. Well, of course I couldn't sell it since God had told me to buy it and make a church out of it. But things ain't gone too well since then."

"What was his name?"

"His name's Valentine. Don't recall his first name right offhand."

"Was it Lenny Valentine?" Dani asked quickly.

"That's the fella. Do you know him?"

"No, and I don't want to. He's not a good man, reverend. What's he been doing to disturb you?"

"Well, I ain't seen him but the once. But there's fellas that keep comin', tough-lookin' men, and they're keepin' people away from the church. Sometimes they even come in and disrupt the service. I found out that some of the people who help us have been threatened too."

"What does he want with the building?" Dani asked.

"He didn't say. We didn't talk long. I tried to talk to him about Jesus, but he just laughed and said he didn't need any more religion than he had."

"So things look fairly grim."

"I hate to complain, and I ain't puttin' God down, but if somethin' don't happen, we're gonna have to close the doors. The man's got half of the congregation scared off."

"So what do you want me to do?"

"Well, I've got to tell you upfront, I can't pay you, Miss Ross."

The simplicity of Flatt's reply touched Dani. She offered a quick silent prayer, then responded, "We won't worry about that."

"That's what I was hopin' for. And I was hopin' you'd come to the preachin'."

"I certainly will." Dani smiled as she rose to her feet. "What time are the services?"

"We start about ten on Sunday morning, and we go until we play out. We meet every night too, about seven o'clock. Be proud to have you come."

"I'll be there, and I'll try to find out what Mr. Valentine has on his mind."

"Thank you, Miss Ross. I appreciate it."

After he left the room, Dani stood there thinking about Lenny Valentine. Everyone in New Orleans knew the man, or at least about him. He controlled much of the vice that paralyzed the city. She knew he was into prostitution and drugs, and she had heard he was investing in some ambitious projects. She thought of the powerful crime lord, rich and influential, buying some of the city officials, and then she thought of the small figure of Reverend Alvin Flatt—alone, poor, and old.

Looking up suddenly at the portrait of her ancestor, she said, "You didn't mind getting involved in lost causes, did you, colonel, as long as you felt that what you were doing was right? If you were here, I think you'd take on Reverend Alvin Flatt as a client and spit in Lenny Valentine's eye! And so will I!"

Two

SITTING ON DOORKNOBS

Fall had brought dark rainy days, leaving the lawns in New Orleans so damp that they were as much water as earth. Within the yards of the inhabitants, desolate trees shaded the faded earth, and the heavy sky overhead was as colorless as the rain itself.

Ben Savage glanced out the window of Dani's moving Cougar, silent and lost in thought. He was watching the trees that had been at one time golden but now were a faded brown.

"What are you thinking about so deeply, Ben?" Dani asked, taking her eyes off the road long enough to glance at him.

"Nothing gold can stay."

"What do you mean by that?"

Savage took his eyes off the moisture-laden trees and turned to scan Dani. She was wearing a simple enough outfit, but it always puzzled him how whatever she wore seemed to take on an extra dimension. Today she wore a light amber skirt and jacket, and a soft, ribbed sweater of the same hue. Around her neck she wore a scarf with a jaguar pattern, and her leather pump shoes with a snake-print insert matched. Everything she wore always matched, and Savage, who had almost no sense of fashion whatsoever, knew she was one of those women born to always wear just the right thing. "Just that—nothing gold can stay." He brushed his hand across the top of his coarse, black hair and shrugged his shoulders. "I read a poem when I took a college course about culture. None of it took on me, as you know."

"I believe I know the poem you mean. Robert Frost wrote it."

"I think that's the guy. Anyhow, I didn't figure it made any sense at first. He's the one who said, 'Nothing gold can stay.' I guess he was talking about leaves or something."

"Yes, he was. He was saying the young leaves have a certain golden hue, but they don't remain that way. They change. I think one line was something like, 'Eden sank to grief.'"

"I always hated that poem. It seemed so hopeless."

"Frost can be pretty hopeless at times. People think of him as a nice old man with a shock of white hair who wrote poems about birds and trees and grass, but he had a very dim outlook on life. I think he was an unhappy man."

"He should have kept it to himself. I don't like to read stuff like that."

"I know," Dani said, and a grin pulled the corners of her lips upward. "You like to read stories with a happy ending."

"That's me. Give me a 'feel good' TV program. That's all the culture I need."

Dani knew that wasn't true, that Savage read more widely than he let on, but she didn't argue with him. The two remained silent until they reached Maribone Street. Ben, glancing at the dilapidated buildings and the many vacant storefronts, shook his head. "Not a very cheerful place to build a church. I still think you're making a mistake taking on that preacher as a client."

"Why do you say that? You've never even met him."

"He sounds like a loser to me."

"He's a very nice man, Ben, and I can't help feeling sorry for him."

"You'd feel sorry for Judas Iscariot."

Dani had a good laugh, and as she turned her eyes on him, there was mischief in them. "Well, Ben, you're a fine one to talk. You're always rushing to help some damsel in distress."

"Am not!"

"You are too. What about that half-drowned kitten you took in?"

"Jane Eyre? Well, that's different."

"It's always different when *you* want to help somebody, but when I do it you call me a softy."

Dani carefully drove along the streets where, despite the rain, a few people were still making their way. It was Sunday morning, close to ten o'clock, and Dani had been surprised when Savage volunteered to go to church with her. His excuse had been, "You don't need to be faunching around alone in that Maribone district."

"Faunching? What kind of talk is that?" she'd replied.

"It's southern talk. Festus used it on *Gunsmoke*, back in the early days of TV."

Now she said, "I'm glad you've come *faunching* along with me, Ben. This is a pretty scary part of town."

The rain had almost ceased now, but it was still drizzling. "Stop in front of the place, and I'll park the car while you go inside. You might melt, but I won't."

Dani appreciated Ben's offer. "I have an umbrella here you can use. That's the church right over there, I think."

Dani brought the Cougar to a halt, slid out, and Ben moved over. When she slammed the door, he headed down the street toward the closest parking spot.

As Dani moved forward she noted that the half dozen people lingering outside seemed tense for some reason. She started toward the door to avoid the drizzle, but two men suddenly blocked her way. She halted abruptly and watched them narrowly. "Hey, what's goin' down, lady?"

The speaker was a tough-looking man in his mid-thirties. He had brown hair in a pigtail and wore only a thin shirt despite the cold. He had tattoos on both arms—a dragon on his left and the U.S. Marine Corps symbol on his right. His nose had been broken, and he had a cold light in his muddy brown eyes.

"Let me pass, please."

"Well, she talks nice, don't she, Sonny? Listen to that. 'Let me pass, please.'"

The other man was huge, younger than the speaker. One of his ears was puffed out as if it were pumped full of fluid, and he grinned strangely. "Yeah, Chino, she talks good."

Dani understood at once that this was part of the hassling that Alvin Flatt had told her about. She turned to move around the men, but the smaller of the two, the one called Chino, quickly reached out and grabbed her arm. "You and me could have some good times, baby. Forget this church bit."

"Let me go, please."

The spectators were watching, and Dani looked around quickly for help. But they were all too intimidated by the two men. She knew it would be hopeless to try to pull away from the man. He yanked at her arm and said, "Come on, we'll go find a place where I can tell you the story of my life. You'll love it."

Dani said more urgently, "Let go of me . . . !" She had no time to say more, for Chino's grip was torn from her arm, and Dani suddenly saw that he was lying on the wet sidewalk. He started to get up when suddenly Ben Savage leaned over and struck him with a judo chop on the back of his neck. Chino went down, striking his face against the sidewalk, and Ben suddenly moved to face the huge form of the big man who stood there shocked by the suddenness of it all. He was evidently a slow-thinking individual, and his eyes were filled with surprise as he turned to the man struggling to get to his feet.

Chino shook his head, and his eyes were cold with anger. "Take him down, Sonny! Bust him up!"

"Okay, Chino." Sonny moved forward, his hands ready for action. He was big enough to destroy anything in his path, but he halted abruptly, for Ben Savage had produced an automatic, and it was trained right on Sonny's eyes. Ben stepped forward, putting himself between Dani and the two men. "You boys want to go to church? We'll get you a seat on the front row."

Sonny was confused but also cautious. There was a steady, relentless light in the eyes of the man holding the automatic. "He's got a gun, Chino. I can't do nothin'."

Chino pulled himself together, shook his shoulders, and stared at Savage. "You're buyin' yourself some trouble, Jocko."

"Move along, Chino. And take Jumbo here with you. Has he had his shots lately, by the way?"

Sonny didn't understand all that was going on, but he recognized the insult. "I'll get you some other time. You won't always have that gun handy."

"I'll always have the gun, Sonny. Now, you two need any help getting out of here?"

The big man turned to leave, but Chino paused for a moment. There was murder in his expression, and his gaze didn't leave Ben Savage's face. His voice was soft as a summer breeze as he said, "I'll be seeing you later, chum."

"Come anytime. We never close. Here's my card." Wanting these toughs to know what type of person they were dealing with, Ben handed the card to Chino, who reached out slowly and took it, not taking his eyes off Ben's face, then slipped it into his pocket. He turned without another word, and the two moved off down the street. The big man didn't look back at all, but Chino turned once and gave Savage a venomous glance.

"Hey, that was cool!" A young black man wearing a pair of rimless glasses was grinning broadly. "You know who those two are?"

"I know *what* they are."

"You're right about that. That's Chino Smith and Sonny Riggs. They're bad men."

"I'm pretty bad myself."

"I suspect you is. My name's Jarvo Davis. You folks comin' to church?"

"Yes. My name's Savage, and this is Miss Dani Ross."

"You folks come on in. I'll get you a five-dollar seat right up front."

"That's kind of you, Jarvo," Dani said appreciatively.

"Maybe I'd better stay out here and see that Bert and Ernie don't come back," Ben said idly.

"If they do, I'll come and get you," a new voice announced.

The speaker was a young boy no more than fourteen. "I'd like to see you point that gun at them two again. Is you the fuzz?"

"Used to be. Just a hardworking private detective now."

"You all go enjoy the music and preachin'. I'll stay out here. If them two come back, I'll come and get you. Maybe you can shoot 'em in the feet or somethin'."

Savage grinned broadly. "You hold 'em, and I'll shoot 'em. What's your name?"

"Henry Jones."

"All right, Henry. You know where to find me."

Dani tried to calm herself down. She never could understand how Savage could burst into violent action and then be in a serene mood immediately afterwards. As she walked into the building following Jarvo Davis, she said, "That's exactly the kind of thing Reverend Flatt told me was going on."

"I may have to discourage those two."

Jarvo turned and said, "I think they'll be lookin' you up. Nobody puts Chino down and gets by with it."

The young black man led them into a cavernous room. It had once been some sort of freight warehouse. The floor, the supporting beams, the walls, and the ceiling were all concrete, and all unpainted. As they approached the front, Dani saw an unprofessionally built stage no more than two feet high. A motley collection of chairs and benches were scattered in front of it. She saw some oak rockers and a few pews with peeling brown paint. Because she was accustomed to the comforts of a well-built church with an attractive interior and exterior design, it took her a moment to adjust to the rough surroundings. A group of musicians stood on the platform. A series of four loudspeakers, not much smaller than Volkswagens, were spaced across the front. "I'll introduce you to the pastor," Jarvo said. "Then I'll have to go. I play the drums."

"I always wanted to be a drummer," Ben said, "but I just don't have the rhythm for it."

At that moment Dani spotted Reverend Alvin Flatt. He was talking to a silver-haired woman who was seated at an old upright piano. The woman was laughing at something he had said, and Dani assumed she was Myrtle, the reverend's wife.

Flatt came toward them, nodding. He was wearing the same outfit he had worn when he had come to Dani's office except the tie was different. It was just as broad and out of style as the one he had worn then, but instead of a bottle of hot sauce it was adorned with Tweety Bird, bright yellow against a blue background. "Well, I'm mighty proud to see you here, Miss Ross."

"This is my friend Ben Savage."

"I'm glad to know you, Brother Savage."

"He done put the run on them two hoods that been scarin' folks off," Jarvo announced proudly.

"You didn't do bodily damage to them?"

"Nothing that couldn't be repaired, Reverend," Ben said.

"I don't think they'll be back right away," Jarvo nodded. "But they gonna come visitin' this gentleman, we know that. I better get to my drums now. You folks enjoy the service. I'm prayin' that the Lord will fall upon us with His awesome power."

"Jarvo's a fine young man. He was dealing drugs six months ago, but now he's given his heart to Jesus."

"That's a great trade," Dani said.

"Come along and meet the rest of the band. Oh, but first come and meet my wife. Myrtle, this is the Miss Ross I told you about."

Myrtle Flatt was short and overweight with silver hair done up in a bun. She had cheerful brown eyes in a round face, and she wore a long dress with long sleeves. Her only jewelry was a wedding ring, and when she smiled she manifested three gold teeth that glinted against the reflected light.

"Why, I'm right pleased to meet you. Alvin told me how nice you were and about you bein' a born-again believer and all."

"Yes, I am. It's so good to meet you, Sister Flatt."

"Most people just call me Mama, and they call Alvin Dad. Some of these poor young 'uns don't even remember their own folks, so I guess it makes them feel good to accept us as their spiritual parents."

The woman's warmth and liveliness pleased Dani. "I know the Lord is going to bless your work here. Not many people come into this area to start a church."

"This is Mr. Savage, Mama," Reverend Flatt said. "I think he's Miss Ross's helper."

"That's what I am. Miss Ross's helper," Ben said with a straight face.

"Are you a believer, son?" Flatt asked cheerfully.

"I guess I'm more what you call a seeker. Miss Ross has been working on me, though."

"Well, you can't run away from God. Old Jonah tried it. He wound up in a whale's belly, but God brought him out again." His blue eyes twinkled, and Flatt winked. "I guess that proves you can't keep a good man down."

Both Ben and Dani smiled at the joke, and then Flatt said, "Come along. We're about ready to get wound up. Dani, if you want to sing a special song for us, we'd be delighted."

"I think I'll pass on that," Dani said quickly.

The seats were filling up now, and everyone was looking curiously at Dani and Savage. They didn't often get visitors from the better parts of town. Wishing she had worn a plainer outfit, Dani made a note not to overdress the next time she came.

"So that's your client. Seems like a nice old man."

"He is. I like his wife too."

Jarvo suddenly began playing his drums in a rather gymnastic fashion. The sticks flashed, and his white teeth were bright against his dark skin as he hit the drums and cymbals with a contagious zeal.

"He's certainly enthusiastic," Savage whispered.

Dani was watching the guitarist, an attractive young woman with blonde hair. She wore a plain green dress that matched her eyes. Like Jarvo she had more enthusiasm than talent. Beside her a young man no more than seventeen played bass. He was at least six feet tall, strong looking, and had a mop of red hair. Freckles were spattered across his face, and he swung his body back and forth as he played the bass.

"Listen to Mama play that piano," Ben said. "Like in a honky-tonk, you know?"

"Her husband told me she learned to play in a honky-tonk years ago."

"A preacher's wife who used to be a honky-tonk woman. Interesting."

The music service was the most unusual that Dani had ever attended. The hymnbooks on the seats were entitled *Heavenly Highways*, but no one used them. Dani knew almost none of the songs they played at first, but finally Sister Flatt began playing a contemporary rendition of "Amazing Grace," making invigorating runs with her right hand while beating out a steady rhythm with her left. The guitar player had a strong though rather husky voice. At least this was a song that Dani knew—her favorite in fact—and she looked it up in the tattered copy of *Heavenly Highways*. She knew the words well, but she knew Ben didn't. The band slowed down so the congregation could join them, and the cavernous old building quickly filled with the words that had been sung millions of times by worshipers all over the world.

> *Amazing grace, how sweet the sound,*
> *That saved a wretch like me,*
> *I once was lost, but now am found,*
> *Was blind but now I see.*

After the last verse was sung, Brother Flatt walked to the center of the platform. All the musicians left, and he stood there, a small man with silver hair and a droopy mustache. He glanced over the congregation, then said, "God loveth the cheerful giver. There's a gallon bucket up here. We don't pass no plate. But if you want to contribute to the work of the church, come by and drop somethin' in. The Lord loveth a cheerful giver."

"Not very high-pressure, is he?" Ben whispered.

"Right, and I respect him for it." Dani knew what Ben did not know—this old man and his wife had put everything they had into this work, and now they were simply trusting God to keep it going. She realized that Ben simply would not be able to understand this. But maybe someday . . .

Dani nervously hoped Reverend Flatt wouldn't publicly introduce her. Holding a worn, black Bible in his right hand, he laid his left hand on it and began reading some Scripture, quoting at least a dozen other passages by heart, including chapter and verse. "Sometimes I put titles on my sermons, and I'm calling this one 'Sitting on Doorknobs.'" A giggle went over the congregation, and the preacher smiled. "You may forget my main points, but I bet you'll remember the title, and hopefully some of the Bible verses I'll give you as we go along. So here we go. Sitting on Doorknobs."

The congregation leaned forward, and Dani cast a look at Ben. He was watching the old man intently, and she wondered what he was thinking. She was sure he thought about God's claims on him often, though he always denied it. She had begun praying for him every day, especially that he would become a Christian. Right now his entire attention was focused on Reverend Alvin Flatt.

"When I was a boy growing up in Texas, we just got by on a forty-acre dirt farm. Since there was twelve of us kids and one mama and one daddy, the groceries got a little bit thin at times. One thing we had plenty of though, and that was chickens. My, we had lots of chickens! We didn't have beef very often, but we had chicken every day. Boiled chicken, baked chicken, barbecued chicken, fried chicken, chicken salad, chicken soup, chicken pot pie. I had so much chicken, I expect I was startin' to grow pinfeathers!

"And we always had eggs too. Eggs for breakfast, eggs for dinner, eggs for supper. A midnight snack would always be a hard-boiled egg. So I remember chickens from my boyhood days.

"Mama always kept lots of settin' hens, of course. Sometimes she'd get a settin' hen that wouldn't lay, and when that happened she'd put somethin' in that old hen's nest. Somethin' that looked like an egg, just to encourage her, don't you see?

"One of my jobs was findin' things that looked like eggs to fool them chickens with, and I found somethin' that worked pretty good. Don't see 'em much anymore, but back when I was just a kid there was lots of china doorknobs. About everybody had 'em back in those days. Out at the junkyard one time I found some old doors that was throwed away. The only good part of 'em left was the knobs. I took 'em all off and took 'em home with me, and I found out that them chickens could be fooled. If a hen wasn't layin', I took one of them doorknobs in there. First thing you know that old hen was sittin' on it, and if anything would work, that would be it."

Dani had never heard preaching quite like this. Flatt's delivery was comical and a bit peculiar. She generally preferred a more sophisticated approach, but she found herself caught up in the story.

"But about them china doorknobs that them hens was all sittin' on—well, not a one of 'em ever hatched. I don't reckon that comes as a great surprise to you, but it must have puzzled them hens a lot. Sometimes I felt kind of sorry for 'em. Sittin' and sittin', keepin' them eggs warm, and not a single little chicken ever came out of one of them eggs. None of them china eggs ever hatched."

Flatt stroked his Bible and was silent for a moment, then went on, "I hate to say this, but a lot of you folks sittin' right here are just like them hens. You're tryin' to hatch somethin' that won't never hatch. Every one of us at one time or another has had a dream that never came to life. Some of you are going to wake up someday and find out that what you've put all your heart into just ain't got no life in it, and it'll never bring nothin' but death."

"My text this mornin' is from the book of Ecclesiastes." He began reciting aloud. "'The words of the Preacher, the son of David, king in Jerusalem. Vanity of vanities saith the Preacher, vanity of vanities; all is vanity.'"

Dani was fascinated as he quoted the entire first chapter of Ecclesiastes. It had never been one of her favorite books, for it seemed hopeless and dark to her. Nevertheless, as the old man repeated the words in his twangy, Texas voice there was power in them. When Reverend Flatt got to the end of chapter 1, he looked out over the congregation. "In chapter 2 we find out about china eggs that Solomon sat on. He claims he tried to hatch them out, and I reckon if you'll listen right good, you'll find yourself in some of these. He says in verse 1, 'I will prove thee with mirth; therefore enjoy pleasure.'" Flatt shook his head, and there was a sadness in his voice. "How many men and women and young people today live only for pleasure? This land's full of them, and at the end what do they have? They go out and have a good time, but when it's over, it's over. I'm not against havin' a good time, and I think God's people ought to have the best time of all; but when it's gone, it's gone. Some of you have been to carnivals where they had cotton candy. Remember? You take a bite of it and there ain't nothin' there. It just melts in your mouth. It ain't like eatin' good old fried chicken or a juicy T-bone steak or corn on the cob. With those delicacies you've got somethin'. But with cotton candy . . . How'd you like to live on that every day? That's what pleasure's like. For a moment it tastes good, but when it's over, it's gone forever."

The preacher spoke about the follies of pleasure for ten minutes and finally said, "Look at verse 3. There's another china doorknob that Solomon tried out. 'I sought in mine heart to give myself unto wine.'" Looking out over the congregation, Alvin Flatt shook his head. "Some of you know what that's like. Some of you have been winos lying in an alley, so drunk you couldn't even stand up. Some of you have lost jobs because of liquor. This country honors the people that make beer and booze, but they're killing our country. When I was a young man I tried liquor, and it brought me nothin' but grief."

Dani leaned forward as Flatt gave statistics of what happens to both young people and older people who indulge in alcohol. *He knows what he's talking about*, Dani thought. He went on to quote from several books she wouldn't have thought he'd read and from sports heroes who had suffered from the ravages of drink.

Finally he said, "In verse 4 there's another china egg. Solomon was the wisest man who ever lived, and he said, 'I made me great works,' then went on to tell what all he'd built. He got to be a rich man and finally said, 'I gathered me also silver and gold. . . . I was great, and increased more than all that were before me in Jerusalem.'

"Who's the richest man in America? Bill Gates, I reckon, is one of them. He's got billions of dollars. I heard somebody say that he had ninety billion dollars before they broke up his company, and now he's down to sixty billion dollars. Poor feller! Only sixty billion dollars! Well, one day Bill Gates will draw his last breath and then he'll stand in the presence of God. You reckon God's going to be impressed with Bill Gates's wealth? I pray for that fellow that he don't put his money first."

The sermon continued, and Dani listened, taking time out only to look around. She found an intensity in the service that she was unaccustomed to. When Flatt got going, there were frequent amens and hallelujahs and praise the Lords, and finally he came to the end of his message.

"I want to tell you about what you can put your trust in. You don't need nothing but Jesus. He's the pearl of great price. He's Heaven's treasure. He come to this earth and lived a perfect life. He died a criminal's death and was buried in a borrowed tomb. But the story didn't end there, praise the Lord. He busted out of that tomb and knocked the devil right into the bottomless pit. And where is Jesus today? Why, friends, He's sittin' at the right hand of God. And what's He doin'?" Here the preacher's voice fell to a whisper, and everyone leaned forward to hear. "He's waiting for the people He died for to come to Him. And why does He want them to come? So He can forgive them, clothe them in a white robe, give them eternal life, and fill them with the Holy Spirit."

Dani felt a sudden warmth as Flatt continued to speak of the magnificence of Jesus Christ. She shot a glance at Ben Savage and saw that he was taken with the strange, unexpected eloquence as Flatt spoke of Jesus in a longing and emotional tone.

Finally Flatt said, "Jesus can give you what you need the most, and that's peace. You can't get it with money or through pleasure or with liquor or dope. Only from Jesus. Back in the days when I was livin' for the devil I played me a lot of poker. The hand I liked best was four of a kind. I can't tell you how many games I won with four of a kind. But I don't miss poker, not a mite. Why not? Because I found a better four of a kind—the Father, the Son, the Holy Ghost, and me! I'm just a weak, frail clay pot; but when I let the Father and the Son and the Holy Spirit have their way with me, why, we're somehow four of a kind—not as equals, you understand, but in the sense of working together.

"And ever since I was converted, I've found that a winning hand is always available if I join up with the Father, Son, and Holy Ghost. Wouldn't you like to have those three on your side? They all three want you. God the Father is looking for the prodigal son. Jesus came to seek and to save that which was lost—that's you! And the Holy Spirit was sent to dwell in you. I'm going to ask you to come down front to meet God. We'll pray with you, even if it takes all night, until Jesus comes into your soul."

The musicians had ascended the platform, and they began to play. As Dani stood with the rest of the congregation, she was aware that many were making their way toward the front. Some were already sobbing, and one huge man lay facedown. Flatt went over to him and began to pray in a loud voice, his hand on the man's head. "O Jesus, save this sinner! Bring him into the family of God. Wash his sins away with the blood of Jesus. Baptize him in the fountain of blood."

The invitation, Dani saw, was going to last a long time. She touched Ben's arm, and he jumped. "I think we can go now, Ben."

The two left, but Dani paused to glance back when they reached the outer doors. She saw that the altar area was covered with people, and she could hear sobs of repentance.

Stepping outside, she said nothing as Ben walked along beside her. Finally they reached the car, and since he still had the keys he unlocked it and then handed them to her. She got inside, started the engine, and moved on down Maribone Street. Turning at the corner she headed for the office to take Ben back to his car.

"What did you think of all that, Ben?"

"Never saw anything like it. That old man is really something."

"He's a genuine preacher of the Gospel. We have to help them, Ben."

"Going up against Valentine could be dangerous. You saw those two. He's got plenty more goons like that he can send out."

"Do you think we should drop the case?"

Ben Savage was silent for a moment, then shook his head. "No, I don't."

His answer, brief as it was, pleased Dani. "All right," she said. "What should we do?"

"Start liftin' up rocks and see what crawls out," Ben said seriously. "With a fellow like Lenny Valentine, something's bound to crawl out."

Three

SIXKILLER

For the next two days Dani tried to put Reverend Alvin Flatt and The Greater Fire Baptized Church out of her mind during non-working hours but was only partially successful. She had a dream about the elderly preacher and his wife, and when she woke up, startled, she decided it was time for action.

The skies were threatening rain, but merchants were getting ready for Thanksgiving as she passed through central New Orleans. Thanksgiving was a special time for her, and she looked forward to spending it with her family. Leaving the crowded downtown streets, she turned north and made her way near Maribone Street. An idea had come to her that morning at the office, and she was using her lunch hour to get it started by talking to a hot dog vendor with the rather odd last name of Oz. She had handled a case for his brother who ran a chain of convenience stores, and she had become quite fond of the vendor.

Dani spotted the hot dog stand and parked the Cougar. She walked over to the portly Oz, who was wearing a New Orleans Saints cap, a brown bomber jacket of World War II vintage, and a pair of cowboy boots. He towered over her, but his round face lit up with a smile. "Well, if it ain't Miss Ross! How are you doin', lady?"

"I'm fine, Oz. I haven't had any of your good hot dogs for a while. Are you still serving?"

"You betcha! Will you have a hot dog or a sausage dog?"

"Oh, one of each, I guess. Have you raised your prices yet?"

"Nope. I've never raised my prices. Hot dogs are a dollar and a quarter, and sausage dogs are a dollar seventy-five. Workin' guys need a break. I know what it's like countin' out the pennies tryin' to have enough to eat on. Lots of folks make a regular stop here. They can't afford a fancy restaurant, you know."

"Your wife still growing the vegetables and making that fantastic relish?" Oz's wife had a secret recipe, and it made the hot dogs especially tasty. "How long have you been at this corner, Oz?"

"Over ten years, missy. I put in my time as a plumber, and then I got out and decided I wanted an outdoor life. I've got it all—fresh air and sunshine and lots of friends."

"And rain too, it looks like."

"I just take whatever comes, missy." The overweight vendor expertly sliced two buns, popped in a simmering hot dog and a sausage, and lathered the tops with relish. "Mustard?"

"Just a bit." Dani waited until he had wrapped them both in wax paper, then put the sausage dog down. Opening the hot dog, she began to nibble at it. "Ooh, that's good," she said, "but hot."

"That's the nature of it, missy. Good to see you again. You solvin' lots of crimes?"

"Not as many as I need to, I guess. How's your brother doing?"

"Finer than frog hair," Oz nodded. He was a talkative fellow and gave Dani a long report on his brother. When he finally stopped, Dani quickly asked, "Do you know anything about Lenny Valentine?"

"More than I need to know. What are you askin' about that scoundrel for?"

"A friend of mine is having some trouble with him."

"Oh, you mean that preacher. Yeah, I heard about that. That's a shame too. Flatt's a nice fellow."

"Yes, he is. Have you heard anything on the street?"

"Lenny Valentine's a bad fellow to mess with. He's moved up fast. I hear he's done some things the hard way to get where he is." Oz's eyes suddenly narrowed. "You reckonin' to help the preacher?"

"I'd like to."

"Well, I hope you can. We need that church down here, with so much drugs goin' down and everythin'. I feel sorry for the poor kids in this neighborhood. They ain't got much chance. That preacher and his crew are doin' a good job."

"Have you heard anything else about Valentine?"

Oz shrugged his beefy shoulders. "Just what everybody else knows. He's buyin' up lots of property around here, and from what I hear he ain't too careful about how he gets it. Friend of mine owned a little shop just off Maribone. She figured she'd stay there until she retired, but Valentine made it so hard she had to leave."

"Did he threaten her?"

"Not him personal. But her windows got broken out twice, and one of them snakes that work for Valentine came by and leaned on her pretty hard. I took my old service .45 over and was gonna educate him, but Emma said that was too dangerous. So she just sold out."

"Do you think she'd testify if it comes to that?"

"She might. I'll talk to her about it. I'd like to see Mr. Tough Guy Valentine put away."

Dani finished the hot dog and took the sausage dog with her, promising to come back more often. As she drove away she filed Emma's name in the back of her mind for later use. Savage had often said, "You have a regular filing cabinet up there. Everything you see or hear or eat or talk about you file in one of those little drawers. Then when you need it, you just pull open a drawer and there it is."

When Dani spotted Merchants Bank just a few blocks away, she pulled into the parking lot. Inside she saw an old friend, Bob Grierson, sitting at his desk. Since he had no customers at the moment, she walked up and smiled at him. "Hello, Bob."

"Well, Dani, good to see you. Sit down."

Dani took her seat and exchanged a few words with Bob, then said, "Bob, I need information about someone. I know you can't give away secrets, but I'm interested in knowing more about Lenny Valentine."

"Lenny Valentine! Why in the world would you be interested in a thug like that?"

"A client of mine is having some problems with him."

"Yeah, well, a lot of people have problems with Valentine. Most of them fold up though. What's your client's name?"

"Reverend Alvin Flatt."

"Oh, yes. I handled the loan when he bought the building."

"Have you talked to Reverend Flatt lately?"

"No. He makes his payments on time, so far anyway. I don't see how though. That congregation can't come up with much of a collection."

"He's on a pretty tight budget, that's for sure. From what I hear on the street, Valentine's buying up a lot of property around there."

Bob Grierson leaned forward, his gray eyes alight with interest. "I guess that's pretty common knowledge. I don't know what he's up to—I don't think anybody does—but he's bought a dozen pieces of property around there."

"Did he finance any of them through your bank?"

"No. It was all cash business. That's strange enough in itself. People don't pay cash for things like that as a rule, but I guess he has the money." Grierson shook his head sadly. "I don't know how he gets away with it, but apparently he makes a fortune off booze, prostitution, and drugs. I guess all that pays pretty well in New Orleans."

"Unfortunately, yes. Bob, would you let me know if you hear anything more about what's going on?"

"Sure will, Dani. Come by more often, okay?"

◆ ◆ ◆

"Lieutenant Sixkiller please."

"Just a minute." A silence followed, and then a new voice said, "Sixkiller."

"Hello, lieutenant. This is Dani."

"Well, I must be getting up in the world to get a call from you. What's up?"

"I thought I'd take you out to dinner tonight."

Sixkiller gasped audibly. "Well, that's a switch. I've been askin' you to go out to dinner with me for weeks, and now suddenly *you* want to take *me* out."

"I thought we might go to Antoine's."

"Last time I went there it took my war pension, but it's your money."

"I'll meet you there at seven o'clock. Is that all right?"

"Sure. I'll have all the crime in New Orleans solved by that time."

Dani smiled and said good-bye. She resolutely put Reverend Alvin Flatt and his church out of her mind and spent the afternoon working hard on other cases. She left at 5, went home, and showered and changed clothes. When she came downstairs her mother, Ellen, said, "Hmm, you have on a serious dress. Who are you going out with?"

"Luke Sixkiller."

Ellen Ross smiled. She was a tall, ash-blonde beauty of a woman and at forty-four had a face and figure that most women half her age would die for. She had grown up in Texas, a state that seemed to produce this sort of feminine beauty in abundance. "I didn't know you were dating the lieutenant."

"I'm not really, but I need to probe his mind a little."

"Well, that dress ought to put him in the proper mood. How much did it cost?"

"Too much." The dress was black velvet with black nylon lace and chocolate sequins on the v-bodice front and back. She reached up and touched the rather spectacular turquoise earrings. "You think it's a bit much?"

"No. It'll give the lieutenant something to think about."

"I'll probably be in pretty early."

"I wouldn't bet on that."

Dani left the house, a few miles north of New Orleans. She took the Lake Pontchartrain Causeway, and in the early darkness she could see pelicans sailing low over the water. Gulls rose from time to time, catching the last rays of fading light. It was a sight that never failed to please Dani, for though she didn't like New Orleans itself, she loved the Gulf close by. She had spent happy days on Lake Pontchartrain fishing for reds.

Exiting, she took 610 through Metairie, then angled onto 10. When she got to the Superdome she turned right and arrived at Antoine's exactly at 7.

Antoine's was one of the better and more expensive restaurants in New Orleans, and Dani came as often as she could. She found Luke standing on the outside chatting with the greeter. The police detective was not a tall man, no more than five-ten, but burly with bulging muscles. He always wore fine, stylish clothing even when on duty, and she suspected he did it to hide his bulk. Luke was wearing a pair of charcoal gray slacks with a single pleat, a salt and pepper sports jacket that managed to minimize his tremendous shoulders, a white shirt that almost glowed with pristine whiteness, and a wool maroon tie. His black eyes were alive as he watched her, and his hair, also black, was neatly trimmed. "Right on time, Miss Ross," he said. "Come along. I'm going to spend lots of your money."

Dani knew very well that Luke would never allow her to pay for the meal. As he led her inside, they were greeted by Louie Doucett, the manager.

"Ah, it's the lieutenant and Miss Ross! So glad to have you here."

"Hello, Louie. How have you been?" the officer said.

"Very well." Louie grinned. "We haven't seen you in a while."

"No. I have to float a loan every time I come here," Sixkiller said with a smile.

"Ah, the lieutenant makes jokes. Come along. I have a fine table for you."

Doucett led them through the room, which had an enormous high ceiling. When he had seated them he lit the candle and said, "What wine will you be having tonight?"

"None for me," Dani replied.

"I forget. Miss Ross never drinks alcoholic beverages."

"Well, I do. Bring me something good, Louie."

"I will choose it myself," he said as he moved away.

"Okay, what are you up to? Trying to corrupt the police department?"

Dani blinked with surprise. "What are you talking about?"

"I've been trying to get you to go out for months, and now *you're* asking *me* out. You must want something."

"You have a suspicious nature."

"It goes with being a policeman."

"Maybe I've just fallen in love with your manly beauty."

"Let's hope so. We'll work on that premise."

The wine came, and they gave their orders to the waiter. For Dani it was always the same. Antoine's made exquisite gumbo—the best in Louisiana, she thought—and with it she ordered blackened red fish and crawfish étouffée. Sixkiller ordered a New York strip and a Cajun stuffed baked potato.

They spoke about their respective work until the meal came. Sixkiller was a good cop—the best in New Orleans as far as Dani knew. The toughest criminals walked around him as carefully as if they were walking through a minefield, and word on the street was, "Don't try to buy Sixkiller. He'll bury you!"

He was the most physical man Dani had ever met. There was a presence to him that seemed to make other men look undernourished. His neck was strong, and his shoulders bulged with muscle. She had gone swimming with him more than once in the Gulf, and many eyes had turned to look at the bronzed body without an ounce of fat and smoothly covered with muscle.

As usual, Dani enjoyed her meal and Luke Sixkiller's company. They stayed until late lingering over coffee, and Dani finally said, "I really enjoy spending an evening with you, Luke. But I also wanted to talk to you about Lenny Valentine."

"I'd like to make fish food out of him and throw him in the Gulf."

"Is he as bad a man as they say?"

"Worse, Dani. He puts on a good front, but deep down he's still a street thug. He started out breaking kneecaps for a loan shark, and by now he's done it all."

"How do men like that keep from going to jail?"

"He did go to the pen once, but by the time he got out he had smartened up."

Sixkiller looked across the table at Dani silently. Finally he asked, "Why are you interested in a creep like Valentine?"

"I have a new client—Reverend Alvin Flatt." She described the situation and concluded by saying, "Luke, couldn't you send an officer down there to keep Valentine's hoodlums from harassing the congregation?"

Sixkiller hesitated, then shook his head. "You're asking the wrong guy this time. We have a new commissioner, Regis Beecham. A political appointee. He was just appointed last week, and he already doesn't like me. Hard to believe, isn't it?"

Dani had an idea of why such a man wouldn't like Sixkiller but knew better than to verbalize it. "That's too bad, Luke."

"He won't be around long. He's got big ambitions—maybe even the governor's race. With him around I don't have much pull. But I'll speak to some of the patrol guys and ask them to watch out during services. When do they meet?"

"Oh, they meet every night."

"That makes it a little harder, but I'll do what I can."

"Thanks, Luke. That's just like you. You're always doing something for nothing to help other people."

Sixkiller moved quickly, reaching across the table to hold her hand. "But the thing is, I always expect to get paid." He winked. "Watch out for me. I might come to collect."

The two left the restaurant, and when they got to Dani's car Luke opened the door for her. Before she could get in, however, he reached out and pulled her close, putting his arm around her. He moved so quickly, there was no opportunity for Dani to resist, and in fact she didn't want to. She sensed his loneliness and felt sorry for him. He kissed her, and she let him, realizing with a slight shock that she enjoyed his nearness. Uncomfortable with sudden second thoughts, she said, "It's time for me to go."

"All right, Dani." Sixkiller's eyes seemed to glow in the dark.

"You're quite a woman. It's going to take some man to keep up with you."

Dani stared at him for a moment, then whispered, "Good night, Luke. You're a good guy."

"I'm going to be more than that to you one of these days if you don't watch out."

Dani smiled at him, and as she drove away, she found herself somewhat disturbed by the encounter. She had always liked Luke Sixkiller, but the kiss had stirred something in her, and she wondered where she was going with this powerful man who was able to affect her so strongly.

◆ ◆ ◆

Two days after her date with Sixkiller, Dani received a call from Reverend Flatt. She recognized his voice instantly and said, "How are you, reverend?"

"Happier than I deserve, Miss Dani. Listen, the church has an annual Thanksgiving dinner for folks who can't afford to eat. I'd like to have you join us if you could."

"I'll do that, and I'll even buy the turkeys for you."

"Well now, that would be downright neighborly of you."

The two talked for a while, and when Dani hung up, she left her office and walked down the hall to where Ben had a small cubicle. For once he was in, and as usual he was wearing an outfit that was less than elegant. He wore a pair of faded jeans, a blue turtleneck sweater, and a pair of white Nikes that were scuffed and the worse for wear. Dani had long since given up trying to advise him on how to dress. "I'm taking up a collection—money to buy some turkeys."

Ben looked up from the book he was reading, closed it carefully, and folded his arms and stared at her. "Why do you need more than one turkey?"

"It's for Reverend Flatt's church, for a Thanksgiving dinner for people who can't afford it."

"Put me down for a few. What does a turkey cost?"

"I really don't know. Come with me. We'll go find out."

The two left the office and went to the nearest supermarket. They piled turkeys into two baskets. "Twelve ought to be enough, I suppose," Dani said.

When they got to the checkout counter Dani pulled out her checkbook, but Ben said, "I'm a little behind in my Thanksgiving dinner giving." He paid for the turkeys, and they left. They loaded the fowl into the car, and when they got in, Ben suddenly turned to her and said, "I hear you went out with Luke."

Though she wasn't sure why, Dani began to blush. Ben's deep-set, hazel eyes were staring at her, and once again she had the notion that he could look right into her mind.

"You're blushing," he said. "Did the lieutenant get forward with you or something?"

"None of your business, Ben."

Ben shrugged and pulled the car into traffic. When they had gone less than a block, Dani said, "Who told you?"

"My sources are confidential."

"Don't you have better things to do than to keep up with what I'm doing?"

Ben turned to her, but she couldn't read his expression. He wasn't laughing, but there was something in his eyes she couldn't understand. "I'm just interested in your love life."

"And why is that?"

"I might want to get married someday and—this might be your lucky day—you're on my list of prospects."

Dani suddenly laughed. "I feel sorry for the woman who marries you."

"Don't be. She'll be getting the bargain of a lifetime."

The conversation lightened the day for Dani, for she knew that Ben Savage had feelings for her, and she also knew that she had more than a casual interest in him. *How can I be drawn to two men at the same time?* Since she had no answer for that, she thrust it aside.

They delivered the turkeys to The Greater Fire Baptized Church of Jesus Christ and promised to come back the next day to help do some of the cooking. As they left, Ben said, "You know, that's not a bad place. If I ever decide to start going to church, it'd be one like that."

After a few moments of quiet reflection Dani said, "I'm glad you feel that way, Ben. One of these days you're going to find the Lord, and one of these days I'm going to shout just like a Pentecostal preacher lady!" She was confident only of the first.

◆ ◆ ◆

When Dani's phone rang at her home the next morning, she answered it before it could disturb anyone else. "Hello?" she murmured sleepily.

"Is this Miss Ross?"

"Yes. Who is this?"

"This is Jarvo Davis. Do you remember me?"

"Of course I do, Jarvo. Why are you calling this early?"

"We've had some trouble down here at the church."

Dani was immediately wide-awake. She sat up in bed and brushed her hair back from her forehead. "What's wrong, Jarvo?" she demanded quickly.

"Well, you know all them turkeys you brought and the rest of 'em that we had that we was gonna cook today for the Thanksgivin' tomorrow?"

"Yes. What about them?"

"Somebody broke into the church, Miss Dani, and they done ruined them turkeys. They poured diesel oil all over them."

Dani Ross had never had a quick temper. She did grow angry at times, but it was a slow process. But now a fury rose in her that was so powerful, she couldn't think for a moment. She sat on the bed gripping the phone so tightly that her fingers ached. Finally she said, "When did you find out about this?"

"When I come in this morning. I was gonna start the fire. We were gonna charcoal 'em, you know, and barbecue some of 'em. But when I got here, the door was busted open. T'ain't much to steal around here except my drums maybe and some other instruments. When I saw them turkeys all ruined . . . well, it just took the heart right out of me."

"It'll be all right, Jarvo. Don't touch anything. I'll be there as soon as I can."

"It's gonna break the reverend's heart. He sure does love to do them turkeys for folks that can't afford 'em."

"I'll take care of that. I'll get some more turkeys out there, but be sure you don't touch anything."

"You gonna come and do some detectin'?"

"Yes, I'm gonna do some detectin'. I'll see you in a little while."

Dani threw on some clothes, brushed her hair just enough to be presentable, and rushed out of the house. As she drove across the causeway, she used her cell phone to call the police department. "Lieutenant Sixkiller please."

It took a few moments, but finally she heard, "This is Sixkiller."

"This is Dani. Luke, I need you."

"What is it, Dani?"

Dani told him what had happened, then said, "Please come on down there. Maybe there'll be some evidence, maybe not, but I know Valentine's behind it."

"He probably is, but not personally. He's too smart for that. I'll meet you at the church."

"Thanks, Luke."

Dani drove furiously, ignoring the speeding limit, but to her amazement by the time she got to the church Luke Sixkiller was already there. She had also called Savage, and as she walked toward the front of the church he pulled up in his classic Studebaker Hawk. He looked concerned. "What's wrong, boss?"

"Somebody broke into the church and ruined all the turkeys."

Savage stared at her for a moment, then nodded. "Let's see what we can do."

They went inside and found that Reverend Flatt had already arrived. He greeted them both and said, "The lieutenant is lookin' at them turkeys. Sure is a mess."

Dani reached out and patted the old man's shoulder. "Don't you worry. We'll get you some more turkeys; those people will be fed."

When they went to the back Sixkiller greeted them. "Hello, Dani. Hi, Ben."

"What have you found?"

"A simple breaking and entry. Of course it's not too hard to break into this place."

"Any clues?" Savage asked.

"None that I've seen yet. It looks like they did a pretty clean job. As far as we can tell, they didn't leave anything behind."

Even as he spoke, Jarvo came in, his eyes huge. "Lieutenant, there's a big can with a little diesel oil in it in the dumpster."

"Did you touch it?" Luke asked anxiously.

"No. I didn't touch nothin'. I seen it though, and I could smell the diesel oil."

"I'll go get it. There may be prints on it." Sixkiller shook his head. "Sure is a mess here."

"Guess we won't be able to feed nobody with these turkeys," Jarvo said sadly.

"Jarvo, you start cleaning up here. Ben, come on," Dani said.

"I know where we're going—to get more turkeys."

"That's right, and this time we'll be sure they get cooked."

At the market when they approached the checkout counter with their baskets full of turkeys, the manager came over to them with a smile. "Looks like you're in the turkey business. Didn't you just buy some yesterday?"

"Somebody spoiled 'em all," Ben said. He related the story of the break-in, and the manager's face hardened. "That's awful." He turned to the woman at the cash register. "Give these folks 50 percent off those turkeys."

"Why, how very nice of you!" Dani said.

"I wish I could give them to you."

"That's all right," Dani said. "We appreciate your help so much."

The two went back to the church and were pleased to see that Jarvo had already gotten the place cleaned up. Several others were working with him, including Jacob Gold, a middle-aged man with iron gray hair. He wore the earlocks of a Hasidic Jew, which he had been, Dani later discovered. "I just came over to help fix the food. I used to be a cook."

"We'll all do whatever we can, Mr. Gold," Dani said. "Ben, will you help too?"

"Sure. Be glad to."

Soon the area designated to be the kitchen was filled with people. Dani enjoyed being reminded that Ben was a good cook. He volunteered to make the pies, and from time to time she would come over to see what he was doing. Late in the afternoon, after he had made at least thirty pies, she said, "Where did you learn to bake pies?"

"From a woman named Ruby."

Curious, Dani inquired, "One of your lady friends?"

"Not really. Just a woman who lived next door to the orphanage where I grew up."

"Where is she now, Ben?"

"In the women's prison in Colorado."

"What for?"

"She killed her husband with a butcher knife." Ben smiled sadly. "She sure could cook, but she had problems that got the best of her."

◆ ◆ ◆

The second annual free Thanksgiving dinner at The Greater Fire Baptized Church of Jesus Christ was a tremendous success. Sixkiller had proven to be a help, recruiting all the off-duty patrolmen and detectives he could to set up tables and chairs and to help serve the meal.

"Kind of a police convention," Ben murmured as his eyes surveyed the scene.

Dani nodded. "It was good of Luke to do this. I love the looks of satisfaction and appreciation on everyone's faces."

Luke came over to stand beside the pair, and as his eyes ran over the room, he said, "Seems like I know most of these people. I've probably arrested a fourth of them."

Tom Bench, who played bass for the band, came over. "Hi, lieutenant."

"Hello, Tommy. You still knockin' 'em out of the park?"

"Doin' my best." Bench was seventeen and a very strong-looking individual with freckles and a homely face.

"Tommy here is going to catch for the Yankees one day. Some professional scouts are already lookin' at him."

"Now, lieutenant, that's a long way off." Bench was an amiable young man. "We sure do thank you folks for helping us out. I could have been in one of your jails, lieutenant, if the reverend hadn't helped me find Jesus."

"I'm glad you're on the right track, Tommy," Sixkiller said.

"Have you hit the glory road yet, lieutenant?" Bench asked, a hopeful light in his eyes.

"Not yet. Think there's any hope for me?"

"Jesus loves everybody, even policemen." Bench grinned and then went back to serving.

Dani enjoyed the meal, and as she was getting ready to leave she went over to her detective friend. "Luke, I'm absolutely furious about the vandalism earlier. Was that can any help?"

"Yeah. The lab already analyzed it. There were prints on it all right, belonging to a cheap thug named Buster Gee. He hires out to break kneecaps and such. We'll check him out."

"Ben and I will investigate from our end too. If we get in over our heads, we'll give you a call."

"Okay, Dani." He reached out and squeezed her arm. "You're a good person, Dani Ross. Watch yourself. Lenny Valentine has a long arm, and I'm sure that he's behind all this."

"I'll be careful. Thank you, Luke. You're a good friend."

A NOT-SO-FRIENDLY VISIT

The next day Dani found Luke Sixkiller sitting at his desk staring off into space. When she entered the room his coal black eyes focused on her, and he got up at once. "Well, you're slumming again, Dani, associating with guys like me. Have a seat."

"How are you, Luke?"

"In what way?"

Dani stared at him as she sat down. She was wearing a simple, pale blue pantsuit with a pair of black alligator pumps. Her new hairstyle framed her face most attractively as she studied him. "What do you mean 'In what way?'"

Luke sat back in his chair and shrugged his thick shoulders. "People say, 'How are you?' But what exactly does that mean? Were you asking how I am economically, psychologically, emotionally, financially, physically? How much time do you have? We'll go through them one at a time."

"I really didn't want that much information." Dani smiled. She was accustomed to the policeman's odd quirks, and she shook her head. "I guess 'How are you?' is a meaningless question, like saying 'Hello.'"

"The only thing worse is 'Have a nice day.' If one more person says that to me, I'm going to break his bridgework."

"You're in a bad mood today."

Luke Sixkiller leaned forward and locked his large fingers together, squeezing them until they were white, then nodded. "I guess I am."

"What's wrong? Anything I can help with?"

"Not unless you can change the whole setup in the world of policemen."

Above Luke's head on the wall was a picture that always fascinated Dani. She knew it was an original oil painting by Turner. She had asked an art dealer what such a picture would cost and had been shocked at his answer. Now she studied it, wondering what had possessed a rough, streetwise policeman like Luke Sixkiller to spend so much money on a piece of fine art. She started to ask him but decided there were sides to Luke Sixkiller she would never comprehend. A part of him was deep and profound, and she hadn't been invited to enter. She just said, "Problems with the department?"

"Always." Sixkiller was dressed dapperly, as usual, today wearing a light blue suit specially tailored to cover the .45 he wore under his arm. His tie was held in place by a ruby stickpin that glittered under the overhead light. "You know, I watch police shows, TV films, and things like that. They always zero in on how cops struggle with alcoholism, mistreatment at the hands of liberals and racial minorities—stuff like that."

"Isn't some of that true?"

"Yeah, I guess it is, but that's not the real problem, Dani. You give a man a gun and the right to use it, and it does something to him."

Outside the window a jackhammer suddenly started up. *Rat-tat-tat-tat-tat.* Sixkiller cast an annoyed glance but shook his head. "They're practically tearing the stupid building down around our ears."

Dani was interested in hearing more of Sixkiller's thoughts. "But policemen have to carry guns, don't they?"

"You ever stop to think about all the power we carry, Dani? Leaded batons, Mace, stun guns, rifles. We have high-powered pistols and steel-jacketed ammunition that can knock the engine out of a car. We have twelve-gauge assault shotguns, scope sniper rifles. We put all that power in the hands of a young man—kid is more like it—who's been raised on television programs and movies with guys like Rambo and the Terminator blowing people away as if they were targets at a carnival boardwalk."

Dani sat quietly wondering where this was headed. Evidently Sixkiller had been simmering for some time. Finally he said, "You know, it scares me, this power we have over people, even the no-goods. Some guys have been blown away, and nobody complained. And if you shoot somebody you thought had a gun and find out he didn't, why, you toss a spare gun at his feet and claim he was trying to shoot you."

The jackhammer rattled again, and Sixkiller shook his shoulders, then ran his hand through his thick, black hair. "I don't know why I'm talking like this. I guess I have my bad days. One day's fine and full of birds singing in the trees. The next day the monsters come out of the closet." He grinned suddenly. "End of therapy session. What do you need, Dani?"

She wanted to help him sort out his feelings but knew he didn't want to talk about it any further that day. "I need to know something about Buster Gee, the man whose prints you found on that oil can."

"I have the info right here. I thought you might be interested in it." He picked it up, but instead of handing it to her, read it aloud. "Well, he's had over forty arrests. Started out young—twelve years old. Spent some time in the reformatory when he was seventeen, then made the trip twice to Angola." Sixkiller studied the paper, obviously repulsed by what he was reading. "He did time in a federal pen for three offenses. He's been arrested for breaking and entering, auto theft, assault and battery, armed robbery. He's done about everything you can think of. Even sellin' stolen food stamps and passin' counterfeit money. He was tried once for murder but got off."

"What a horrible life!"

"Yeah, ain't it though." He handed her the sheet and watched as she ran her eyes down the fine print. Her eyes were sharp and alert, and her face showed a quiet confidence he always found pleasing. Her complexion was fair and smooth and rose-colored, and he liked the shading of her skin. He knew she liked a good laugh but also became angry at the injustices she saw around her. He looked away as she turned her eyes toward him. "What do you think, Luke?"

"About arresting him? We can do that. It wouldn't come to much though."

"Why not? You have his fingerprints."

"That's not enough in this day and age. He'll get a hotdog attorney who'll make all kinds of motions, probably get some social worker to claim that he went wrong because his mama didn't change his diaper quick enough. The courts are so jammed up with blow-away murders that they're not going to pay much attention to a guy who attacked a bunch of turkeys. It would get laughed out of court, Dani."

Dani suddenly leaned forward, her eyes filled with feelings Sixkiller couldn't understand. "I wish you weren't so bitter, Luke. I know your job is hard, but there's goodness in the world too, people who honor God and want to follow His ways."

"I know that's true because I see it in you, Dani Ross. I guess I just need to learn to roll with the punches. Trouble is, I don't learn very fast. Sometimes I think I don't learn anything. I just go on doing what I have to do, not because I'm smart or because I have any plans. I just lean forward and run straight at what's in front of me." He summoned up a smile, though it took an effort. "There's no use hanging onto a dead horse or nursing bitterness about it. No sense looking back either. When a thing's done, it's done." He slapped the table with his hands. "I don't know why I'm talking like this. Let's go down to the zoo and watch the monkeys. Anything to give ourselves a break from reality."

"Some other time, Luke. I have something I need to do now."

"And I know what it is. You and Savage are going to try and roust Buster Gee." He rummaged through the mass of papers on his desk, came up with a notebook, and ripped a page out of it.

"You can find him in one of these places. Don't let Ben shoot him, though. I couldn't get away with ignoring that."

"Thanks, Luke." She rose as she put the paper in her purse, then asked curiously, "How's the new commissioner turning out?"

"He is cordially hated by every detective in the New Orleans Police Department. Give him time and he'll have the uniformed cops hating him as well."

"Do you think he'll stay?"

"Long enough to ruin a few lives. Then they'll promote him so he can do the same thing in a larger sphere. Now, how about going out with me tonight?"

"Not tonight, but give me a call sometime soon, okay?"

As Dani left she felt depressed. Luke Sixkiller was a strong man, but his job was wearing him down. She had noticed the same thing several times during the past few months, and she prayed now that he wouldn't become like some policemen she'd known, totally calloused toward any human suffering.

◆ ◆ ◆

As Dani sat beside Ben, she enjoyed the feel of power in the Studebaker Hawk. Ben had found the old sports car rusting out under a huge oak tree on a farm. He had bought it for a hundred dollars and spent several years restoring it. Now as she leaned back against the black leather, she ran her hands along the seat. "I love this car, Ben."

"Old is better."

"Not always."

"Yes, always! Old is always better than new, small is always better than big, and real coffee is always better than instant coffee." He turned to look at her, his hazel eyes amused. "I've seen a lot of changes in this world since I've been around, Dani—and I've been against every one of them."

"I suppose you'd like to go back to having the outhouse in the backyard instead of indoor plumbing."

"That would be a small price to pay if we could have things like they used to be. Remember when you could call a company or business and get a human being instead of a menu?"

"Vaguely."

"Do you remember when you could take a youngster to the movies and not see a car blowing up, raw sex, and garbage-mouthed actors?"

"I do yearn for those days, but some new things are better."

"Name one."

Dani laughed. "Now that you've asked me, I can't think of one. How about sliced bread?"

"You don't remember when bread wasn't sliced."

"My granddad told me they used to have to slice their own. And during what he called the Big War, meaning World War II, he said that you couldn't buy real butter. You bought some kind of artificial butter, and it was white like lard. It came with a little packet of food coloring. You had to mix it up."

The two were making their way toward one of the less attractive areas of New Orleans, and Dani looked around at the men and women walking down the street. It was growing colder, and many were wearing coats and sweaters.

"Is that it over there?" Dani said. She pointed to the sign that simply said, "Pool."

"Sixkiller said it was under a beat-up old gym, so I guess that's it." He eased the Studebaker into a parking lot and sat back. "Why don't you wait here in the car? The decor of a pool hall somehow doesn't go with your outfit."

"The pool hall will have to take me as I am."

"You may hear a rude remark when you enter. The gentlemen inside aren't accustomed to ladies like you."

"I'll survive. Come on, Ben."

Ben got out of the car, locked it, then shook his head. "I don't expect people will be stealing my hubcaps. Not a very big demand for Studebaker hubcaps these days."

As the two walked toward the pool hall, they passed a woman

who looked like she had been in some sort of cosmetic disaster. Her blonde hair was shaved on one side and dyed orange on the tips; she wore black fingernail polish. She also wore a pink top, black vinyl shorts, funky glasses with red frames, and earrings made from chrome .38 cartridges. "There are some ideas for your next party, boss." Ben grinned slyly.

Dani didn't answer but stepped through the door as he held it for her. Her eyes swept the interior, which was dominated by a long bar with a brass rail. On it were gallon jars of hard-boiled eggs and pickled pig's feet.

A faint hissing sound filled the room, created by wood-bladed fans hanging from the ceiling. The pool tables were lighted by overhead lamps contained in tin covers. Some elderly men were playing dominoes at a table, and the air was thick with the smell of draft beer, gumbo, chewing tobacco, and cigarette smoke.

A young man, obviously a weight lifter, held his stomach in and tensed his muscles so they showed clearly through his thin cotton T-shirt. "Hello, folks. You want to shoot a game?"

"No thanks," Ben said. "We're looking for someone."

"Who might that be?"

"A fellow named Buster Gee."

"Yeah? Well, he's right back there shootin' a game by himself. You cops?"

"No." Ben grinned. "We don't want any trouble. Just a little talk with Buster."

The young man stared at them. He had one blue eye and one brown eye thanks to a tinted contact, giving him an odd appearance. His neck was so thick, it was impossible to tell where it began, and his pectoral muscles made his chest puff out like a pigeon's. "Okay. You need anything, I'll be at the bar. No trouble though."

"No trouble," Ben assured him.

Ben and Dani approached the solitary shooter, then paused as he lined up the balls and stroked the cue ball smoothly. It traveled over the green felt, nudged another ball so it fell obediently into a pocket. The shooter then moved into perfect position for the next

shot. He turned and stared at Ben and Dani. "You want somethin'?"
he demanded.

"Just some conversation if you don't mind, Buster."

"I don't know you guys." Buster Gee was a nondescript-
looking individual, scrawny almost to the point of skeletal thin-
ness. He had deeply sunken eyes, a broken nose, a fish-like mouth
turned down at the corners, and fingers longer than usual. If
there was an attractive part of Buster, it was his hands. Dani
thought, *He'd probably make a great violinist with long fingers like
that.* She knew, however, that such fingers were handy for other
things too, like opening safes.

"My name's Savage. This is Miss Ross. We'd like to have a short
talk with you if it's okay."

"About what?" he demanded. His eyes were a pale gray or light
blue. They seemed flat, as if curtains had come down over his eyes.
Whoever said, "Eyes are the mirror of the soul" had never met
Buster Gee.

"A friend of ours is having some trouble, and we think you
might be able to help us with it," Dani said quietly.

Gee's eyes turned to take in Dani. He swept her up and down,
then shook his head. "I've got my *own* problems. You can take care
of your friends."

"That's what we're trying to do," Dani said. "It might be better
if we had this talk in private."

"There ain't gonna be no talk." Gee turned and began shooting pool. Dani and Ben exchanged glances. Both of them stood
there silently. The silence didn't seem to bother Gee, who just kept
playing. When he drew his cue back for a shot, Ben simply reached
out and held the stick motionless. Gee turned around, his face suddenly flushed. "What do you want? Are you cops or somethin'?"

"In private," Ben said, releasing the cue stick. "Look, Buster,
you're going to talk to us one way or another. We could have come
to your room after dark, but that wouldn't have been nearly so
pleasant. Why don't we just keep this on a friendly basis?"

Gee hesitated, studied the two, then shrugged. "Okay, so talk. But right here."

"We know you poured diesel oil on the turkeys over at the church on Maribone," Dani said quietly, watching the man's face.

"Prove it."

"Not hard to prove," Dani shrugged. "You left the can with your prints on it in the dumpster."

"I don't know nothin' about it."

"Lieutenant Sixkiller thinks you do. I told him we were going to have this talk. You know the lieutenant?"

"Yeah, I know him." Gee was less cocky now. He fidgeted, then laid the cue down on the table. Jamming his hand into his pocket, he shook his head. "What do you two want?"

"You're a two-time loser, Buster. One more time, and you go to Angola *beaucoup* years," Ben said. "Why go to that place over a bunch of turkeys?"

"All right, so I done the turkeys. I'm tellin' you, but I won't confess it to the cops. I doubt you two are wired."

"We're not wired. All we want is to find out why you ruined the turkeys."

"I don't like church. I don't like God. I don't like that preacher. That's why I done it."

"That's *not* why you did it," Dani said. "Somebody hired you to do it, Buster."

The small man seemed to shrink before their eyes. He drew his mouth back in a grimace of fear and said, "Look, I can't go to Angola. I can't take that place. If they nail me, I'll be in for twenty years."

"You should have thought about that before you messed up those turkeys."

"Okay, okay. What do you two want?"

"Just tell us who hired you."

"I can't do that. He'd shred me."

"There are other towns you can move to. Tell us who hired you, then hit the road," Dani said.

Buster Gee was trembling with fear, and after a long hesitation he said, "Look, here's the deal. I'll tell you who hired me, but you can't tell nobody I said it. Okay?"

"Agreed," Dani said quickly.

"And Sixkiller can't come after me. Okay?"

"Not for this," Dani agreed quickly.

"Okay." Gee hesitated, then said, "I was paid by Chino Smith, but don't tell him I told you. He'd make fish bait out of me."

"We'll keep our word, Buster," Dani said. "But if I were you, I'd look for another line of work." She hesitated, then suddenly reached into her purse. "I'd like for you to have this."

"What is it?" Gee recoiled as if she were trying to hand him a poisonous serpent.

"It's part of the Bible."

"The Bible?" Gee seemed to flinch at the word, then shook his head violently. "I don't need none of that religion stuff."

Dani shoved the small Gospel of John into his pocket. "Read it. Jesus died for you. He loves you even if nobody else does."

Savage watched this closely, not liking what he was seeing. Dani turned and left the poolroom, almost every eye on her. When they were outside, Ben said, "You never give up, do you? You really think God can do something with Buster Gee?"

"There but for the grace of God goes Dani Ross—or Ben Savage."

"Guess you're right there, boss, but . . . What now?"

"I think we'll pay a visit to Mr. Lenny Valentine."

◆ ◆ ◆

Ben stopped the Studebaker outside the closed iron gates. "The place looks like the Taj Mahal," he murmured.

The two of them had come to the most exclusive residential section of New Orleans. The houses there under one million dollars were considered low-rent. Lenny Valentine's home was set back behind the wrought-iron black fence amidst tremendous live oak trees that dipped their huge branches to the ground. The ponderous trees had their own grace and serenity. Spanish moss, used to stuff mattresses during the Depression, decorated the trees, hanging down like strands of fine lace.

A man suddenly appeared at the iron gate. He slipped it open, stepped outside, and came around to the car. "Yes, sir, can I help you?" He was a well-built Latino with hard, shiny, black eyes.

"We'd like to see Mr. Valentine," Ben said.

"You got an appointment?"

"No, I'm afraid not, but people usually like to see representatives from the IRS."

The flat eyes changed suddenly, and the man nodded. "Wait here please."

"Why did you imply we were from the IRS?" Dani said.

"Because I want to get through the gate."

"But he'll be expecting a real IRS agent."

"Another one of his dreams gone smash." Ben grinned. "You worry too much about little things. Worry about big things like where we're going to have supper tonight and whether I'm going to let you kiss me good night at my front door."

The two sat there and watched as the man disappeared into the house. He came back almost at once and swung the gates open. "You can park right over there, sir."

"Thanks a lot," Ben said.

He parked the car in a circular driveway. The house was massive and ornate. It was a three-story, red brick building with four huge white columns decorating the front and black shutters on each side of the numerous windows on all three floors. On the second and third stories a black wrought-iron balcony ran the full length of the front of the house, bringing the charm of New Orleans architecture to the building. The six stairs leading to the front doors were made of the same brick as the house and had been constructed in a half circle leading up to the house. Hanging pots of geraniums, ferns, and other plants decorated the front porch, and two large, white statues of lions flanked the front doors.

"It's not as big as that white house in Washington," Ben said as they got out of the car. "But then it's not a lot smaller either."

The gatekeeper had followed them, and Dani could see the imprint of a gun under the sports coat that he wore. "Go right up. Someone will meet you at the door."

"Thanks," Ben said and gave him a flashing smile. "Come along, Miss Snodgrass."

Dani giggled. "Snodgrass?" she whispered.

"I always wanted to date a woman named Snodgrass. Irma Snodgrass was my second grade teacher, and I was madly in love with her. Let's see . . . She'd be on Medicare by now, I suppose."

Ben rang the doorbell, and it opened almost at once. A tall, patrician-looking man wearing a severely cut black suit said, "You've come at a bad time, sir. There's a party going on at the indoor pool."

"I'm sorry that we have to disturb Mr. Valentine's social life, but . . ."

The butler clearly wanted to ask them to leave, but the earlier mention of the IRS made that inadvisable. "This way, sir and madam."

Ben and Dani walked along the Italian marble floor, glancing at the pictures on the wall. Most of them were modern art, and as Dani passed by an original Dufy, she nudged Ben. "That should be in a museum."

"This place *is* a museum. It's not very homey, is it?"

Their guide led them down three twisting corridors and then through a pair of large eight-foot French doors with sparkling water on the other side. When they stepped inside, Dani whispered, "That's the most enormous indoor pool I've ever seen."

"It's not as big as the Gulf of Mexico," Ben said. "But what the hey."

A rather short man, somewhat overweight, was coming up out of the pool. He shook himself like a seal, walked over to a chair, and grabbed a white robe. He slipped it on and stared over at the pair, then nodded as they approached. "You're from the IRS?"

"No, we're not," Ben said quickly. "There must be a misunderstanding. Are you Mr. Valentine?"

"Yeah. My man said you told him you were from the IRS."

"No, I didn't. When he wouldn't let us in I just said, 'People usually admit IRS agents.' He took it from there."

Lenny Valentine looked somewhat like the old movie star Edgar G. Robinson. He had dark hair and dark eyes and heavy jowls. There was a dangerous quality about him, and he said, "Lex, show these people out."

A tall, thin man with a sallow complexion moved toward them. He had hazel eyes, a knife-blade of a mouth, and straw-colored hair cut very short. "You two, out!"

"That's not very neighborly, Mr. Valentine," Dani said. "We do need to talk to you."

"Who are you?"

"My name's Dani Ross. I'm a private investigator. We're looking into a case that involves you. I'm hoping it can be settled amiably. Otherwise it could be rather . . . messy."

Lex Noon stepped forward and seized Dani's arm. "You heard what Mr. Valentine said. Come on."

He started toward the French doors when Ben suddenly stepped forward and, with a lightning-like move, reached under Noon's coat. His hand came out with a shiny Beretta. He pointed it almost casually at Noon, then said pleasantly, "You have a license for carrying this, Lex?"

Noon seemed to freeze. He dropped his hold on Dani's arm and stared at Savage, his face absolutely still, but his hazel eyes glittering.

Dani glanced at Valentine and saw his mouth forming a startled O. A movement caught her eye, and she looked over to see a woman in a pale blue robe suddenly stand to her feet. She was holding an infant in her arms and had on large, oversized sunglasses that seemed to cover most of her face. She was staring at them with an expression of shock, drawing her lips back in a peculiar way. But Dani had no interest in her. Dani turned to face Lenny Valentine.

"You ought to hire better help, Lenny," Ben said. He removed the clip from the Beretta and with a swift motion ejected the shell. It hit the tile and rolled along, sounding very loud in the silence. Ben handed the Beretta back to Noon and stood there waiting, his eyes alert.

"You're a pretty talented guy. What's your name?" Valentine said.

"Ben Savage."

Valentine was staring at the two. "Never mind, Lex," he said. "Take a break."

Noon whirled suddenly and walked away. He went over to stand beside the woman, who hadn't moved.

"What do you two want?"

"I'll give it to you straight out, Mr. Valentine," Dani said. "You're trying to hassle a client of mine—Reverend Alvin Flatt."

"Never heard of him."

"Now, now, Mr. Valentine, you can do better than that. You made an offer on the building that he's using for a church. When he refused to sell, you sent your hoodlums to hassle him. I have already brought this matter to the attention of the NOPD. We've come here on a mission of peace. Please leave Reverend Flatt alone, or it might grow unpleasant for you."

Lenny Valentine suddenly seemed to be choking. His face reddened, and his eyes began to bulge. "Unpleasant? I'll show you unpleasant! Now get out of my home!"

"Certainly," Dani answered. "Here's my card. If you want to discuss this matter further, I'd be glad to see you anytime. Come along, Mr. Savage."

Dani walked determinedly toward the door, and Ben followed her. He gave one quick look over his shoulder at Noon, who was standing still as a statue, his eyes burning with hatred.

When they were outside, he said, "I'm not a gypsy, but I see a dark man in your future, and he has ill will toward you."

When Dani didn't answer, he opened the door for her, then got inside and started the engine. "I'm not sure we handled this one right. We made Valentine look bad in front of his hired help."

"No, you made his hired help look bad. That man is evil."

"Yes, I think he is."

"Did you see the woman? I wonder if she's his wife."

"I don't know, but one thing is sure. You and I both better keep our doors locked from here on in."

"WHAT IS LOVE ANYWAY?"

"Hi, Ben." Angie Park looked up from her computer and studied the detective carefully. "I see you caught another yard sale."

Savage was wearing a pair of brown chinos worn thin with use, a blue T-shirt, and a much-used flight jacket. Plopping himself down in a chair, Ben put his feet up, crossed his legs, and stroked the Nikes that appeared to be relatively new. "Beware of any enterprise that requires the wearing of new clothes," he said cheerfully.

"Is that an original Ben Savage proverb?"

"Well, I wasn't the first to say it, but I've always believed it. Clothes *don't* make the man." He reached across the desk, opened the globular glass candy jar, and plucked out a peppermint. He plopped it into his mouth and tossed the cellophane wrapper into Angie's wastebasket. "What's goin' down, Angie?"

"Well, Dani seems pretty uptight."

"About what?"

"I think it's about that preacher."

"Reverend Flatt?" Ben leaned back in his chair and closed his eyes. "I'm kind of worried about him myself."

"What's going on, Ben?"

"It's like the David and Goliath story, Angie. Right off the top of my head I'd say the preacher doesn't have any more chance of hanging on to his church building than I have of flying to the moon."

Angie leaned forward and placed her chin on the heel of her palm. She was wearing a light green linen dress with a scooped neckline, short sleeves, and a matching jacket. On the bodice was a single, painted white tulip, and the hem of the ankle-length dress was edged with tulips and butterflies painted in pastel colors. She looked very pretty actually, but as usual there was sadness in her eyes. "Ben," she said, "what do you think about cosmetic surgery?"

Savage's eyes flew open, and he sucked on the peppermint for a moment before answering. "You talkin' about man stuff or woman stuff? If a man gets his ear cut off, I guess he ought to get a substitute put on."

"That's not what I mean."

"You thinkin' about gettin' an overhaul?"

"What's wrong with that?" Angie's tone was defensive. She stared defiantly at Ben and said, "You get a haircut to make yourself look better, don't you?"

"Yeah, I do, but if they had to put me to sleep and do it with scalpels, I think I'd just let it grow long." Savage spoke quietly, and his thoughtful hazel eyes were fixed on the secretary. He had come to really care about Angie, and he knew that her experiences with men left a great deal to be desired. Finally he said, "You're really thinking about doing this?"

"I talked to Dani about it, but she was against it."

"Pretty smart woman, that boss of ours. Especially in your case. You're already a good-looking woman."

"I'd look better if I got a few things done."

"It's what's inside that counts." Savage reached over, grabbed another peppermint, and went on. "I heard that in some commercial, I think, but for what product I have no idea. It's pretty true of human beings though. You know that as well as I do."

"You wouldn't do it, Ben, if you were me?"

"It's pretty hard to crawl into somebody else's skin, Angie. And women think differently from men. They act differently too. When you go out shopping for a pair of shoes, you probably take half a day and look at a dozen pairs. I go in and say, 'Give me a size ten and a half regular black,' and I'm out of there in minutes. I don't think either way's best. They're just different."

Angie sat back in her chair and tapped her chin with a yellow pencil. She had learned to trust Ben Savage's judgment, so she said, "Come on, Ben, can't you give me a little bit more than that? I mean, I'm asking for advice."

Savage grinned. His squarish face looked strong and tanned and healthy in the sunlight coming through the window to his right. "Most people, when they come asking me for advice, don't really want to know what I think. They want me to agree with what they've already decided to do."

"That's not fair, Ben!"

"Okay, okay—here's what I really think. If I were you, I wouldn't do it." He seemed to struggle for a moment, then clasped his hands together and stared down at them thoughtfully. "I had a friend up in Colorado. Had a fine wife. I'd always been kind of skeptical of these marriages that are said to be made in Heaven, but that one made me think. They really seemed to have it all put together, Angie, and then the sky fell on them."

"What happened?"

"She was in a car wreck and got terribly burned. It was a miracle she got out alive. She had third-degree burns over most of her body, and her face was scarred. I went to see her in the hospital, and her husband, Buddy, told me that I couldn't show any emotion or shock. Just keep a poker face." A memory flashed across Ben's mind, and he shook his head. "I don't guess I did too good a job of it. When I saw Helen for the first time, I would never have recognized her. Seeing her that way shook me up, I can tell you."

"What happened, Ben?"

"Buddy stuck with her. This was over five years ago, and she's still having operations. She was a real beauty, Angie. Skin like a baby's. Perfect features. Not much left of that now."

"And her husband stayed with her?"

"Yes, he did. Whenever I meet people who think they're having a hard time, I think of Buddy and Helen and how he just kept loving her."

"What about her? Did she ever get over it?"

"I don't think she ever completely did, but she was a Christian, and she kept telling me that she couldn't complain to God since He'd been so good to her. That shook me up too." He gazed at Angie, then added, "They were always a handsome couple, and now he's handsome and she's not. But they're still together, and that's kind of a miracle to me."

"Isn't she afraid another woman will take her husband away now that she's lost her looks?"

"I don't think so. Buddy's proved himself, and Helen knows that he loves her—not her smooth skin or anything like that—nothing on the outside."

The office was quiet for some time. Angie sat quietly thinking over what Ben had said, and Savage knew better than to interrupt her. He knew physical appearance was a big thing to many women, but he hated to see Angie get caught in that trap. He finally said, "You know, I was terrible at English all the way through school. I couldn't make head or tail out of most of the poetry they made me read. I cheated most of the time and read some scholar's interpretation instead of figuring out the poem for myself. But there's one poem that I really understood."

"What was it?"

"One of Shakespeare's sonnets. You want to hear it?"

"Yes, I do."

Savage quietly recited the words of the poem, keeping his eyes fixed on Angie as he spoke:

> *"Let me not to the marriage of true minds*
> *Admit impediments. Love is not love*
> *Which alters when it alteration finds,*
> *Or bends with the remover to remove:*
> *O no! It is an ever-fixed mark*
> *That looks on tempests and is never shaken;*
> *It is the star to every wandering bark,*
> *Whose worth's unknown, although his height be taken.*
> *Love's not Time's fool, though rosy lips and cheeks*

Within his bending sickle's compass come;
Love alters not with his brief hours and weeks,
But bears it out even to the edge of doom.
If this be error and upon me proved,
I never writ, nor no man ever loved."

"Why, that's beautiful, Ben!" Angie exclaimed. "I'm surprised at you."

"Don't be too surprised. It's about all the poetry I know."

"Tell me what you think it means."

"Well, I like those two lines at the beginning. 'Love is not love which alters when it alteration finds.' Those two lines always stuck with me because one thing is always sure with a man and a woman—there are going to be alterations. She may have peachy skin and thick, glossy hair, but one day that skin will be dry, and the hair will be gray or white. And he won't keep that athlete's body. That'll be altered too. He'll get a potbelly, his legs will get skinny, his neck will shrivel up until it looks like a turkey's. There'll be alterations."

"That's right," Angie said slowly. "And the poem says that though those things will come, real love doesn't change."

"Right. And later the poem says, 'Love's not Time's fool, though rosy lips and cheeks within his bending sickle's compass come.' When you see an old sex goddess who's lost it, it really comes home to you. We're all going to get old, Angie, but some people keep on loving no matter what happens. Like my friend Buddy loving his wife Helen."

"I guess love in Hollywood is one thing, but real love is altogether different."

"You're right."

"What is love anyway, Ben?"

Savage threw up his hands. "Who am I? Ann Landers?"

Angie gave him a shy smile. "Well, I'm surprised you know a poem that beautiful. It must mean something to you."

"What do you think I am? Just another pretty face? End of

counseling session." Ben suddenly grew serious. "I like you, Angie, and you ought to like yourself. If some guy likes you just because you got the cosmetic surgery you knew would get his attention . . . well, you deserve better than that. But if he loves you for who you really are, that's another matter."

At that instant the door to Dani's office opened, and she came out. "Don't you two have anything to do?"

"Yes, and we're doing it," Ben said lazily.

"What were you talking about?"

"The cosmos. Time in space."

"Is that all?" Dani said scornfully. "Don't you have any work to do?"

Just then the phone rang, and Angie picked it up, glad for the interruption. "Ross Investigations. How may I direct your call?" She listened for a moment, then said, "Just a moment please. It's for you, Dani."

She took the phone. "This is Dani Ross." She listened intently as the two watched her, and a disturbed look came over her face. "I'll be right there. What room did you say? Thank you."

Handing the phone back to Angie, Dani said in a terse voice, "It's Alvin Flatt. He's been in an automobile accident."

"What! How is he?"

"I don't know. I'm going over to find out."

"I'll go with you," Ben said quickly.

For once Dani didn't argue, and the two of them left. Angie sighed deeply. "'Love is not love which alters when it alteration finds.'" A wistful look came into her eyes, and she touched her cheek with a tentative hand and shook her head, thinking thoughts that had long been dormant.

Ben drove Dani to the Baptist Hospital, weaving in and out of traffic. "Maybe he's all right," he said. "Did they say how it happened?"

"No. I didn't ask. I guess we'll find out when we get there."

Ben swerved to avoid a semi, then jerked the Studebaker back into the proper lane. "I hope he's okay."

Dani didn't answer. She seemed preoccupied, and her face was tense. Savage said, "You know, things happen so quickly. A guy bends over to tie his shoelace, and when he straightens up, the whole world's changed for him."

Dani looked over at him. She studied his face thoroughly for a moment and then said, "You're right, Ben. We don't know what's going to happen from one minute to the next. So I guess the only thing to do is to be as ready for it as we can."

"But how can you be ready for some tragic event you don't know is coming?"

"I read somewhere that Buddhists imagine a little bird perched on their shoulders, and it keeps on whispering in their ear, 'Is today the day? Am I ready? Am I doing all I need to do? Am I being the person I want to be?'"

"I think you'd know more about that than I would, with your faith and all." The two didn't speak for some time, but just before Ben pulled into the street where the hospital was located, he said, "I've been thinking a lot about the reverend."

"And?"

"I was telling Angie that his situation is like David going up against Goliath. I'd like for us to give the preacher all the help we can. He's got a hard row to hoe."

As Ben pulled over to the curb, Dani nodded. "It's the hard things that make us what we are. A book that's easy doesn't help you much. It's the difficult books that we learn from. Raking leaves is easy, but all you get is leaves. But if you do some tougher digging, you just might find diamonds."

"You're getting philosophical on me, boss. I'm just a hired thug."

They both got out of the car and hurried into the hospital. Dani stopped at the desk. As soon as they had their passes, she and Ben walked together to the elevator. Neither of them spoke on their way up; there seemed to be little to say. Finally Ben commented, "I never know what to say to people who have been hurt or have experienced a great loss. "

"It's not the words we say but the caring in our eyes that counts."

Finally the elevator stopped on the sixth floor, and they hurried down the hall. When they found the room, Dani knocked. A faint voice answered, and the two entered. Alvin Flatt lay on his back on the hospital bed. His left leg was in a cast, and his face was plastered with bandages. His wife sat beside him, her eyes filled with fear. She said at once, "Oh, Miss Ross, it's so awful!"

"What happened?" Dani asked, going over to stand across the bed from Myrtle.

"It happened so quick, I couldn't see it." Flatt's voice was faint, and Dani suspected he had been given considerable medication for pain.

"He was on his way to church. When he crossed the street, this car appeared from nowhere and ran him over. The driver didn't even stop."

Dani glanced at Ben, and a silent communication passed between them.

"Did the police come up with anything?"

"No. They asked us all kinds of questions, but Alvin didn't even see the car. And there weren't any witnesses."

"Daughter—" Dani looked down to see that Flatt's eyes were on her. He looked old and sick and frail. He raised a hand that had known much hard work, and she took it at once. His fingers closed on hers. "What is it, reverend?"

"I ain't one to question God," he whispered faintly. "But I been layin' here thinkin' about what's going to happen to the church with me out for a while." He seemed to struggle, and his eyelids were heavy. "I think the Lord's been talkin' to me, and I'm askin' you to help."

"Why, I'll do all I can, Dad." The word *Dad* slipped out of her mouth easily because everyone else in the church referred to Flatt as Dad.

"I don't have nobody to stand in for me, but you was studyin' to be a preacher before . . . You've got to help those people."

Dani felt a sense of alarm, for she knew he was asking her for more than a small favor. She was sure Ben's eyes were boring into her, but she refused to turn and look. "What do you want me to do?" she said quietly, though she knew the answer.

"I want you to be the preacher until I'm able to get back. Will you do that, daughter?"

Time seemed to stand still, and Dani's mind raced. *How could I possibly fill in for this man? I'm no preacher. I'm not even supposed to be. And besides, I have a detective agency to run. I can't possibly do this.*

She was aware of Alvin Flatt's faded blue eyes fixed on her. His hand trembled as he held onto her waiting for her reply. She felt torn. She knew that according to what the Bible taught, women were not to be elders or pastors. There were so many other valuable ministries they could perform, but not that. And yet she felt such a kinship with this dear minister of the Gospel that she sincerely wanted to help him and his fledgling church. *Lord, I don't want to do anything wrong. I want to serve You in the right way. And yet my new friend needs someone to fill in for him during his recuperation. If what I am about to do is wrong in Your sight, please forgive me. And please encourage the hearts of those dear believers despite my misstep.*

"All right," Dani said slowly, nodding. "I'll do the best I can."

"The anointing will be on you, daughter," Flatt said, and his grip relaxed. His eyes closed, and a peaceful expression came across his features.

"Bless you, darlin'," Myrtle cried. "He's been worried sick about the church, but I know you'll do real well. I'll be right there with you, and we'll all do all we can for the Lord."

Dani felt she had made a terrible mistake, but she saw no way to back out without leaving the church and Reverend Flatt high and dry. When the doctor came in to check the patient's condition, he assured Dani there were no internal injuries, though at the preacher's age even a fractured leg was serious.

"He'll have to have constant care. Of course, his wife insists she can do all that. Is he a relative of yours?"

"No, he isn't."

"I thought he called you 'daughter' a moment ago."

"He calls most younger women that, doctor. He'll be all right then?"

"Oh yes. I'm sure he will."

Ben had stood listening to all this, saying nothing. Finally, when Dani was through, she looked at him, and the two left the hospital. When they were in the car, she said, "Take me back to the office, Ben. I need to go home and talk to my parents."

"Right."

When Ben pulled up in front of the office to let Dani out, she said almost fiercely, "Ben, you have to help me. I can't do this alone."

"Sure, boss."

"What I mean is, you have to take over the agency. I'll be down at that church a great deal."

Surprise came across Ben's face. "Do you think I can do it?"

"Of course you can do it. You have to do it. As a matter of fact," she said almost bitterly, "you'll do a lot better job running the agency than I will preaching at that church. I'm no preacher."

Ben reached over and took her hand. He held it tightly for a moment and then to her surprise brought it to his lips and kissed it. It was a courtly gesture, and he had never done such a thing before. "You'll do fine, boss," he said. "Now go to it."

Stunned by Ben's gesture, Dani was still for a moment, then lifted her eyes to his. "You don't think it was an accident, do you?"

"Nope. Definitely not."

"It had to be Valentine."

"No doubt. At least he had it done."

Dani nodded slowly, then moved to leave the car.

"Watch yourself, boss. If he did it to one preacher, he'll do it to another."

Six

NO JOB FOR A LADY

Lenny Valentine ran his hand over the hood of the low-slung automobile and gave a brief sigh of pleasure. He was wearing a pair of dark blue slacks and a white knit shirt, and there was a glow in his dark eyes as he studied the vehicle. He was a man who loved possessions, and automobiles were his passion. He had in his special collection a Mercedes, a BMW, a Porsche, a Ferrari, and now he had acquired a Jaguar. He studied the sleek lines and the glow of the new automobile and was lost in the pleasure of the moment. It was not the driving of the cars that he wanted so much as possession—ownership, the feeling that they were *his*. The fact that the average person could not afford one of these cars, much less half a dozen, was a mark of triumph to him.

Five feet away Lex Noon leaned against the brick wall that surrounded the courtyard. Green vines draped the ancient wall, and exotic flowers bloomed with a luxurious growth common to the semitropical climate. Noon studied Valentine for a moment, his face expressionless, then lifted his gaze to study the wall. *Got to check the security system. That wire along the wall probably needs to be replaced.* His attention drifted as a bright green parakeet flew over the wall and landed on the fountain, perching on the rim. The water overflowed into a larger pool. The sound made a pleasant gurgling noise. Noon fixed his eyes on the bird for an instant. He was a cold-blooded killer, so smart that he hadn't been sent to prison yet. He had been tried many times but never convicted. He had no affection for anyone, though he had a great loyalty to the man who paid him.

As he studied Valentine, his mind ranged freely as he considered the many details that made up the kingdom of the short, over-weight man who moved around the car, pausing to touch it, stroking it as a man might stroke the smooth flesh of a woman. True, he had no emotional ties to Valentine, but Noon had developed a code of his own, and his number one ethic was, "Be loyal to the one who pays you." Noon was a cold, efficient man, tall and thin. He had an unhealthy look, a sallow complexion, but this was deceiving, for he was strong and faster than the strike of a cobra. His appearance actually helped him, for men continually underestimated him, thinking him to be sickly, and Noon encouraged this by assuming some of the other aspects of ill health.

"What do you think, Lex?"

"Fine automobile. You want to take it out for a spin?"

"Later this afternoon maybe. Come on." Valentine turned to the short black man who stood in the shadow of the wall awaiting his orders. "Check everything out one more time, Benny."

"Yes, Mr. Valentine, I'll do that."

"Come on, Lex. Let's go have a drink."

The two men walked out of the courtyard that bordered the six-car garage. They walked under a balcony enclosed with orna-mental, black wrought iron and entered through a side door. Neither man spoke until they reached an enormous room with win-dows all across the front, allowing the golden sunlight to stream in. The bar flanked one wall, and an olive-complected young man with a pair of watchful, dark eyes said, "Fix you a drink, Mr. Valentine?"

"Yeah. Dig out some of that Heineken beer."

Valentine did not ask Noon if that suited him but threw him-self down in a strange-looking chair made entirely of stainless tubular bars that supported a canvas seat. "I don't know why this thing's so comfortable. It looks like a torture machine out of the Middle Ages," he observed. "But it sits better than anything else I've got." He looked around the room furnished with modern furniture; the walls were filled with modern paintings from the Cubist School.

Noon took the brown bottle from the young man but did not sit down. He rarely sat down. Something inside him drove him constantly. He placed the bottle to his lips and took a tiny sip, watching Valentine quietly.

Valentine didn't sip—he guzzled. Tilting the bottle, his throat worked convulsively, and he drank until it was two-thirds empty. He waited momentarily, then belched mightily and held the bottle up. "That's good beer. A lot better than anything I had when I was growing up."

"It should be, the price it costs."

Valentine suddenly laughed. "You're going to gripe about a three-dollar bottle of beer? And don't tell me again what a tough time you had growing up."

Noon didn't smile, for he *had* come up the hard way. He'd grown up in the worst section of Chicago and had fought his way up in a world of human piranha. If there had been any gentleness in him, it had been forced out of him during those years. Now nothing remained but the hard core of self-survival and loyalty to the man who paid him. "No sense throwing money away," he said.

Lenny Valentine drained the rest of the beer, then waved to the young man. "George, give me another."

"Yes, sir, Mr. Valentine."

Valentine waited until he got the second bottle, then said, "What's going on with that preacher?"

"Alvin Flatt? Not a whole lot. He's a tough old bird. Most guys would give up after getting a dose of what Chino gave him. He could have killed him when he ran him down."

That was not the answer Valentine wanted. He lowered his head, and the double chin made a pouch. He did indeed look a great deal like the actor Edgar G. Robinson, who had played an Al Capone-like character in the early days of the movies. There was a cruelty in his eyes and a coldness that reminded people of the eye of a tiger shark. "So Flatt's playing tough," he said. "Maybe we better hit him a little harder."

"You want me to put the pressure on?"

"I shouldn't have to tell you that, Lex. You know how much is riding on this deal."

"All right, Lenny. If that's what you want . . ."

Noon took a tiny sip of the Heineken until a thought that had been forming in his mind came into focus. He spoke slowly, but there was a different note in his tone. "We can hit the preacher, but that Savage guy . . . he's trouble."

"Savage? He's nothin'."

"We'd better clip him, Lenny."

"Not until we have to."

Noon didn't like the decision but filed the information deep in his brain. "All right. You're the boss."

"We have to get that property though. Keep the pressure on. I've got to have that building. It's in the very middle of the plan. Without it I've got nothing, Lex."

"All right." Noon thought for a moment and then nodded slightly. "That preacher will give up. Everybody else has. If he don't, there'll be one less preacher in the world to clutter up the landscape."

The phone beside Valentine rang, and he picked it up quickly. "Yeah, this is Valentine." An annoyed look came to his face, and he spoke to Noon. "It's the hospital. They called me, then put me on hold. How do you like that? Give me one of them cigars over there, will you, Lex?"

Lex moved over to a mahogany box, opened it, and lifted out an enormous Cuban cigar. He picked up a platinum knife, trimmed the end, then handed the cigar to Valentine, who stuck it in his mouth and waited until Lex lit it. He puffed light blue clouds of smoke as he stoked the cigar, and when it was glowing he leaned back against the canvas and waited. Finally he said, "Yeah, doc, this is me. What's the word on my wife?" He listened quietly, his expression unchanged, and finally said, "Okay. Do the best you can." He hung up without a formal good-bye, then puffed on the cigar for a moment. Turning to Lex, he said, "Maria ain't doin' too good. The doc don't think she's going to make it."

Noon didn't respond. He had no feelings for Maria Valentine, and he knew no comment was expected. Any love that Valentine had entertained for his wife had disappeared long ago. He had never been faithful to his wife even when she was healthy. Since she had been diagnosed with cancer and had gone downhill very quickly, he had been even more involved with other women. Most of these affairs were not serious, but Lex was well aware that though it was never spoken, Maria Valentine's death would be a relief to her husband. He went through the motions of hiring the best doctors, the best care, but it was all a façade.

Lenny looked up and studied his lieutenant. He hadn't expected any expression of condolence, and now he whispered so quietly that only Noon could hear, "It'd be good if she went quick."

Noon felt strained to make some reply. "We all got to go sometime."

◆ ◆ ◆

One of the things Dani did like about having her office in the French Quarter was that she was never far away from a good place to eat. Everything was available in the way of cuisine, and now as she walked down Bourbon Street with Luke Sixkiller on her left, she suggested, "Let's eat at Tricou's."

"Sounds good."

Sixkiller glanced at Dani, wondering why she'd called him, but knowing that she would get to whatever was on her mind soon enough. His eyes moved from point to point as they moved down the street. It was unlikely there would be anything for him to handle, although he did pass three drug dealers, all of whom caught a glimpse of him and seemed to melt away into invisibility. The word was out in New Orleans that Luke Sixkiller was a hard man, and the criminal element avoided him as much as possible.

FOUR OF A KIND 83

The Tricou house had been built as a home and an office by a doctor in the early 1800s. It was one of the finest examples of the architecture of that day. The carriageway, the L-shaped courtyard that had been slave quarters, and the stables were still very close to their original state. The smell of freshly cooked food came to them as the two took their seat in the courtyard, and a middle-aged, black waitress smiled at them. "Good morning, Miss Ross."

"Hello, Helen. What's good today?"

"King creole can't be beat. I mixed it myself. Shrimp, alligator, sausage, and crawfish tails all sautéed in creole sauce. You'll like that."

"All right, I'll try that. What about you, Luke?"

"I think I'll have some jambalaya."

"Yes, sir. A full order?"

"All you can carry."

Dani smiled as the waitress left, then leaned back in her chair. "I like this place. The food here is better than at Antoine's or some of the more expensive places."

The two talked about food for a moment, and as they spoke Luke studied Dani without appearing to. She was, to him, exactly what a woman should be. Her eyes were wide-spaced, and their gray-green color seemed to have no bottom to it. They opened up into her soul, so it seemed. She was tall and shapely, and something about her pulled at him constantly. Tough as he was, Luke Sixkiller knew that this woman had something for him that no other woman had ever had, and as she spoke he studied her face, a mirror that changed as her feelings changed. He knew also that she had an inner toughness, and from the first time he had met her, he had been certain she could handle anything that came her way.

Dani glanced up suddenly and found Luke's eyes on her. She smiled slightly, saying, "Every time I buy you lunch I want something."

"Okay, so I'm on the take. What'll it be?"

Dani leaned forward, and her voice dropped slightly. "I need help, Luke. I'm worried about the church."

Sixkiller sat there silently. "Yeah. I've been thinking about that. A funny thing happened."

"What was that, Luke?"

"The captain called me in. He hinted around that I ought to stay away from that church."

"Why would he do that?"

Sixkiller's obsidian eyes were half-hooded, but his lips pulled together for a moment, then relaxed. Shrugging his shoulders, he said, "Somebody got to somebody high in the organization."

"Do you think the captain is in on it?"

"No, he's a good man. But there's money in this, Dani. And where there's money, all the rules go out the window."

"Well, thanks anyway, Luke."

Sixkiller leaned over and took her hand with one swift motion. He held it for a moment, looked down at it, then reached over with his other hand and drew his forefinger across the top of her hand. He did not release her, and Dani was intensely aware that he could close his grip and easily crush her bones. In a way it gave her pleasure to know that she was in his power. She'd never felt this way with any other man, and it troubled her at times.

"I'll do what I can off-duty, but no official help."

Sixkiller released Dani's hand and leaned back, and as Helen approached with their drinks, he said, "There's something wrong with this, Dani. Something's rotten in the state of Denmark."

"This isn't Denmark, Luke."

"I know, but that's all the Shakespeare I know. Keep your eyes open. Make sure Ben's with you as much as possible."

She smiled up at Helen and nodded. After the woman left, Dani said, "Thanks, Luke. It's good to know you're here."

"Good old Uncle Luke." Sixkiller's broad lips turned upward at the corners, and he lifted his glass of tea. "Here's lookin' at you, kid." As Dani lifted her glass, he said, "That's what Bogart said to Ingrid Bergman in *Casablanca*. I've been practicing my Bogart impersonation."

Dani smiled. "It's fine. Now I'll have to start working on my Bergman impersonation."

◆ ◆ ◆

One of the assets that Ben Savage possessed that made him a good detective was the ability to blend into practically any background. At five-ten and 175 pounds he didn't draw attention because he was neither overly large nor small enough to be noticeable. His smooth muscles and tightly knit framework were covered by a pair of faded jeans and a light blue cotton shirt open at the throat. He wore no hat, and his black hair was neither excessively long nor short. His face was Slavic and squarish. Traversing the streets of the French Quarter, he could have been taken for a tourist or a working man. He was like a chameleon, somehow taking on the attitude and appearance of whatever crowd surrounded him at the moment.

As he moved along, Savage took note of the drug dealers, prostitutes, and pimps who seemed to spring up like mushrooms in New Orleans, but they weren't what he was looking for today. He had been walking for twenty minutes when suddenly he spotted a man leaning against one of the wrought-iron, black lampposts. Drifting toward him, Ben smiled. "Hello, Hack. What's happening?"

The man he spoke to, no taller than him, had obviously been ravaged by time and circumstance. Hack Beardon was one of the lowlifes that could easily be found on the streets of New Orleans. His eyes were almost pulled together by scar tissue, and his nose had been broken more than once. If this hadn't identified him as an old prize fighter, his puffy left ear would have. And if that had failed, his voice would have given him away. When he spoke, it was as if he had gravel in his throat.

"Hey, Ben. Nothin' much."

"Come on, let's get somethin' to eat. I'm starved."

"Sure thing, Ben."

Actually Savage wasn't even hungry, but he knew that Beardon's "territory" included the area where Reverend Alvin Flatt's church was located. He also knew that despite his unprepossessing appearance Hack Beardon was intensely aware of his own world. Ben had used him often as a source for finding out what went on beneath the surface of that section of New Orleans.

"What's your fancy today, Hack? I can eat anything."

"I could eat some Tex-Mex."

"Okay. Will Juan's Fine Burritos be okay?"

"Sounds great, Ben," the gravelly voice rumbled.

The two men made their way to the restaurant on Magazine Street. The tables were covered with checkered tablecloths; candles in old wine bottles dripped red, yellow, and blue wax. A saucy young Mexican girl with flashing brown eyes took their order. Hack ordered a multi-combo platter and Ben a burrito.

When the waitress left, Ben dipped a large chip into the red sauce and bit into it. His eyes immediately began to water. "That's hot!" he said.

Hack grinned out of his slitted eyes. "You just ain't no man, Ben. Let me show you." He scooped up an enormous amount of the hot sauce on a chip, opened his mouth, and dumped it in. His expression didn't change for a moment, then he grinned. "That ain't hot. There just ain't no men no more."

Ben laughed. "You're right about that." He liked Hack Beardon. Beardon had fought before his time, but the story of his battles against Tony Zale, the middleweight champion, were legendary. Hack had been one tough fellow, not always within the bounds of the law. Ben knew Hack was used on a few knee-breaking assignments by bookies whose clients were behind in their payments. To Savage this didn't seem so bad; some sent hoodlums with guns to make their collections.

Ben waited patiently, realizing that Hack was really hungry and apparently couldn't eat and talk at the same time. The hot, spicy Mexican food seemed to flow off the platter as Beardon enjoyed his food to the max. Ben ate his burrito and washed it down with a tall glass of iced tea, then urged Hack to have some dessert.

"Let's try some of that fried ice cream. It ain't bad."

Ben ordered the ice cream, and by the time the waitress brought it, Hack was talking steadily.

"What you need, Ben?"

"Maybe I just need your company."

Beardon's broken mouth stretched into a wide grin. "Yeah, sure."

"Seriously, Hack," Ben said, "I'm having some trouble finding out what I need to know about Lenny Valentine."

Hack's expression instantly changed. "Stay away from him, Ben. He's one of the real bad ones."

"What's he doing?"

"Well, he ain't dealin' dope no more. He's buyin' up property—nobody knows what for. Some of the spots he's buyin' is pretty low-rent."

"Maybe he's gone legit."

"Not him. My old man said Valentine bought a mule once that he knew wouldn't live much longer, just so he could kick him a time or two. You watch him, Ben. There's some guys pushin' up daisies that didn't." Hack took a large spoonful of ice cream and let it soak its way down his throat. His sharp brown eyes went back to studying Savage. "Funny you should ask about him. He put the skids on a buddy of mine not too long ago."

"What'd he do?"

"My friend's name was Trumbo. We was in jail together for a while. A real good guy. He met this woman named Bertha through the mail, while he was still doin' his time. They wrote each other, and she come to visit him. I never could understand that."

"Understand what, Hack?"

"Why a woman would start up a romance with a guy in the clink. A lot of women do it though. The inmates know just what these lonesome women want to hear. They ought to be romance writers. One guy was sixty-five years old, but he was gettin' mail and money from four or five women all over the country. He was gonna get out soon, and he was gonna marry one of 'em. Hack shook his head and moved his shoulders restlessly. "It seems like women would have better sense."

"What about your friend?"

"Oh, yeah. His name was Jack Trumbo. Anyhow, this woman named Bertha wrote him, and she came to visit a few times. Finally she married him while he was still in jail. I got to stand up with him. The chaplain arranged it all. She was a pretty good woman too."

"So what happened to Trumbo?"

"He bought a place when he got out, cleaned it up, and started a washateria. Done good too. But then Jack had to sell it."

"What do you mean he *had* to sell?"

"You know, Ben—somebody put pressure on him."

"Valentine?"

"His name never came up, but it was him all right. When Jack refused to sell, they sent some guys around and busted him up."

"Did he blow the whistle?"

"Not Jack. Who would listen to an ex-con anyways?"

"What's he doing now?"

"Him and Bertha got a place in Belle Chasse. About five miles past Gretna. You know the place?"

"Yeah, I know."

A ghostly smile came onto Hack's face, and his gravelly voice rattled out, "Funny thing—his wife's a blacksmith."

Savage blinked with surprise. "You mean . . . she shoes horses?"

"That's right, Ben. A real blacksmith." He leaned back, grabbed a toothpick, and began to pick his teeth. "It shouldn't be too hard for a trained detective like you to find a female blacksmith. Couldn't be too many in Belle Chasse."

◆ ◆ ◆

Savage crossed the arching bridge and took Highway 18, heading for Gretna. He stopped once and looked at a phone book, but there was no blacksmith listed. He went into a convenience store and asked the clerk, "I don't suppose you know where the Trumbos live?"

"Jack Trumbo?" The girl was overweight and had a rather poor complexion, but she had a pair of lovely, warm brown eyes and a well-shaped mouth. "Sure I know. His wife Bertha is a blacksmith."

"That's right."

"Go on down to the second light and turn left. It's way off the road really, back in swamp country. Everybody knows the Trumbos out that way."

"Thanks a lot." Ben gave her his best smile and winked, then went back to his car. He had to ask twice more, but finally he saw a sign that said, "Blacksmith." He pulled up in front of the old barn, noting that the house beside it had been freshly painted and that someone had done a good job of planting flowers in an orderly fashion. The house was made of cypress; to the left was a large pasture where several horses were grazing.

The door to the barn was open, and he could hear a ringing sound of metal being struck. When he entered, the darkness troubled him for a moment as he came in out of the bright sun. But then he made out a figure standing at an anvil banging on a bar.

He stood there waiting, and when the woman stopped, he said, "You Mrs. Trumbo?"

The woman turned quickly. She was wearing a leather apron that came down to her knees. She had a mop of deep blonde hair, and her eyes were alert as she said, "Didn't hear you come in. Can I help you?"

"My name's Savage. Mrs. Trumbo, isn't it?"

"Yes. Just call me Bertha."

"Well, I'm Ben. I'm a private detective."

The woman stared at him, then grinned. "I've never met a private detective before."

"I never met a lady blacksmith before."

"I guess we're both endangered species. Let's go sit on the porch."

"I don't want to interrupt your work."

"I'm all through here for a while. How did you find me?"

"A fellow named Hack Beardon told me about you and your husband—and your bad luck."

Something changed in the woman's expression, and she studied Ben carefully. "Wasn't much luck involved with it. Come on."

The two went up on the front porch where she motioned him toward a wicker chair. "I'll get us some tea."

Ben sat down, and the woman came back soon with a full pitcher of iced tea. He noticed the strength of her forearm; her hands were as hard and callused as any man's he had ever seen.

The woman laughed. "Everybody's curious why a woman would want to be a blacksmith."

"It *is* a little bit unusual. As a matter of fact, I don't think I even know a male blacksmith. How did you get into this kind of work?"

"Oh, I was about fourteen." Bertha Trumbo sat down and sipped her tea. "My uncle was a blacksmith. I would hang out at the shop, and he taught me a few things. Then after I grew up I tried being a sales clerk, but I didn't like it. So I kept coming back to my uncle's. He owned this place. Back then a horseshoe cost two dollars and a trim cost a dollar. Today shoes cost—hmm, forty-five to 125 dollars a horse."

"That much?"

"Yep. Anyway, my uncle taught me, and I like the job."

"Your husband's not here?"

"No. He went to the dog races."

"Hack said he got beat up."

A hardness came across the woman's face. She was a sweet-faced woman, fairly attractive, although oversized. "I wanted to shoot 'em, but I didn't have a gun. I tried to help Jack, but they knocked me down too."

"Who was it?"

"I don't remember their names, but they was just frontin' for Lenny Valentine anyway. Everybody knows he's tryin' to buy up all the property in those blocks. Somebody ought to shoot him."

"Somebody probably will someday. What did his goons say Valentine wanted with the property?"

"They didn't say, but they weren't regular businessmen, that's for sure. They carried guns. They tried to act straight, but they weren't."

"You go to the police?"

"No. What good would that do? Valentine's a big man, and we're nobodies."

"You're not nobody, Bertha. Anybody who can shoe a horse is not a nobody."

The two talked for some time, and after Ben had obtained all the information he could, he said, "You ever get hurt in your work?"

"Sure. Anybody that works around horses gets hurt. They step on your feet, and sometimes they kick. I shoe about ten horses a day, and I like doing it. Jack's had a rough time, but he's almost over that beating he took. I'm gonna take care of him. He's a good man. Did Hack tell you how we met?"

"Yes, he told me."

Bertha searched his face for something, Ben wasn't sure what. "People think a woman is crazy to marry a prisoner, but I'd prayed for a husband for a long time, and that's just the way it worked out."

Ben smiled. He liked this woman. "Jack's a lucky guy," he said. He stood to his feet. "Thanks for the tea." He hesitated for a moment, then said, "Would you testify if we get more to go with this?"

"You mean you might find a way to get Valentine?"

"We might."

"Yes, I'd testify. Just let me know. That man shouldn't be allowed to hurt people like he does."

Ben left thinking about Bertha and Jack Trumbo. He had always been irritated with women who got involved with inmates, but this woman was the real goods. As he sped back toward the city, he thought, *I hope you and Jack make it, Bertha.*

Seven

AN OLD ACQUAINTANCE

Closing her eyes, Dani leaned back in the worn office chair and tried to organize her thoughts. She had always been good with numbers and adept at arranging business matters. But now, after spending almost two hours at the church going over the books of The Greater Fire Baptized Church of Jesus Christ, she had reached an impasse.

The room was quiet except for a large fly that persisted in buzzing high around the room, then dive-bombing her. The old air conditioner barely managed to circulate the hot air. Reverend Flatt's battered old desk had been painted a gruesome shade of pink for some reason—perhaps that was the only paint available. The desk had three drawers on each side, all of them stuck shut in the humid air. Dani had further aggravated herself by tugging at one of the drawers so hard that the handle came off in her hand. The walls were covered with calendars and pictures reflecting Reverend Flatt's taste, many of them from funeral homes, and almost all of them faded with age.

Dani had gone through the contents of a four-drawer filing cabinet. Reverend Flatt had been faithful to save *everything*. Not only bills, invoices, and matters pertaining to the business of the church, but letters, notes, old bulletins from his first days at another church, all mixed in with pictures and mementos of the life of the Flatts.

Dani had worked very hard and finally had succeeded in sorting out those items that pertained to the immediate financial needs of the church. Using the calculator she always carried in her purse, she had fought courageously to bring some sort of order out of the chaos, but after a hard struggle she was ready to give up.

"There's no way that I can make anything out of Brother Flatt's figures," Dani whispered aloud just as a loud knock sounded on the door. Sitting up, she brushed her hair into place, reached for a tissue, and mopped the perspiration from her forehead. "Come in," she said as cheerfully as she could.

The door opened, and Jarvo Davis came in with the light, bouncing walk that so characterized him. "Hey, preacher lady!" he grinned, his teeth white and flashing against his dark skin. "We all ready to begin today's Sunday service. There's a good crowd because everybody missed not having church for the last few days."

Dani flinched slightly at the words. She wasn't sure she was up to this. She put her hands flat on the desk, pressed hard against them, then shook her head. "I'm just not ready, Jarvo. I can't do it."

Jarvo gave her a surprised glance. He was a bundle of energy and, by God's mercy, had escaped the ravages of his previous addictions. Growing up in the Calliope Project, he had somehow managed to survive, although he had fallen into dealing drugs. He had been converted soundly under the preaching of Reverend Alvin Flatt, and he longed to be a preacher himself. Coming over to stand across the desk, he gave one of his little sideways hops and flung his hands out in excitement. "You're gonna do great, Miss Dani. Everybody's excited about it. The place is packed!"

Jarvo's excitement intimidated Dani even further. "I don't suppose you'd care to preach for me, would you, Jarvo?"

"Oh no, not this time. Course I wants all the practice I can get, but this is your first sermon, and we're all waitin' to hear you. Hey, I'll bet you're gonna get out of control!"

Dani laughed at the expression. "You think that would be good?"

"What I mean by that is, in some churches everything's all *under* control. It's all spelled out on a piece of paper, and everybody's afraid they're going to get off by a few minutes, that somethin' will interrupt. But I think God likes it when our little plans don't

work out. One time we had it all planned to have a nice preachin'
service and had a good band in here and everythin'. It was all
planned down to the last minute." Jarvo's white teeth gleamed,
and he snapped his fingers with a sharp clicking sound. "But it
didn't happen that way. Brother Flatt got up to preach and couldn't
say a word. Then the Spirit of God fell on the place, and everybody
began cryin', and some people just fell on their faces. Never did
get no preachin' that night, but I reckon there must have been fifty
people come into the kingdom. That's what I mean. Maybe that'll
happen this morning."

Dani smiled wanly and got to her feet. "I hope so. But I'm not
a preacher, Jarvo."

Jarvo shifted and fidgeted for a moment as Dani came around,
then said, "Miss Dani, I always pray for Reverend Flatt before he
preaches. You reckon I could pray for you?"

"Please do," Dani said gratefully.

Reaching up, Jarvo put his hands on her shoulders. He prayed
a fervent prayer for the power of God to fall upon Dani, and when
he ended with a loud "Amen and glory to God and the Lamb forever!" she smiled. "Well, if my preaching is as good as your praying, we'll really see something."

"It's gonna be better than that. Come on now. I hear the band
warmin' up."

Dani and Jarvo walked out of the small office, and as they
entered the auditorium, Dani saw that the place was full. The band
began to play, and as she moved forward, she was conscious of
many eyes upon her. She knew she was totally unable to do what
Reverend Alvin Flatt did, and fear came over her. It swept over her
like a wave, and suddenly she wanted to turn and flee, to run away,
leaving The Greater Fire Baptized Church of Jesus Christ without a
preacher!

But as she reached the low platform, Jarvo, after grabbing his
drumsticks, saw her face and knew what to do. He was a sharp
young man, and he came forward and whispered, "God has not
given us the spirit of fear but of power, love, and a sound mind.

God's gonna be with you, Miss Dani." He went at once to the drums and nodded. Carla Jo Ingram struck a chord on her guitar. "Let's go, fellas!" she said, and instantly the band seemed to explode. Tom Bench, freckles and all, stood tall and strong, playing bass, and Jarvo beat the drums so fast that the sticks were a blur.

Dani was learning once more to be sensitive to the presence of God and His Spirit. She had been in cathedrals and mega-churches that cost millions of dollars and yet lacked a demonstration of the power of God. But here in this low-ceilinged, old storage building, dusty and molded with age, she suddenly felt that God was truly there with her. She didn't know the song the people were singing, but Carla Jo's clear voice rang out as she sang into her microphone. The battered speakers picked it up, and the simple words soon implanted themselves in Dani as the congregation sang them several times.

The song service greatly encouraged Dani. As she sang, she faced the congregation, and her eyes moved from face to face. There were many dark faces there, some black as night, others olive, and probably half a dozen nationalities in all. Some of the faces were ravaged with disease, but many more were filled with a hope that Dani knew had brought them to this place. It was a poor congregation indeed, but Dani suddenly knew that God had put her here to help them.

The singing lasted for thirty minutes. "That was good singin'. I know it pleased the Lord," Jarvo said, smiling. Sweat glistened on his brow, and his clothes were damp, for there was no air conditioning but only hand fans that beat the hot air futilely. "We've got a special treat. Brother Flatt is doin' good, and he covets your prayers. He'll be back with us as soon as the Lord raises him up." Turning slightly, he waved the microphone and said, "We got a new preacher this morning. This is Reverend Dani Ross. She's gonna fill in for Brother Flatt until the Lord raises him up. Why don't you give a clap offering to God for sending such a fine lady preacher to tell us the Word of God."

Dani moved forward nervously, her Bible in her hand. Now that the moment had come, she was unsure how she would react. But as she surveyed the faces of the congregation, a spirit of love came upon her. Suddenly this wasn't just a speaking engagement; she truly felt love and concern for these people. When the applause died down, she smiled and began to speak into the microphone. It was rather awkward holding her Bible in one hand and the microphone in the other. The pulpit was rather battered and tilted slightly, but she laid her Bible on it anyway. "I'm sure we're all praying a lot for Brother Flatt to be back with us soon. He asked me if I would come and help until that day comes, and I promised that I would. But Brother Jarvo is a little bit wrong in his introductions. I'm not a preacher. I'm just a believer. I don't have any title such as 'Reverend' or 'Bishop' or anything like that. I come to speak to you today because of the one thing we have in common—Jesus Christ is the Lord of my life, just as He is the Lord of your lives. Most of you, that is."

Dani briefly expressed her pleasure at being there, then said, "I'm reminded of a story I heard once about an Indian preacher. He preached for a congregation, and the offering was given to him that day. Someone asked him how much it was. 'Two dollars,' the Indian preacher said. 'Well, that's not much money,' came the reply. The Indian minister simply said, 'Okay. I not much preach.'"

She waited until the laughter died down, then said, "That's me I think. Not much preach, but it's free. I don't have the nerve to charge for what I'm doing right now. One thing I am, though, is an accountant, a bookkeeper of sorts, and I would encourage you to share and have a part in the offering. Your gifts will not go to me but for the ministry here at this church. This work needs support, and God will reward you as you give." She hesitated, not wanting to say any more about money, then plunged right into her message. "I am not a professor or a theologian. So this morning I am going to simply read a portion of Scripture and make a few remarks. If you have a Bible, turn to Matthew chapter 20, beginning at verse 30 and going to the end of the chapter." She waited until the rustling of the leaves of many Bibles quieted and then began to read.

"'And, behold, two blind men sitting by the wayside, when they heard that Jesus passed by, cried out, saying, Have mercy on us, O Lord, thou Son of David. And the multitude rebuked them, because they should hold their peace; but they cried the more, saying, Have mercy on us, O Lord, thou Son of David. And Jesus stood still, and called them, and said, What will ye that I shall do unto you? They say unto him, Lord, that our eyes may be opened. So Jesus had compassion on them, and touched their eyes; and immediately their eyes received sight, and they followed him.'"

As Dani finished reading, she said, "Would you pray with me?" Everyone, she saw, bowed their heads, and she followed suit. "O God," she said, "many of us have great needs this morning. Needs that can't be met except in You. So as we read these words and look up to You, I pray, dear Lord, that You would meet the needs of my own life and the needs of every person in this service today, and I ask this in the name of Jesus."

A loud amen rolled like a wave over the congregation, and Dani began to speak with confidence. She held the microphone in her right hand and from time to time gestured with her left. "This is a typical incident in the life of the Lord Jesus. I doubt if any of us could imagine Jesus on a desert island all alone. That is so unlike the picture that we get out of the Gospels. Of course, from time to time He would withdraw from the multitudes and go off alone to pray to His Father. But He always came back and threw Himself into the busy life that He lived in the sight of men.

"In this particular incident I would call your attention first to the fact that there were people here who had a great need. It mentions two blind men, and being blind in the days of Jesus was even more difficult than in our own day. Now private and federal agencies help those who have lost their sight, but that was not so in that day. The blind had no option but to go out and beg. It was a hard, difficult life. In a way these two blind men represent each one of us in some way or other. Many of us who are not blind have needs that are just as pressing. Some are bound by drugs; others are the victims of abuse. Poverty stalks our land even in these days of plenty. Some have never gone to bed at night with a full stomach."

Dani saw heads nodding with agreement and knew she had hit a nerve. She went on to talk about how hopeless the blind men must have felt. Then she lifted her voice and said, "But verse 30 says, 'When they heard that Jesus passed by they cried out saying, Have mercy on us, O Lord, thou son of David.'

"Isn't that marvelous? It is to me." Dani's eyes sparkled. She had no idea what an attractive picture she made. She was wearing a simple dark gray dress with very little jewelry—only two small pearl earrings. But her appearance was full of life as she talked about how wonderful it was that those men had someone to call on, just as people do today.

"I want you to notice that verse 31 says that the multitude ordered them to hold their peace. There'll always be something or someone that will keep you from coming to God, but I want to urge you this morning—don't listen! When your friends make fun of you, ignore them. They need God too. Run to Jesus. These two blind men, when an obstacle came, simply cried out louder and more urgently saying, 'Have mercy on us, O Lord, thou son of David.'"

Amens resounded through the congregation as many felt the presence of the Lord. Dani went on to talk about how Jesus stopped and called out to the two blind men. "Then He asked them a most peculiar question in verse 32: 'What will ye that I shall do unto you?'" She put her hand on the Bible, held the microphone close to her lips, and spoke almost conversationally. Everyone listened quietly. "That sounds like a rather foolish question, doesn't it? I mean, Jesus knew they were blind. He knew all about them, as He knows about all of us. And yet He asked, 'What will ye that I shall do unto you?' Wouldn't it have been foolish if they had said, 'We want a new donkey' or 'We want a new suit of clothes'? That's the trouble with most of us today. We ask God for the wrong things. They asked for the *right* thing. They needed sight, and that's why they answered, 'O Lord, open our eyes so we can see like other people.'"

Dani spoke for some time about how important it is to realize that there are two kinds of needs—superficial and real. She spoke about the sadness of people wasting their lives on trying to meet the wrong needs when their real need is spiritual, in their hearts.

She glanced down at her watch and was shocked to see that she had been speaking for over thirty minutes. Not wanting to go on too long, she said, "I want you to look at verse 34, the last verse of this chapter. Every time I read it, it brings tears to my eyes, although it's so simple. 'Jesus had compassion on them.'" Dani felt the tears in her eyes. "The fact that Jesus, the Creator of the universe, has compassion on us—that always touches my heart. He had compassion on me when I was lost and undone, and He came to my heart, and He drew me to Him, and He forgave me of all of my sins. He put my feet on solid rock, and now each day I have to look to Him to keep me from falling and to protect me from the tragedies that surround me. I don't know how to give an invitation," she said quietly, "but I do know two things. First, I know that many of you out there have a need. Your life is fragmented, broken to pieces. And you're sitting amidst the wreckage thinking, 'There's no help for me. I've gone too far.' But there is help for you, for Jesus still has compassion. That's the second thing. You have a need, but Jesus has compassion; He cares. These blind men received their sight, and Jesus can meet your need too. He can give you the peace or courage or guidance or provision you need, and most of all, forgiveness of all your sins. I'm going to ask you to come forward so Brother Jarvo and I and others can pray with you. If you will have faith in God, you will receive what you need, just as those blind men received their sight."

Dani hadn't noticed, but the musicians had moved into place. They began playing softly, and Carla Jo Ingram, an ex-prostitute, began singing with her sweet but powerful voice. It was one of the old hymns Dani had grown up with—"Softly and tenderly Jesus is calling." The old words, sung so many times in so many churches and camp meetings, were clear and sweet, and people began to leave their seats and move to the front. Some of them simply fell on their faces before the altar. Jarvo left his drums to pray with seekers, and the elders of the church joined him.

Dani lifted her eyes and saw a woman partly hidden in the darkness way in the back. She was well-dressed and wore sunglasses and a hat that covered her brow so that her eyes and features could not be seen. She obviously wasn't poor. Dani keenly felt that this woman needed her. She took a step and started to go to her, but the woman suddenly turned and left. Dani felt a sense of loss as if she had missed some great opportunity. "God be with her," she said. "Whoever she is and whatever her needs, I pray that You will meet them."

♦ ♦ ♦

"Well, I hear you set the woods on fire."

Alvin Flatt was sitting in a chair in his hospital room wearing his tattered, faded robe, but his eyes were bright and alert. His left leg, in a cast, was resting on a low stool. Myrtle Flatt poured Dani some iced tea and served homemade pralines. Reverend Flatt had begun talking as soon as she sat down. "I got good reports—many lost sheep brought in, and the Spirit of God moving with power." Flatt beamed at her. "Have another praline."

"Oh, I'd better not. I have to watch my figure."

Flatt winked at his wife. "Go ahead; fatten up a little bit. There'll just be that much more of you for some man to love."

Dani laughed suddenly. "Well, I'll have just one more, but then I'll have to quit. I can resist anything but temptation and pralines."

"We heard about the service," Myrtle Flatt said. "I wish I could have been there. I'm comin' tonight."

"It was a good service, praise the Lord. I was scared to death, though."

"Ain't no need of that from what I hear. Everybody in the church and even out on the street's talkin' about it. You held up the Lord Jesus, and that's all anybody can do. That's what John the

Baptist did," he said excitedly. He waved his hand back and forth in the air. "All he did was say, 'Behold the Lamb of God.'"

"Now you quiet yourself, Dad," Myrtle said. "You're gonna get too excited."

"Let me alone, woman! I can get excited if I want to."

Dani nibbled at the praline, which was delicious, and finally said, "I hope you'll be able to come back soon."

"So do I. I'm frettin' too much in this here place." Reverend Flatt reached up and stroked his cavalry-style mustache, and his pale blue eyes gleamed. "Can't tell you how much Mama and me appreciate you steppin' in."

"Well, I'm doing what I can. Of course, it's going to take a miracle for the church to keep going. I've been looking over the books, and things don't look good."

"God owns all the banks," Reverend Flatt said. "He's not gonna let His work go down."

Dani wanted to have faith, and she certainly didn't want to discourage the Flatts, but just before coming there she had gone over the books again. She knew the church was in dire need, and if some cash didn't come in, the mortgage would fall through, and Lenny Valentine would be able to buy the land for a bargain price.

She stayed for over an hour, amazed at Alvin Flatt's command of both the Old and the New Testament. She finally rose and said, "I have to go now."

"The Lord be with you and protect you, missy," Reverend Flatt beamed. "I believe you've come to the kingdom for such a time as this."

◆ ◆ ◆

When Dani arrived at the office, she found Ben sitting on Angie's desk and said with some irritation, "You'll have to start paying rent if you keep hanging around here. Why aren't you out working?"

Ben moved off the desk and winked at Angie. "The boss has been eatin' raw meat again."

"Never mind that. Come into my office and update me on all our cases so I can see if we can pay the bills this month."

As Ben gave her his reports, she saw that he had organized them as well as she could have herself. She hadn't realized he had this kind of ability and looked at him with a new respect. "Well, congratulations, Mr. Savage. I didn't know you were the management type."

"I'm not." Ben shrugged. "I don't like it. I want you to come back and be the boss and just let me be the hired muscle."

Dani sat down, and a look of discouragement swept over her.

"What's wrong? You got the mullygrubs?"

Dani managed to smile faintly. "That sounds like what I've got all right. Oh, Ben, things look so hopeless!"

Savage gave her a surprised look. He had seen Dani Ross in some tight situations, and rarely did she show any discouragement. But now he saw that her shoulders were slumping, and she was gnawing on her lower lip, a sure indicator, he had learned, of frustration.

"Want a shoulder to cry on?" he suggested hopefully.

Dani glanced up and tried to smile. "Thanks for the offer. I just might take you up on it."

The buzzer on Dani's desk sounded, and when she flipped the switch she said, "What is it, Angie?"

"Mr. Lex Noon to see you."

Dani and Ben exchanged serious glances. She answered, "Send him right in."

"I wonder what he wants," Ben murmured. He turned to the door, and when Noon came through, Ben moved slightly back against the wall, facing Noon. His eyes were half-hooded as he examined the face of the killer.

"Hello, Miss Ross," Noon said. He was wearing a white shirt and charcoal slacks. There was an air of cold confidence about him as always. He looked coldly at Savage but didn't speak to him.

"Hello, Mr. Noon. What can I do for you?" Dani inquired.

Noon smiled without changing the expression in his eyes. "Mr. Valentine would like to see you."

"You came to make an appointment?" Dani asked.

"He's a little busy. He'd like to see you at his place if it's not too much trouble."

Dani studied Noon's face, then remembered what Ben had said about him—that he was a killer without a conscience. "He thinks no more of a human life than you or I would think of a fly," Ben had said. She shifted her glance to Savage, who nodded slightly. "You mean right now?"

"Yes. I have a car outside. It shouldn't take too long."

Dani rose from her seat. "All right." She went out the door followed by the two men, and when the trio reached the street she saw a long black limousine. Noon opened the door, and Dani got in, followed by Savage. Noon stepped inside after them, then shut the door. "All right, Benny."

As the limousine pulled away from the curb, Dani looked around and remarked, "Everything in here but a swimming pool."

"It's pretty fancy all right," Noon said. "I don't care for it myself."

"Your boss does though," Savage said. He had placed himself directly across from Noon. There was an alertness about him, Dani noticed, the same kind of care a man would have when in a cage with an extremely powerful and dangerous animal. She took her cue from Ben and studied Noon carefully. "Do you have any idea what this is all about, Mr. Noon?"

"Mr. Valentine doesn't take me into his confidence that much. I just work for him."

"How's business?" Ben asked.

A smile touched the hoodlum's thin lips. "We're doing very well, thank you." He hesitated for a moment, and then his eyes locked with Ben's. "Mr. Valentine likes it when things go smoothly. When they don't, he, uh, well, he gets upset."

Ben tilted his head to one side and studied the hired killer. "And when he gets upset, you take over. Is that right, Lex?"

"Pretty much."

Dani listened, knowing the exchange was potentially deadly.

Both men, she knew, were quick and agile. Ben was not vicious, but she knew he would do whatever was necessary to protect himself and especially her.

Wanting to deflect the conflict, she quickly asked, "Do you like baseball?"

"No. Do you?"

"Not much. I go to a game now and then."

The conversation continued in that vein, but all of them knew there was more going on inside the limo than small talk.

When the car pulled up in front of Valentine's house, Noon stepped out, opened and held the door for Dani and Savage, then said, "We shouldn't be too long, Benny."

"Yes, Mr. Noon."

Dani followed Noon and was in turn trailed by Savage. When they arrived at the huge indoor pool, Valentine was sitting at a table alone. Over to one side was the same woman Dani had seen before. Dani realized this was the same woman she'd seen in church. She wasn't dressed the same but wore the same sunglasses, and Dani recognized the hair. Lex announced, "Here they are, Mr. Valentine."

"Thanks for coming here. I could have come to see you, but I've been a little busy lately."

Dani smiled slightly. "I can see that," she said somewhat sarcastically.

Valentine gave her a sharp look, then laughed. "Okay, so I'm lazy. Whatever. Have a seat. George, let's have a little service here." One of the servants came over and nodded at the two.

"What'll you have? Just name it, George can fix it."

"Iced tea for me," Dani said.

"Do you have any decaf coffee?" Ben asked.

"Yes, sir."

"I don't care if it's good or bad, just make it big and hot."

The servant grinned. "Yes, sir."

Dani sat across from Valentine. He had been swimming, and his black hair was plastered down, his skin damp with water and perspiration.

"I won't keep you long, Miss Ross," Valentine said. "I've been thinking, and it seems to me that we might get together on a little business deal."

"What's the deal?" Dani said sharply.

"You get right down to business, don't you? All right, here it is— I want to do something big right in the heart of town . . ."

Dani was listening carefully to everything Valentine said. She knew she had to tread carefully. He was crafty, vicious, and capable of anything just to get his way. At the same time she was aware that Ben had turned to face Lex Noon. The two men had not taken their eyes off one another. They both acted as if they were keeping an eye on a bomb that could go off at any moment.

"Here's the deal," Valentine said. "I'm buying up property in town, and I'm gonna tear down most of it and make a new mall. It'll be like nothing else. Minneapolis has the biggest shopping mall in the world. I ain't tryin' to beat that, but I do have big plans. Lex, bring them papers over here, will you?"

"Yes, Mr. Valentine." Lex disappeared, and the drinks arrived. "You want sugar and cream for that, sir?"

"Real men just take it black," he replied.

Noon came back with a large roll of white paper under his arm. He laid it out on the table and pinned the edges down with some fancy paperweights. Heaving himself out of his chair, Valentine came over and waved his hand at it. "That's what the architect has come up with. You can see it's got everything—cafes, restaurants, shops, even a place to leave the kiddies with paid help. It'll knock out a lot of the ugly part of the city. You'd be in favor of that, wouldn't you, Miss Ross?"

Dani was studying the map. It was a big operation, undoubtedly worth millions of dollars. Lifting her eyes, she said, "Impressive, Mr. Valentine. But I wonder . . ."

"You wonder what?"

"I'm careful about tearing old things down. Once they're down, you can never replace them. In Atlanta there's not a single trace of the battles that took place there during the Civil War. *Nothing* was saved. People would liked to have kept some reminders, you know what I mean?"

Valentine stared at her. "These are slums I'm talkin' about. Who wants to celebrate a slum?"

"Some buildings there go back a hundred years or more. They need to be saved. Renovated, sure, but not torn down."

"You don't want progress then."

"Not at just any price," Dani said.

"Some of these people might not want to sell," Savage interjected. He sipped the coffee as he stared at Valentine. "I met a couple of people recently, Jack and Bertha Trumbo. They didn't want to sell."

Dani saw the name register with Valentine, but the big man said at once, "I don't know 'em, but I've offered to buy most of these places."

"The Trumbos didn't want to sell," Ben repeated quietly. "So somebody beat Jack up and scared the woman so they'd change their mind."

Lex Noon's eyes flickered toward Ben, and he said quietly, "Sometimes it's wise, Savage, to go with the flow."

"If George Washington had gone with the flow, you'd probably be speaking with an English accent and be bowing down to the king and queen." He laughed to himself as he pictured the absurd scene in his mind.

A quietness fell on the room then, and the tension was palpable. Valentine stared at the two for a while and finally said, "All right, we've been playin' games here. You know eventually I'm gonna get the property where that church is. I've offered to buy it, but that fool preacher won't sell. Go back and talk some sense into him, Miss Ross. He's gonna lose it one way or another. There are plenty of other places he can build a church."

"But God told him to build it right there," Dani said quietly.

"God ain't told nobody nothin'!" Valentine snorted. "Look, this can be easy or it can be hard. The easy way is, I'll pay any price that the preacher asks, but he refuses to set one." Valentine's eyes were hot with anger.

Dani knew it was dangerous to cross him, but she wasn't about to give in to him.

"You go back and tell him that it'd be smart just to sell and go start a church in another part of town. I'll even help him find a place if that's what he wants. I've got property all over the city."

Dani decided that it was time to go. "I'll pass the word along, but I wouldn't count on the results you want." She rose to her feet, and Ben did the same. She turned to leave, but at that moment the woman, who hadn't uttered a word, said, "Hello, Ben."

Surprised, Dani turned and saw that the woman had approached. She took off her glasses, and her eyes were fixed on Ben Savage. "It's been a long time, Ben," she said quietly.

Everyone's eyes turned to Savage. Valentine said, "You know him?"

"A long time ago I did."

Dani's gaze went to Ben, and she saw that he was pale and was staring at the woman. He seemed unable to speak but finally cleared his throat and said in a tight voice, "It's been a long time, Florrie."

Valentine stood, his gaze shifting between the two. "What's all this, Florrie? Did you two know each other?"

"A long time ago."

Dani remembered the name. Ben had told her when they were captives in madman Maxwell Stone's silo about how he had been in love with a young woman named Florrie during his circus days. And she could see now that Ben Savage still had feelings for her. She studied the woman carefully. She seemed to be in her late twenties and had very black hair, large brown eyes, and a heart-shaped face. Her lips were sensuous.

Ben acted as if he were just coming out of a trance. "Are you ready?" he said, and Dani joined him at once. They left the pool area and returned to the car. Lex Noon came with them, saying nothing. Everyone was silent as they got into the car. Noon said, "Take Miss Ross back to her office, Benny."

"Yes, sir."

Noon watched as the limo pulled away and then turned quickly and went back to the pool. He had studied the exchange carefully, and when he got back he saw anger and suspicion on Lenny Valentine's face. Florrie was speaking as Noon approached. "It was a long time ago, Lenny. Long before I knew you."

Valentine stared at her silently. When he spoke, his voice was low, but Noon heard the threat in it. "You're *my* woman. Forget about other men. Forget about Savage."

Florrie said tightly, "I have to go take care of Tommy."

Valentine's eyes followed Florrie, and he turned to say, "Do you think we can get those two to make things go our way, Lex?"

"They're pretty determined. Isn't there some way we can develop the mall without the church property?"

"No." Valentine stared at his lieutenant. "We may have to get those two out of the way. Is that a problem?"

Lex Noon thought for a moment, then shook his head. "No problem, Lenny. No problem at all."

Eight

A TIME FOR COURAGE

Ellen Ross lifted the strips of turkey bacon out of the frying pan with a spatula, placed them on a plate, then stared at the neat stack. She began to put four more pieces in the skillet, and as it sizzled, she began to fill small glasses with fresh orange juice. Suddenly two strong arms encircled her waist and squeezed her.

"Dan, stop that! I'm cooking."

"Which is more important—cooking or making a husband happy?"

"Can't I do both?" Ellen turned, put her arms around Daniel's neck, and gazed up at him fondly. She was a tall woman, but not as tall as he. The recent heart attack he had suffered had caused her to love him more than she ever had, which was considerable even before.

"No, I don't think you can do both," Daniel answered. He leaned over and kissed her on the lips, then shook his head. "It's like eating out. You can either have fancy decor or good cooking, but you can't have both. Not at the same place."

Ellen was pleased that he was jocular, for he had been rather sober lately. She knew he was worried about not getting back to the office, forcing Dani to take all of the workload on herself. She said briskly, "I'll tell you what, I'll fix breakfast first, then pay attention to you the rest of the morning."

"Sounds like a winner." Daniel glanced toward the door. "Dani's sleeping late, isn't she?"

"She came in sometime after 1 last night. She must be exhausted."

Daniel Ross always had a serious face, but now an expression of dismay stretched the muscles even tighter. The heart attack had drained him of strength, and he wasn't the man he had once been. He had always been able to do anything he pleased physically, and he hated being tied to a schedule that did not permit this. "I think I'll go down to the office today. I can at least do some of the book work."

"Angie's taking care of that, and Ben."

"I want to do *something*. I feel so useless."

Ellen reached around his waist and hugged him tighter. "You *can* do something. You can spend time with me. You know, Dan, for the first time in our marriage you're paying more attention to me than you are to the business."

"I guess that's true, isn't it? Too bad a man has to have a heart attack to show him what the real values are." He glanced upward at the sound of footsteps. "That sounds like a herd of elephants running across the floor."

"It's just Allison."

"I don't see how one fifteen-year-old can make so much noise."

"She's just a healthy girl."

"Here, let me cook the eggs," Daniel offered.

"All right. I'll make the toast and fix the grits."

As the two were preparing breakfast, Dani was slowly getting dressed. She had less interest in clothes than most women perhaps, and this morning she pulled on a pair of brushed cotton jeans and a blue shirt. She was fastening a wide leather belt around her waist when the door burst open, and Allison darted inside. "Can I come in, Dani?"

Dani smiled, for Allison was already inside. It was her way of entering a room. "Sure, honey. That's a cute outfit you have on. Is it new?"

"This old thing? I've had it for years. I got it at The Teen Shop. Do you like it?"

"I sure do." The outfit did look very good on Allison. At the age of fifteen she was just beginning to fill out; she had been worried about her looks and her figure, as most girls are when they pass from girlhood into womanhood. At times Allison fell into despair over such momentous things as a pimple on her chin. Such a tragedy was the end of the world, and nothing anyone could say could ease her sorrow.

She plopped down on the chair, watching as Dani started arranging her hair. "Have you got a minute?"

"Sure. What is it?"

"Well, there's this boy . . ."

Dani listened as Allison described a young man named Greg Holmes. Greg, it seemed, was seventeen and a combination of George Clooney, Brad Pitt, and Superman.

"Every girl in school is just gaga about him, Dani."

"He sounds really cool."

"Well, the thing is, he's asked me to go out with him."

Dani had finished her hair, and now, laying the comb and brush down, she turned to smile at her younger sister. "Well, of course he did. Why wouldn't he?"

"Oh, Dani, don't be silly! I mean he could date any girl in school, and he chose *me*."

A premonition began to grow within Dani, and she went over to brush a lock of hair back from Allison's forehead. "What's the matter? Aren't you happy about his interest?"

"Sure. It's great. But . . . well, I don't know if I ought to go out with him or not."

"Why not?"

"Well, he's—" Allison broke off, and an embarrassed look swept across her face. "I don't know if I ought to do it because—well, he's had sex with a lot of girls."

"I see." Dani hesitated, not wanting to drive Allison into an unfortunate position by preaching at her. "You could always say yes to a date but no to sex."

"That's hard sometimes, according to what some of the girls say. He's pretty insistent."

Dani wanted to launch into an impassioned sermon about the dangers of a girl putting herself into the power of such a young boy. Resisting the impulse, she said quietly, "I had the same problem with Harold Jenkins."

"Harold Jenkins?"

"Yes. He was my Greg Holmes when I was your age. All the girls were crazy over him. He was the ideal, and finally he asked me out." Dani smiled at the memory. "I spent two months' allowance buying an outfit, and I didn't sleep a wink the night before our date."

"What happened?"

"Just about what you would guess. I spent the night fighting him off. Every time we were alone he pawed at me. Eventually he drove out to the lake and parked. It was pretty grim, Allison. He meant business, and he wasn't used to having girls say no. Finally I gave him a crack across the mouth and got out of the car. He drove off and left me there, and I had to walk home, a five-mile walk late at night. But it was good for me because I learned something. Guys like that are always going to be around, and they're always interested in themselves, never in anyone else."

Allison was watching Dani carefully and didn't move for a long time. Dani wondered if she'd gone too far by telling such an obvious story, but finally Allison lifted her head, firmness in the clean lines of her jaw.

"I'm not going out with him."

"I think that's very wise, Allison. There are lots of nice guys around if you look hard enough for them."

Allison stood up and squared her shoulders, but there was regret in her eyes and something almost like fear. "All the girls will think I'm nuts. I've already told them that he asked me."

"Those who truly respect you and care about you will respect your judgment, Allison." She put her arms around her sister and held her tight. "I know it's hard, but everything worthwhile is hard.

Last week I read that the ancient Scottish poets would lie blind-folded with a stone on their bellies to compose their poems, but most of our poets today are comfortable and produce nothing worthwhile."

Dani stood there as Allison clung to her, wondering, *Was I this vulnerable when I was her age? Yes, I guess I was. I think every fifteen-year-old girl is.* "Come on. Let's go downstairs and eat some breakfast."

"All right," Allison said. She appeared to have settled the mat-ter in her mind. As the two came down to breakfast, Dani watched for some sign of grief but saw none. *Nice to be able to make that sort of shift. Most of my problems were not that simple.*

As they sat down to eat, Dani asked, "Where's Rob?"

"Oh, he's gone off with Jason on a trip to Baton Rouge," her dad answered.

Dani caught the note of disapproval in her father's voice.

"Did he go on that dumb motorcycle?"

"I'm afraid so. I wish those things were outlawed."

Rob Ross had passed into his motorcycle phase. He had man-aged to scrape together enough money to buy a well-used Harley, and he spent all of his time either working on it or riding it around at speeds entirely too fast in everyone's judgment except his own. Dani shook her head. "I wonder what the enticement is in those things?"

"What do you mean?" Allison said with a puzzled look.

"I mean . . . well, have you ever ridden on one of them?"

"No, I never have. It looks like fun though."

"They're like something out of a medieval torture chamber. They're uncomfortable. The wind seems about to blow you off. You can't relax. You're either holding onto the handlebars or onto somebody else who is holding onto the handlebars. You have to lean in the direction of the turn. You get sunburned. And if it rains, you get drenched."

"I think it's more fun that that," Allison said firmly. "At least Rob says it is."

"He has to defend his idiocy," Daniel Ross grumbled. "I got on one once behind a guy when I was about his age, and I vowed to God that if I ever got off with all my arms and legs, I'd never get on another one."

Ellen was passing out more scrambled eggs. "So what's the attraction of it?"

"Oh, the danger, I'm sure. And there's something romantic about it, I guess." Dani shrugged. "It's like climbing mountains. Only those who do it know why. To the rest of us it looks silly."

Wanting to change the subject, Ellen Ross said, "How did the service go last night?"

"Oh, it went well. A big crowd was there."

"Can I come tonight, Dani?" Allison asked eagerly.

"Sure. You can go with me. I'll come and get you."

"No need to do that," Daniel said. He put a mountain of grits in his mouth, wishing he could still eat eggs like he could before the heart attack, then mumbled, "We'll all come down."

"Don't do that. I'm already as nervous as a long-tailed cat in a room full of rocking chairs," Dani protested.

Ellen Ross laughed. "You'll just have to put up with it. I'll bring some of our friends with us too."

"How are things going? Still a tight squeeze financially?" Dan asked.

"It's *impossible*. If God doesn't work a miracle, the bank will fore-close on us in a month. I don't see any way out."

Daniel Ross stared at his daughter. She was much like him in appearance, more so than she was like her mother. She had the same rangy frame, wide shoulders (for a woman at least), and patri-cian features. "Well, hang in there, daughter. God will bring you through it."

Dani smiled and gulped down a few more bites, then rose and said, "I have to run. I have some errands to do."

"We'll see you tonight," Ellen said. "Preach a good one."

Dani hurried outside, got into the Cougar, and backed it out of the driveway. She loved the feel of the power of the car, although it was nothing like the cars some of her friends drove. She wondered what it would be like to drive a Lamborghini or a Dodge Viper, then laughed aloud. "That would be like Rob riding a motorcycle. It would just be showing off, for me at least."

As she headed down Highway 10 toward Lake Pontchartrain, she thought dourly of the the church's hopeless financial situation. At times she was almost tempted to tell Alvin Flatt to accept Valentine's offer. He could relocate the church somewhere else in the city. She had hinted at this to the skinny preacher, but he had shaken his head stubbornly. "God didn't tell me to go noplace else. I'm doin' what God says, Miss Dani. Until He tells me different, I'm stayin' right there."

The traffic grew heavy as Dani pulled onto the causeway. People were headed to work in large numbers, as always, and Dani had learned to drive defensively. As she sped along, she glanced out at the pelicans sailing parallel to the causeway. As always, she took pleasure in watching their precise formation. "They must take turns leading," she said aloud, then shook her head with a half laugh. "If I don't stop talking to myself, they'll lock me up."

Halfway across the causeway she began thinking about Ben Savage and Florrie Contino. She had been waiting, ever since Ben had first seen her, to find out more, but Ben had closed up as tight as the doors on a tomb. He wasn't a talkative man in any case, but since that moment he had become almost as silent as the Sphinx.

Dani remembered very clearly the one time Ben had ever spoken of Florrie. It had been during the period when they were trapped in a silo at the mercy of a maniac. Ben had been strong through the whole experience except one time when he seemed to break down. They had been alone, and he had told her how his father had died before he was born and that his mother was in a mental institution. And then he had begun speaking of his early life. He had been placed in an orphanage, but when he was twelve years old he was adopted by some circus performers, the Flying Rudolphos, a trapeze act. They had taught him how to be a flier, and that had become his life—a life he loved. She remembered how he had explained his relationship with Florrie. As she drove along the narrow concrete strip over the blue waters of Lake Pontchartrain, she could almost hear his voice as he spoke.

"I lived for nothing but getting up on the trapeze. I had a lot of natural ability, and so eventually Hugo, a friend of mine, was my catcher, and I was doing the flying—me and Florrie. She was a little thing, all steel wire and nerves, a niece of the Rudolphos. We grew up together along with Hugo. There were other girls, but none of them meant anything to me. It was Florrie from the beginning. She always wore white with sequins forming a rose. Because she was only nine when I came, I never thought of her as a woman until one day when I caught her as she came out of Hugo's hands. She looked at me without a word, but I loved her from that moment.

"I guess I must have been blind not to have seen it, but Hugo loved her too. For a long time I dreamed about how it would be when Florrie and I married. All I cared about was her and the flying. Then one day Tony took me aside and told me, 'Everybody knows it but you, Ben. Hugo and Florrie are in love.'

"Well, that kept eating at me, and I tried to talk myself into leaving, but I couldn't. I hated Florrie, and Hugo too, but I never showed it. One day Hugo said, 'Florrie and I are getting married next month.'"

Then came the only time she had ever known Ben to be overcome by emotion. He had put his face in his hands, and choking sobs gathered in his throat. She had asked, "Ben, what happened?"

After a painful delay he answered, "We were ready to do the last pass. Hugo would be holding Florrie. I'd do a double, and Florrie would pass under me as I came out of it. It looked dangerous, but it really wasn't. That night as I was at the top of my backswing, I saw Hugo, and I hated him! Something happened to me—and something went wrong with the timing. I came at the two of them, and I hit them like a cannonball. We all three fell, and Florrie and I hit the net. Hugo caught just the edge of it. He tried to stop himself, but he couldn't. He hit the floor and—he broke his back, Dani, and he died a week later."

Dani remembered the stark agony and tragedy in Ben's eyes as he had said this. She had put her arms around him, and he had clung to her. "It was an accident," she had whispered. "You can't punish yourself forever."

Dani knew that Ben had never gotten over the death of his friend Hugo, and she also understood clearly that he had never gotten over the youthful love he'd had for Florrie Contino.

A sense of helplessness swept over her. This was one of those things she longed to rush in and fix but could not. She shook her head and thought about Ben, about how strong and able he was, and yet his past had reached out to strike him down like a phantom. A line she had read somewhere formed in Dani's mind: *"Living is more dangerous than anything: it's terrible to be alive."*

"He has to break free of this! He's got to overcome it," Dani whispered. She couldn't say why, but she knew that somehow Florrie Contino posed a threat for Ben Savage. And she knew that in some mysterious way, what happened to Ben happened to her, Dani Ross. They had maintained a love-hate relationship ever since they had met, and she knew deep in her heart that if Ben Savage were hurt, she would be too.

She struggled futilely to drive the thoughts from her mind, finally looking up to see that she had driven almost automatically to the church. Parking the car, she walked toward the church, noting the faces of the people. She had learned to recognize the drug dealers and the hookers, and her heart went out to them. She saw five-year-old kids who, short of a miracle, would do as the others had done—go into crime, ending up dead or in the penitentiary.

As she approached the church, she thought, *If Valentine builds a mall here, that won't help these kids. They'll just be forced into another neighborhood that's as hopeless as this one.* As she greeted Jarvo, who was talking with a group of young people in front of the church, Dani suddenly knew there could be no retreat, no discharge from this war. She would go on with it no matter what the cost.

NO ESCAPE

Stepping into the office, Luke Sixkiller darted a wary glance at Captain James Hennessey. Hennessey was a tall man, lanky and lean, somewhat resembling Abraham Lincoln. He had the same gaunt face and deep-set eyes. A coarse shock of dark hair fell over his forehead. His countenance was usually sober, for years of police work had given him a cynical view of life. Nevertheless, there was also a glint of warmth in his brown eyes, and he had proved to be a fair man to all who served under him—not always a characteristic trait of a police chief in a large city.

"Sit down, Luke."

"Thanks, captain." Luke lowered himself into one of the worn, maroon leather, upholstered chairs and crossed his legs. He said nothing more, though as always when Hennessey called him into his office, he became unusually alert. This was not the first time he had been sent for. Usually Hennessey had a bone to pick with him, primarily because Sixkiller was an aggressive policeman. This trait sometimes brought him into conflict with social workers and liberal newspaper reporters. As Luke leaned back and clasped his hands together, he waited for the trouble to start.

"How have you been, Luke?"

"Fine." Sixkiller grinned. "Did you bring me in to get a progress report on my personal life?"

Hennessey was signing papers. He hesitated and looked up, then gave Luke a steady glance. "I just like to know how my men are getting along."

"Do you mean economically, socially, psychologically, or what?"

Hennessey grinned, and his whole expression lightened. He laid the pen down, then stretched mightily. He had tremendously long arms and had been an All-American basketball player at North Carolina. "Just in general, I suppose."

"I'm fine, captain." Somewhat puzzled, Luke leaned forward and asked, "Come on, captain, I know you didn't bring me in here for a casual chat."

"You're right. I've had a complaint about you."

"Nothing new about that."

"That's right too." Hennessey smiled, his face breaking into a mass of wrinkles around his eyes. His lids narrowed until they were mere slits. "We have a pretty good department around here, Luke."

"Sure we have, captain. Except for splits on religion, race, creed, color, and a fight to the death to climb up the ladder, we're just one happy family."

Hennessey shook his head in mock despair. "You Native Americans take a pretty dim outlook on things, don't you?"

"Come on, captain, let's get to it. What am I in here for? I feel like I've been called to the principal's office."

"I got a call today from the commissioner. He gave me a general hint that you're spending too much time on that church business. You know, Reverend Alvin Flatt?"

Concern showed itself in Sixkiller's eyes. "The commissioner has time to notice little things like that?"

"No, he doesn't, which worries me."

"Something's wrong here, captain."

"Yes, there is, Luke. I just don't know what. You know I don't like to be told what to do, even by the commissioner."

"My guess is that somebody pretty high up called in a favor from the commish."

"I think you're right, but I don't think it's Valentine. He doesn't have that kind of pull, not with the NOPD." The captain looked to see Luke's reaction.

"You never know about a guy like that. He has a lot of money, and money is power. Somebody real important said that one time."

"I've said it myself, but anyway, the commissioner wants you to drop the case."

"Are you ordering me to stay away from that church?"

"No, Luke. I just wanted to pass on the message." Hennessey leaned back and studied the muscular Luke Sixkiller. "I have my own theory about this. I'm a trained investigator, you know."

"So what do you think?"

"I have a feeling that you're in love with Miss Danielle Ross. Am I right?"

Sixkiller grinned widely and shook his head. "Well, you're welcome to your own opinion, which may or may not be on target, cap."

"Come on, Luke, tell me the truth. Where are you in regard to Miss Ross?"

"I'm nowhere, but it's not my fault. I keep asking her out, but she keeps turning me down. But you know us Native Americans. We never give up."

"Well, I admire your taste." Hennessey picked up his pen and held it over another paper. "Okay, you've been told, and that's all I'm going to say. But if I get another complaint, I'll have to take it seriously, Luke."

"Anything else, captain?"

"No. You can go back to your crime fighting now."

◆ ◆ ◆

Late one night Florrie Contino stood to the far right of the large window. She held the drapes open a few inches and peered into the courtyard below. The greenish glow of the mercury light illuminated the area, giving it a rather ghostly aspect. Nothing seemed to be stirring, but Florrie was well aware that the security at this place was better than at most government institutions. She leaned forward and searched the shadows near the wall. Lenny usually kept

two large Dobermans there. They were vicious animals, and Florrie
was terrified of them. She had heard the trainer say, *These dogs
aren't pets, Mr. Valentine. You don't want them getting friendly. You
want them ready to tear somebody's throat out.*

Both dogs had gotten sick two days earlier and were at the vet's,
and their absence had induced Florrie to make a decision. She had
been thinking about leaving Valentine for weeks, and she felt this
was her chance.

A sudden movement caught Florrie's eye, and she quickly drew
back, but then she saw it was only a bat. A considerable colony of
them lived somewhere nearby. The bat shuddered and threw itself
from side to side, catching mosquitoes or bugs of some kind, and
Florrie watched it until it rose and disappeared above the glow of the
mercury light.

Glancing down at her watch, Florrie saw that it was just eight
minutes past 3 A.M. She had not slept at all but had walked the
floor until she had grown weary. Lenny had gone to New York for
a day or two, and she knew tonight was her best opportunity to
make her escape.

From somewhere far overhead she heard the muted sounds of
an airplane. She pressed her face almost against the glass of the
window, but she could see nothing except three or four faint stars.
She realized she was procrastinating, dreading the moment when
she would take Tommy and try to flee this awful place. The idea of
getting away had come to her often, but it had taken her weeks to
convince herself to actually attempt it.

Letting the curtain fall back, she walked across the room sound-
lessly, her feet sinking into the thick carpet. She stood over Tommy's
crib, and by the faint glow of the night-light she saw that he had
his thumb in his mouth as he often did. Reaching out, she
smoothed his silky dark hair back from his forehead, love for her
son sweeping over her. It was the one area of tenderness left in her
life, and as her fingers ran over the head of the sleeping infant, she
was assailed by thoughts of the past. She didn't weep, for she had

cried herself out long ago; but the painful memories were almost unbearable.

Turning quickly, she walked up and down the room, waiting until 3:15, the time she had selected to get away. Familiar with the various security measures, she knew the only opportunity to leave undetected was at 3:15, when the security systems were recycling. She'd have only a minute or two, but that was enough. Since the dogs were not here, she could leave unnoticed, though fear still kept her nerves on edge.

Tommy made a faint noise, and she quickly went to look at him. He was still asleep, breathing evenly with both hands flung high above his head.

There was nothing to do but wait for the right time to make her move. Memories of the past flooded in again, and she knew that coming into contact with Ben had brought it all back. She had seen him when he came there with Dani Ross to visit Lenny. He hadn't recognized her because she was wearing sun glasses and a hat that covered her face. Her heart had nearly stopped when he walked in.

Seeing Ben Savage had brought back so many unwanted memories. Even now as she stood in the semidarkness of the room, she thought of the time when she and Ben had been fliers with the Rudolphos in the circus. That period of her life was the one bright and shining memory for Florrie. The years when she and Ben were growing up had been good and sweet. She had been innocent and in love—not with Ben, of course, but with Hugo. Strangely, she had almost forgotten what Hugo looked like, but for some reason she had never forgotten Ben. The two had never worked together after Hugo's death. Ben had simply disappeared, and Florrie had been deeply unhappy. She remembered now with a stab of pain how she had left the safety of the circus and the love of the Rudolphos and had gone to Hollywood to make a name for herself. It had been an unsuccessful move, for Hollywood, like New York, had more than enough young women wanting to become stars.

Those had been terrible years—a time she wished she could

forget. She had begun to drink heavily and had even experimented with drugs—not hard-core, but enough to frighten her. She had gone downhill morally and finally accepted a part in a play that was going on tour. The play had folded in New Orleans, leaving her stranded along with the rest of the cast.

Glancing at her watch, Florrie saw that it was nearly 3:15, and she wondered if she would have the courage to go through with this. She knew all about Lenny Valentine's cruelty and how he had no mercy on anyone who crossed him. If she were alone, she would have tried leaving long ago, but she had been afraid for Tommy.

Tommy . . . She went back and looked down upon the sleeping infant. Strangely enough, though Lenny Valentine was his father, Florrie never thought of him in that way. She knew Valentine had an obsessive desire for a son, which his wife had not been able to give him. She also knew that he planned to marry Florrie as soon as Maria died.

At one time that possibility would have appealed to her. She thought back about how he had met her when she was a hostess at a restaurant. When they first went out, she had been impressed by his money and power, though there was nothing about him physically to draw her. He had courted her, and finally she made the mistake of agreeing to live with him. She quickly found out that he was totally manipulative, obsessive, and possessive; she was merely one of his possessions. When she became pregnant, he offered to pay for an abortion. But after Tommy was born, Lenny changed his mind. "This is my son," he said. "We'll get married as soon as Maria dies."

At first this had seemed an easy way out for Florrie, but the more she found out about Lenny and the more she grew to love Tommy, the more ill-advised marriage to him seemed. Lenny would make Tommy into the same kind of man he was, and Florrie hated that idea!

Florrie looked nervously at her watch. Fourteen minutes after 3. "All right," she whispered, "it's time to go, Tommy." She hadn't bothered packing her own clothes, for she could buy new ones later.

She put her purse over her shoulder, then the diaper bag, then wrapped Tommy in a warm blanket. She had dressed him for travel before he went to sleep, and now she began walking toward the door. As quietly as she could, she opened the door, then started down the hall. Her room was on the second floor, and she was grateful for the thick carpeting in the hallway. Her heels made no noise as she descended the steps. Moving quickly, she turned toward the back door. The kitchen floor was Italian tile, and the taps of her heels sounded like a pile driver in the silent room. She almost choked with fear, but she swallowed hard and passed on through the door that led to the garage.

Closing the door behind her with her free hand, she moved through a short hallway, then stepped into the garage. She didn't dare turn any lights on. She moved toward the Mercedes, Lenny's gift to her. Suddenly the lights overhead came on with a blinding glare. Uttering a startled cry, Florrie whirled around.

"Hello, Florrie."

Lex Noon stood just inside the door that led outside from the garage. He was fully dressed, no surprise to Florrie since the man never seemed to sleep. She stared at him, her heart racing.

"Let us go, Lex," Florrie whispered.

Noon shook his head. "I can't do that, Florrie. I don't believe in much, but I'm loyal to the guy I work for. He's not a nice man, but I take his money, and I'll do what I'm told."

Florrie knew her only hope was fading. "Please, Lex. I—I can't stay here any longer."

Noon moved closer, very little expression on his face. "Look at it this way. If you give Lenny the boy, he'll probably let *you* go. All he wants is a son. He'll find somebody else to be the mother."

"I can't do that."

Noon didn't move but just stood there. "Everybody has to make the best of things, Florrie."

"I'll get away, Lex. One way or another."

"Lenny will never let you do that. You know how he is." Despite his words he felt sorry for the woman, and he saw the tears running down Florrie's face. A faint spark of compassion suddenly rose deep inside him, surprising him. For a few moments he considered letting her go, but he knew he couldn't. For better or worse he had tied himself to Lenny Valentine. In a softer voice he said, "Maria's not going to make it, and Lenny wants a son. He'll marry you if you stay here. Don't try to fight him, Florrie. You know what he's like when he's crossed."

Florrie didn't answer, having given up all hope. She knew now that she would never get away. She turned and without another word made her way back to the house. When she reached her room, she sat on the bed trembling and holding Tommy. He made soft protesting noises as she hugged him tightly.

"I'm sorry, Tommy. I'm so sorry!"

Ten

MARGIE'S LAST CHANCE

The rising flood of clear and brilliant sunlight outlined the jagged skyline of New Orleans. As Dani walked down Maribone Street toward the church, she thought about how fresh and clean everything seemed even in New Orleans—for half an hour at least. During this brief period the city was bathed in morning's freshness; the coolness was sharp and crisp. She knew that the ugliness of human beings would quickly be obvious again in the rougher sections of the city. The rich could conceal their passions, greed, and lust behind beautiful buildings, 500-dollar suits, and thousand-dollar dresses; the poor had nothing to conceal the evil in their hearts.

As she walked along the street, she noticed the upturned faces of a group of young black girls playing hopscotch. Their faces were filled with distrust, suspicion, and the beginnings of hatred. She saw a large yellow dog with an incredibly long face come slinking out of an alley. A tomcat trudged along shadowing the dog as if considering mayhem. He apparently thought better of it and turned back until he was swallowed up by the darkness of the alley.

A sound startled Dani, and glancing upward she saw a bird of some sort perched on a lamppost with his feathers fluffed up. He puffed his chest out and anthemed the day as it began in the Crescent City. Dani recalled a poem by Thomas Hardy that spoke of an ancient thrush, worn and tattered and near death; the poet said the bird sang a joyful song that it could not understand.

Reaching the hospital, Dani turned into the lobby, at this hour of the day as quiet as a cathedral. She moved to the elevator, and when it opened with a creaking sound, she got on and punched the appropriate button. As the door closed, a man and a woman hurried on. The two positioned themselves to stare at the door wordlessly. Dani wondered why people never spoke on elevators, at least in big cities. An impulse came to her then, and she turned and smiled brightly at the couple. "Good morning. It's going to be a nice day."

The couple, acting in tandem, cast their eyes sideways toward Dani, then nodded and mumbled something. It almost seemed as if they were robots with no will of their own.

When the elevator stopped, Dani got off and walked down the corridor. Nurses, nurses' aides, and interns were going about their duties looking surprisingly cheerful for people with such difficult jobs. *I could never get used to facing suffering every day*, Dani thought. *But I suppose you'd have to get used to it or you'd go insane.*

As she continued on, she thought of how much love it would take to fill all the empty lives on this one single floor of only one of the many hospitals in New Orleans. As she glanced into one room and saw a woman with white hair sitting motionless in a wheelchair, her eyes staring blankly ahead, Dani thought, *Who is she? What's her name? What's she doing here? Could I help her in any way?* She had passed by quickly and caught only a glimpse of the woman. It was one of those glimpses that she knew she would keep in her mental scrapbook. She knew the memory of that woman would return some night as she lay on her bed unable to sleep or as she drove along the Pontchartrain Causeway. Dani wondered suddenly if God was telling her to give that woman a word of encouragement. It grew so strong that she abruptly came to a stop in the middle of the hallway. *Was that thought from You, God?* Years before, an older Christian had told her, *If you feel you must do something, ask God if you are hearing His voice or merely your own. If your heart has peace about doing it, go ahead, trusting Him to use you.*

Feeling rather foolish, Dani turned and retraced her steps. She approached the room and stepped inside. "Good morning."

The elderly woman had been dozing, but she came awake instantly. She had a pair of eyes as brightly blue as the periwinkles that grew in the woods beside Dani's house. Dani saw that despite her age she was alert. "I hope you're well today," she said.

"Why, good morning, dearie. How are you?"

"I'm just fine," Dani said. "I was just passing by on my way to see a friend and wanted to wish you a good day."

"Why, how neighborly of you!" The woman had a good smile. Time and trouble had etched themselves into her features, but there was still a warmth in her that most people lacked. Dani reached into her purse and brought out a small booklet. "I'd like to leave this with you. I think you would enjoy reading it."

"What is it, dearie?"

"Oh, it's just a book about how people found the Lord in different ways. It's very interesting."

"Why, I'd be glad to read it. My son's coming to see me later. He's a minister. I'll bet you're a Christian too."

"Yes, I am," Dani said with a smile. She laid the book on the nightstand. The old woman stretched her hand out, and Dani took it. It felt weak and fragile. The bones felt no stronger than the bones of a bird to her. Yet there was life in those amazingly blue eyes. "God bless you, dearie," the woman said. "It's good to meet one of God's people. May the Lord be with you this day."

"And with you," Dani said.

She turned and left, feeling that she had done something right. It had taken her a long time to learn to be obedient to the little impulses that came to her at times. Sometimes she misread the situation, but she knew it was better to make a mistake and offend someone once in a while than to miss a chance to be a blessing to someone who needed it.

When she came to Flatt's room she knocked on the door, and at once he said, "Come on in out of the weather!" She had learned that he always called out this greeting, whether it applied to the present situation or not.

Smiling, Dani pushed the door open and saw that the preacher was wearing a red and white checkered, flannel shirt instead of a hospital gown. He had on a pair of loose-fitting pants that covered the cast on his left leg, now resting on a low stool. A pair of crutches leaned against the bed. "I'd get up and greet you, but it's a little awkward."

"That's all right, Dad," Dani said. "I just came to visit."

"Well, sit yourself down, and I'll have room service bring us some coffee."

"Room service?"

"Sure enough. There's a nurse here named Gertrude. Got her broke in right good." He pushed the button, then continued to talk rapidly, mostly about going home. He broke off when a very large, muscular nurse weighing 200 pounds or more suddenly appeared in the doorway. Her face was round, and she scowled slightly as she said, "Well, what is it this time, Mr. Flatt?"

"Me and my lady friend here would like two cups of coffee. I'll have mine black. How about you, daughter?"

"Black is fine."

"This isn't a hotel," the nurse scowled.

"Oh, come on now, Gertrude, you know you like to wait on me. I'm not askin' for cake or pie. Just for a little coffee."

The nurse stood there as if torn between two opinions. "All right," she said grudgingly, "but I don't want to hear another word out of you until noon."

"I ain't promisin' nothin'." Reverend Flatt smiled. When the nurse left, he said, "She's gonna find the Lord. I been workin' on her. I'm gettin' out tomorrow, so the Lord's gonna have to do some fast work. Pray for her, daughter."

Dani promised to do that and listened as Flatt began to tell her more about Gertrude. He knew the names of her two ex-husbands and the present one, as well as the ages and conditions of her four children. He knew that her mother had emphysema in Chicago and that Gertrude was worried about her being so far away. He also knew that she had gone to a revival meeting when she was sixteen years old and had almost gotten saved.

"She'll come around. I reckon that's why I'm in this hospital—to lead Miss Gertrude to know Jesus."

Dani loved to listen to the old man. He had read books she wouldn't have dreamed he'd even heard about. Some in science, some in philosophy, and even a few modern novels. He had read numerous books dealing with the Bible. She listened for half an hour, saying little herself while they had their coffee. When Gertrude came in to check on her patient, the preacher told her he was sure she'd get saved by the next day.

"What if she's not saved by tomorrow?" Dani asked curiously after Gertrude left. "Won't your prediction's not coming true make her skeptical?"

"Never thought about it. I believe the Lord told me she's gonna be saved, and we can't withhold information, can we now, daughter?"

Dani took a deep breath and knew she had to say something about another topic. "Dad, I've been thinking about the church. There are other places in the city that need ministry too. Why don't you just sell out to Valentine and go someplace else?"

"Because God ain't told me to do that," Flatt said simply. "He told me to plant a church right there, and that's what I'm gonna do."

Dani sat there silently, knowing further argument would accomplish nothing. Flatt reached over and patted her hand. She saw that his hands were twisted with the beginnings of arthritis, and her heart went out to him. Here he was an old man, penniless and not well, with an aging wife, and yet he was willing to take on one of the most powerful men in all of Louisiana.

"Don't ever give in to your fears, daughter. The Lord Jesus ain't told us to do that. The trouble is, most of us would like to take the easy way. You remember when Jesus told Peter that He was going to Jerusalem to die, and Peter had a fit! He said, 'Lord, You can't do that!' Remember what Jesus answered?"

"Yes. He said, 'Get thee behind me, Satan.' I've always thought that was a little harsh."

"It appears that way, but Peter had missed out on the main

thing Jesus came to do. He didn't come mainly to work miracles or to heal people or to raise the dead, although he done all them things. He came to die. And here was Peter telling Jesus to try to get out of what the Father had told Him to do. I've always felt that me and Peter are a lot alike. Always in hot water. Always talkin' too much. Makin' mistakes and havin' to repent over 'em."

Flatt fell silent, and Dani didn't speak for a while. Finally he said, "I only have one brother. He got sick—cancer it was—and the doctor told him he wouldn't make it. When I talked to him about it, he said, 'I'm asking God to heal me. And if I die of this thing, I'm gonna die believin' God. With my last breath I'm gonna keep askin' God, and if He don't choose to heal me—well, that's *His* business.'"

Flatt paused, and Dani sat very still. She could hear someone out in the hall singing a Neil Diamond song, a welcome change from the usual bland piped-in music in the hospital. Finally she quietly asked, "What happened to your brother?"

"He done just what he said. He died, but he went out believin' God."

"How wonderful!" Dani whispered.

"Tim never believed just in what he saw. He always believed in what God said, and I learned something from that. If you're gonna lose, lose trustin' God. After all, you'll only lose in this life. I'm gonna keep on believin' that God is gonna give us that place, even if they pick me up and carry me out on the street. I'm gonna thank God for the victory while they're totin' me out!"

◆ ◆ ◆

Dani couldn't get Alvin Flatt's words out of her mind as she drove to the church. It was ten o'clock in the morning, and she parked and went inside to find Jarvo sweeping the floor. He came over to greet her and said, "Come here, Miss Dani. I want you to meet somebody. The kingdom of God has done got bigger."

Dani smiled at Jarvo. He was an amusing fellow, sharp and full of worldly wisdom. Streetwise and having dabbled in many things that he shouldn't have, he still had a good spirit.

Jarvo led her to the room they used to counsel people, where a young woman sat waiting. There was a tough look about her. She was wearing an especially skimpy miniskirt and a revealing blouse. She had on too much makeup, and her hair was dyed blonde.

"This here is Margie. She just done become a servant of the livin' God. Ain't that right, Margie?"

"I guess that's so." Margie sized up Dani with one brief glance. "You don't look like you belong in this part of town."

"Oh, she does! She's the preacher until Reverend Flatt gets back."

"Preacher?" Margie exclaimed. "I didn't know there were women preachers."

"Oh, I'm not really a preacher, Margie." Dani smiled. "I'm just helping hold things together until the pastor gets back. What's this about your becoming a Christian?"

"Well, it's right enough if Jarvo's tellin' me the truth."

"I'd like to hear about it," Dani said, sitting down opposite the girl. Margie had been reading from Jarvo's Bible, the only orange Bible Dani had ever seen. Jarvo had told her that he had dyed it so he could recognize it easily. "Well, I don't like to talk about it much," Margie muttered.

"You don't have to if you don't want to," Dani said quickly. "But I'd be glad to hear about it."

Dani's voice and smile seemed to encourage the young woman. She began to tell about her life. When she was sixteen she had run away from an abusive stepfather. She had hit the streets of New Orleans and had gone downhill taking the easy way—drugs and sex and all that goes with them. She shook her head saying, "I got beat up and sick of living like that, so I decided to kill myself."

The words struck Dani hard. "Kill yourself? That's tragic."

"I was dying anyway. Every morning I got up hating to get out of bed, and all day I tried to drink myself or dope myself so I couldn't feel anything. But I couldn't get rid of the pain."

Jarvo took a seat beside Margie, his black face alive with interest. "Go on and tell her what happened, Margie."

"Well, I decided to get enough pills to put myself under, and I was on my way to make a buy. But I passed by this place here, and I heard music. I stopped and listened, and somethin' changed in me. I didn't know what it was. I went inside to hear who was playin', and there was Jarvo and this little band. They were singin' about Jesus, and I don't know why, but it got to me. I began to cry, and Jarvo heard me. He came over and brought me in here, and he read to me out of the Bible. Then he prayed for me." Margie looked up, tears glistening in her eyes. "And I done what he said. I called on Jesus, and somethin' happened. I'm a mess, but I know somethin' happened when I prayed to Jesus and asked Him to forgive me."

Dani was touched by the girl's story. She began to tell her she had done the right thing. "And we'll help you, Margie. I know it's hard to change, but we'll all help. That's what this church is here for."

Margie looked at Dani, then turned toward Jarvo. Finally she dropped her head and said, "If this church hadn't been here, I would have been dead by this time."

Dani straightened up; the young woman's words had hit her hard. *If this church hadn't been here, I would have been dead by this time.* She had been questioning Flatt's determination to keep the church in this specific place, but here was a young girl who would have died if this specific church was not in this exact spot. Obviously God was in the whole situation—the band playing at that particular moment, Margie passing by and hearing the music just then. Margie had found Jesus Christ because the church was *here.*

Dani once again felt that God had spoken to her. *All right, Lord,* she said in her heart, *I'm a slow learner, but I know now that You want this church in this place, and I'm going to do all I can to keep it here. I'm going to do what Brother Flatt's brother did. I'm going to keep believing You until Lenny Valentine carries me out of here on a stretcher!*

Eleven

A LITTLE MORE PRESSURE

All of Lenny Valentine's employees had learned to read his moods even though they could be as unpredictable as the wind. Valentine could go from cheerful good humor to out-of-control rage in a matter of minutes. As George wiped the bar glasses, he kept his eye cautiously on his boss. Valentine was in a bad mood, and George knew better than to aggravate him in any way. He asked in a soft voice tinged with echoes of Mississippi, "Do you want somethin' to eat, Mr. Valentine?"

"No! Bring me a bourbon."

"Yes, sir. Comin' right up."

Valentine was sitting in his modernistic chair staring blankly at the wall opposite him. He took the bourbon from George, gulped it down, then handed the glass back without a word. His mouth was turned down in a sullen look, his eyes half-hooded and glittering fiercely. He looked up at the sound of approaching footsteps, and when the door opened and Florrie came in carrying Tommy, his countenance grew somewhat less ferocious. He walked over to where Florrie stood and gazed into the face of the child. Tommy stared back at him with wide-open eyes, already dark brown. He had a mop of dark hair also. Staring at Valentine, he reached a chubby hand upward. Lenny grinned, his mood lightening. He put his finger out, and when the infant grasped it, he said, "That's my boy." He stood there admiring the clear eyes and ruddy complexion and let the baby hang on to his forefinger. Finally he looked up to ask Florrie, "Where are you going?"

"I'm taking Tommy to the pediatrician."

"What's wrong with him?" Valentine's voice was sharp, and he stared at Florrie critically.

"Nothing's wrong with him. It's just time for his six-month checkup."

"Okay. Before you go, let me hold him a minute."

Florrie was reluctant, but she had no choice. She surrendered Tommy to Valentine, then stood watching as he walked back and forth. She knew that if there was any real affection in Valentine, it was for their son; and though in one sense that was a good thing, it was also a threat to her. She had quickly learned that Valentine had no more affection for her than for his other women. She was one of his possessions, as were all his lovers. But she knew that he saw Tommy differently. Florrie had quickly recognized how badly Valentine longed for children, particularly a son. She had heard him complain often enough about Maria's failure to give him children, especially boys, and now as he walked back and forth, dark thoughts came to her. *I'll never be able to get away. Not unless I leave Tommy behind.*

Valentine held the infant out to her and said, "Benny will take you now."

"I can put him in the car seat. Benny doesn't have to go with me." She was sure he wouldn't accept this but decided she might as well try.

"No. I don't want you going alone." He leaned forward and studied Tommy's face intensely. "He looks like me, doesn't he?"

As a matter of fact, the baby didn't look like Valentine in the least. He took all of his major characteristics from Florrie, but the underworld leader was unwilling to see this.

Without warning, Valentine grabbed Florrie's arm in a crushing grip that made her gasp. "Don't try to run out on me, Florrie. You know what I'd do if you ever did that."

Across the room Lex Noon had been standing quietly, as he usually did. The scene caught his attention, and he wondered how Florrie would handle it. His hazel eyes were inscrutable as he watched the two; he already knew the scenario that would follow.

Florrie didn't answer except to say, "You're hurting my arm, Lenny."

Valentine gave her a mean look, then released her arm and shrugged. "Lex, go with her. Carry the baby stuff. Florrie, stop off and get some toys for Tommy after he sees the doctor."

Florrie said as she turned, "Maybe a gun, so he'll be like his daddy."

Lenny Valentine was a heavy man, but he moved quickly enough to make even Noon's eyes blink. Jerking Florrie around, he slapped her across the cheek with a meaty hand. The impact left a red imprint on Florrie's face, and she gasped in pain.

"You'd better watch your mouth, baby! Now get out of here."

Florrie turned, and Noon picked up the diaper bag. He didn't speak as he led Florrie to the car. He opened the door of the Jaguar, allowed her to get inside, then said, "You don't have to go, Benny."

"Yes, Mr. Noon."

Getting behind the wheel, Lex started the engine and opened the garage door with the remote. He opened the steel gate between the stone walls the same way, then eased the Jaguar onto the street. He didn't speak except to ask the way to the pediatrician's office.

Sitting in the back, Florrie answered Noon curtly. Her face was still red with the force of Valentine's blow, and a sense of shame came over her, as it always did when he mistreated her. She glanced at Noon's face in the rearview mirror hopefully, but she knew he would never help her.

Fifteen minutes later they reached the pediatrician's office. It was a yellow building set back off the street, flanked by tall, live oaks draped with Spanish moss. Noon parked the car, got out, and opened the back door. Picking up the diaper bag, he waited for Florrie to get out. As they started down the walk, he spoke for the first time. "Don't stir him up, Florrie. I thought you'd learned what he was like. That crack about the gun could have gotten you a real beating."

"Did you tell him about my trying to get away?"

"No."

"Why not?"

"Because you didn't get away with it."

"Lex, help me!"

Noon turned his head but didn't break step. "I can't do that, Florrie." His voice was clipped and short, his mouth as tight as a steel trap. He opened the door, and they entered. He moved beside Florrie as she walked up to the desk and confirmed the appointment. She came back, and the two of them sat down in tubular steel chairs with orange padded seats. There was an array of magazines on the coffee table, but neither of them picked one up. Lex sat quietly and from time to time glanced around the room in habitual caution. He always suspected everyone of being up to something. The waiting room was half filled, and the two had to sit there for half an hour. Once Florrie said, "I have to change Tommy."

"All right." Noon rose and went with her to a room pointed out by the receptionist where there was a changing station. He stood silently as she efficiently removed the disposable diaper and quickly fastened another one on. Then she picked the baby up and kissed his chubby cheek. "That feel better, Tommy?" she whispered.

With a gurgle, Tommy doubled his fist and struck himself in the eye, then chortled as if he had done something clever. Florrie laughed and then turned to Noon, who was watching this with interest. "You never had any children, Lex?"

"Me? No. What would I be doing with a kid?"

"They're just about all we have to leave behind."

"Then I guess I'll leave nothin'. I'd hate to put a kid out in the world like it is today anyway."

Florrie had no answer for this, so she walked back into the reception room. She hadn't been seated more than five minutes when a nurse came out and called, "Mrs. Contino?"

Florrie rose and turned to ask, "Are you going in with me?"

"No, but be sure you come out the same way you go in."

Noon crossed his legs and waited patiently. A woman in her mid-thirties with red hair was seated two chairs down. She wore an expensive-looking dress, and a large solitaire diamond flashed from her left hand. "Why didn't you go into the doctor's office with your wife?"

The remark amused Lex Noon. "It makes me nervous," he said, turning to face her.

"Well, you have a beautiful baby. He looks just like you."

Noon laughed to himself. "Thanks," he said quietly. To cut off further conversation he picked up a copy of *Travel and Leisure* and began to leaf through it. The woman offered no more conversation and finally went inside when her name was called. Lex put the magazine back and sat as still as a picture for the next thirty minutes. Finally the door opened, and Florrie came out carrying Tommy. He moved forward at once, took the diaper bag, and asked, "Everything all right?"

"Yes. He's fine."

◆ ◆ ◆

The jangling of the phone caught Lenny off guard. He jerked slightly, then reached over and snatched the receiver. "Hello! Yeah, this is me. Why are you callin' so late?" He listened carefully, then said impatiently, "Yeah, yeah, I know. Listen, things are goin' good. When do we go for it?" Again he listened intently, and anger swept across his broad face. "Who told you that? This preacher ain't nothin'!"

Across the room George silently fixed a sandwich. The signs of anger on Valentine's face were clear, and as he had done many times, George thought, *I have to get away from here. Someday I'll get into trouble if I keep working for this guy, trouble I won't be able to get out of!*

"I know the jerk is sitting right in the middle of the project! You think I'm stupid? I'm telling you, I'll handle it." He shook his head as he listened and finally said, "All right, I'll nail it down, but you better be ready with the rest of the dough." Lenny listened for a moment, then snapped, "You told me that a million times. Nobody knows you're backing me. And listen, don't try to back out. That wouldn't be very smart." He slammed the receiver down, then stared at the picture on the wall. It always angered him for some reason. The Jackson Pollock painting consisted of dribbles of variously colored enameled paint thrown at random onto the canvas.

Lenny had once seen an article about Pollock, along with a picture of him at work. The painter, mounted on a ladder, was pouring paint out of enamel cans pierced with an ice pick. The article had stated that when the paint dried, Pollock chopped the canvas up into different sizes and sold the paintings for unbelievable prices. Valentine remembered paying 200,000 dollars for this one. *It's a bunch of garbage! I could do better myself.*

"George, go get Chino. He ought to be around here somewhere."

"Yes, sir."

After George left the room, Lenny pulled a beer out of the refrigerator. Pulling off the cap of the brown bottle, he drank half of it, his throat contorting like a snake swallowing a rat. He did not look particularly intelligent, but he had a steel trap for a mind. Thinking over his conversation with his "silent partner," he was not in a happy mood.

The door opened, and Chino Smith walked in. He was wearing a pair of tan gabardine twill pants and a tight-fitting T-shirt that showed off his muscular arms. "Yes, boss, what is it?"

"Sit down. I have a job for you."

Chino Smith sat down on the chair Valentine indicated and listened carefully as he got his instructions.

◆ ◆ ◆

As Florrie got out of the car, she waited until Noon shut the door, then said, "Thanks for not telling Lenny about what I did."

Noon shrugged but didn't answer. Florrie studied him for a moment, then asked, "Don't you get tired of what you do?"

The question surprised Lex. "What should I do—sell insurance?"

"At least it would be honest."

"Honest? You're a funny one to talk like that. When did you get so holy?"

"I'm a fool, that's what I am. I'd give anything to walk away from all this, but I can't. Lex, you can leave any time you want to." She waited for his reply, but he had no more expression on his face than a statue. She knew she was talking about something Lex Noon had long ago forgotten, if he had ever known it, and wearily she said, "Forget it, Lex." She turned and walked through the door, knowing that Lenny would want a report. She went at once to the living area, where Lenny was waiting. He demanded immediately, "How's the kid?"

"He's fine. No problem at all."

"That's good," Lenny said. He cocked his head to one side saying, "What toys did you get?"

"I forgot. I'll go back and get some."

"Never mind. We're going to eat out tonight."

"All right, Lenny." Glad to get away, Florrie turned and walked out of the room. As soon as she was gone, Valentine said, "Lex, we have things to talk about."

Noon followed Valentine to a small room down the hallway. It was a war room, more or less, and contained nothing but a desk and three chairs. The walls had no paintings or ornamentation whatsoever. The room was soundproof, and Noon checked it periodically to be certain it wasn't bugged.

Noon turned to Valentine and asked, "What's up?"

Valentine, however, wasn't ready to talk business. He opened the drawer of the desk, pulled out a cigar, trimmed it with a pen knife, then lit it with a platinum lighter. He put the lighter back in the drawer, shut it, then drew on the cigar, sending blue smoke upward. When it was glowing well he said, "Florrie ever say anything about me?"

Noon was caught somewhat off guard. "What do you mean?"

"What do I mean? I mean, does she ever talk to you about me?"

"Why should she talk to me? I'm just hired help."

Valentine clamped his teeth down on the cigar, considered Lex's answer, then leaned back in his chair. Noon sat down across from him and studied his boss, who appeared to have forgotten the question. Suddenly Valentine doubled his fists and pounded the surface of the desk. "She was fun at first, always the best lookin' dame in any room she went into. But now she acts like I'm poison."

Noon listened as Valentine voiced his frustrations. It was not unusual for his boss to do this. He trusted no one as much as he did Lex Noon. This was, however, the first time he had ever brought up his relationship with Florrie.

Finally Valentine grew silent. His mind worked rapidly, and Lex wasn't surprised when he said, "She'll try to get away, Lex. Keep an eye on her."

"Sure." He hesitated for a moment, then said quietly, "There's lots of women out there, Lenny. Why do you want to hang onto one who wants to get away?"

"That's my kid, that's why!" He rolled the cigar around in his mouth nervously, took it out, and stared at it as if it had some cryptic meaning. The silence grew in the room, filling it with an almost palpable presence. Finally Valentine said, "That's my son. I've got all this money, but what's going to happen to it when I'm gone? I need a family. I want Tommy, and I want more kids." He jammed the cigar back into his mouth, saying, "Too bad about Maria. I'm really sorry, but there hasn't been anything between us for years. When she dies, I'll marry Florrie. That's the way it is."

Knowing it was useless to argue with Valentine, Noon shrugged and sat there silently. He was surprised to find that he had a touch of pity for Florrie Contino. He had seen women come and go often, for Valentine always had at least one in the wings. To Noon they had been merely actresses on a stage. He had known that none of them would last long. But he was surprised to discover that he had compassion for the small, dark-haired woman. He had thought himself past that and could not decide whether to be irritated or relieved that he was still able to care about people. He pushed the subject into a back compartment of his mind and listened as Valentine abruptly changed the subject.

"I talked to my partner. Things are all set, except for that church."

"Who is this partner of yours, Lenny?"

"Can't tell you that. It's part of the deal that he be kept out of it."

Noon found that insulting. "I'm not much for talking out of school, you know."

"Sure, sure. I told him that. He said nobody could know."

"His name will be on the papers. Then people will know."

"He's smarter than that. His part of the deal is set up with a dummy corporation with some fancy name that nobody will recognize. That's not your business, Lex. But something else is."

"What is it?"

"We have to shake that preacher out of the tree."

"He's a pretty stubborn guy."

"Yeah, he is, but it's the woman who's holding things together."

"The Ross woman?"

"Sure. Flatt ain't got the money to make the mortgage payment. I found out that much. When he fails, the bank takes over, and then I'll be allowed to buy the place."

"You mean the fix is on at the bank?"

The question amused Valentine. "Sure. You think banks are owned by angels? They're as quick to make a buck as anybody else, and they ain't always too careful about how they do it."

Lex said, "Flatt might get some help. Borrow the money maybe."

"I been keepin' close tabs on him. The Ross woman is all he's got, and I sent Chino to take care of her."

Lex Noon shook his head. "Bad move, boss. Chino is stupid."

"Of course he's stupid. But he's tough, and he does what he's told."

"But if he gets caught, he'll talk. Besides, the woman has seen him before, and so has Savage. Remember?"

"Sure, I remember, but they won't even see him this time. Don't worry about it, Lex."

"Did you tell Chino to ace her?"

"No. Nothin' like that. That raises too much of a stink. I don't like killin' a woman anyway."

"First time I ever heard you state a difference."

Valentine shot a glance at Noon, wondering if the hazel-eyed killer was making fun of him.

"What do you think I am, an animal? Now listen, here's what's going to happen . . ."

Twelve

BAD NEWS

"It looks like I'm superfluous around here."

Dani had been going over the affairs of the office with Angie and had been pleased to find that things had gone very well without her. Now she glanced with satisfaction at the papers Angie had scattered all over Dani's desk. "I may as well quit and let you and Ben run the office."

Angie was pleased at the compliment. "Ben's worked hard. He doesn't like keeping up with the records and so on, but he's been real good at it anyway."

Leaning back at her desk Dani suddenly noticed something different about Angie. "You have your hair fixed differently than usual."

Self-consciously Angie reached up and touched her hair, which was much shorter now, making her face look fuller. "I found a new hairdresser. Do you really like it?"

"You look great."

Angie paused for a moment, then tentatively added, "I went to the bank yesterday to see about a loan for my surgery."

Afraid that Angie was setting herself up for a disappointment, Dani gently responded, "I wish you'd think twice about that. It's very expensive, and I don't think you need it."

"You keep on saying that, but have you noticed how scarce men are? This may be my last chance."

"Men aren't all that scarce."

Not liking Dani's words, Angie showed a rare flash of temper. "Not for you. You have Ben and Luke running around after you with their tongues hanging out."

"Nicely put, Angie."

Instantly Angie knew she had stepped over a line. "I didn't mean it that way, but with your looks you'll always have guys interested in you."

Angie was an attractive woman, but Dani knew she had some deep hurts. She'd experienced disappointment after disappointment in her choice of men. There was a pleading quality in Angie's voice as she spoke. "I'm getting older every day, and I want a home and a family and kids."

"Every woman wants that."

"Some don't, but I do."

Dani asked, "Didn't you tell me that Hal's been married before?"

"Yes. It didn't last long though."

"Why did they break up?"

"He says they just weren't compatible."

A frown crossed Dani's face. "I *hate* that word."

"What word?"

"Compatible. It's a catch-all phrase for anyone who wants to get out of a marriage. It doesn't mean anything."

Angie became defensive. "Well, sometimes two people just don't get along."

"Then they need to find that out *before* they get married. Marriage isn't like a business partnership. It's a covenant ordained by God. The man and the woman become one when they get married. Break up a business partnership and it could be messy, but breaking up a marriage is worse. It leaves cripples behind—emotional cripples. You've seen enough of that."

"Hal said his ex-wife was impossible, that nobody could live with her."

"Did she marry again?"

"I—I don't know."

Dani realized she couldn't get Angie to change if she didn't want to. Hoping to defuse the tension and leave open the possibility of talking with Angie about this on another day, she changed the subject. "This all looks good. I'm going to work for a while today and try to catch up on some loose ends."

"All right. I'll be at my desk if you need me."

As soon as Angie left, Dani crossed the room, pulled her cell phone from her purse, and called Luke Sixkiller.

"Hey, Dani. What's happening?"

"I have a favor to ask."

"Let me have it."

"I'd like to know something about a policeman named Hal Borman."

"Such as?"

"Well, it's a personal matter. My secretary's been dating him, and I'd just like to be sure he's an up-front guy. If you can find out anything about him, including his former marriage, and let me know, I'd appreciate it."

"Okay, Ann Landers, I'll see what I can do. I don't know him myself, but I'll ask around and get back to you."

"Thanks, Luke."

"Dinner tonight?"

"Maybe tomorrow before the service. I have to be down at the church early tonight."

"Okay. I'll pick you up at 5 tomorrow. Maybe you can call church off for a night, so we can go to the wrestling matches."

"No way!"

"Hey, it's Texas Championship Wrestling! It's educational."

"I'll bet! I'll see you tomorrow."

Dani hung up the phone and went back to her work. Five minutes later someone knocked. "Come in," she said. The door opened, and Ben stepped inside. He went over, plopped himself down in the chair, and said, "How are things with Reverend Ross?"

Dani didn't respond to his mild gibes. "I'm fine," she said. "Ben, you've done a good job keeping the office going. I appreciate it. Maybe I can squeeze a raise out for you pretty soon."

Ben smiled and started to answer, but the buzzer sounded. "What is it, Angie?" Dani asked.

"Phone call. From a man who won't give me his name."

"I'll take the call."

Picking up the phone, Dani said, "Danielle Ross speaking." A male voice she didn't recognize said, "You have problems, Miss Ross."

"Who is this?"

Ignoring the question, the man said, "You've been annoying some people, and it's got to stop."

"If you don't give me your name, I won't talk to you."

"You think a lot of your brother, Miss Ross?"

Dani was silent for a moment. Ben was watching her face intently. "What about my brother?"

"If you care for your brother, I'd suggest you back away from Alvin Flatt."

For a moment Dani couldn't answer, then she said, "You stay away from my family!"

"Your brother's had a little accident." Dani's hand tightened on the phone until her fingers grew white. "If you hurt my brother—"

"Oh, he's all right—for now. You know where the interstate crosses Pearl River?"

"Yes."

"Take a right turn just before you go onto the bridge. Go a quarter of a mile and you'll see an abandoned shack over on the right. You'll find him in there."

"If you've hurt my brother—!"

"He's all right, but if you don't back off from this church business, he won't be the next time. You have a sister too, don't you? Pretty good-lookin' kid. You wouldn't want anything bad to happen to her. Or your parents. Your old man had a heart attack not long ago. It would be too bad if somethin' shook him up, wouldn't it?" The voice grew harsher. "We're not playing, Ross! You back away from that church and leave it alone or it's curtains for your family." *Click.*

"What's wrong?" Ben demanded.

"It's Rob—he's in trouble. Come on."

◆ ◆ ◆

Dani turned the Cougar onto the narrow road that led back into a swampy-looking area. "He said it was a shack over on the right."

On their way there Savage had tried to help Dani not fear the worst but was unsuccessful. "That must be it," he said. "It's the only one I see."

Dani nodded. The small structure covered with aluminum siding sat off the road in the woods. It looked more like a hunter's cabin than anything else. The windows had been broken out, and the weeds had grown waist-high all around the yard. Dani pulled the car up and got out instantly. She moved toward the house, but Ben said, "Wait a minute. We don't know what's in there." He pulled a nine-millimeter from under his arm and said, "Let me take a look."

Dani followed closely as Ben climbed the steps. "Watch out. These steps are rotted out," he whispered. He stood to one side of the door, pulled it open with a swift gesture, then dashed inside.

Dani mounted the creaky steps and entered. Light filtered through the window on one side, and her heart nearly stopped when she saw Rob lying on the floor. As she fumbled her way through the partial darkness, she stumbled over the remnants of a broken chair and fell onto her knees. Ben was already kneeling beside the young man.

"He's tied up with some kind of wire," Ben said. Dani saw that silver duct tape covered Rob's mouth and eyes. She pulled the tape off his eyes and was relieved to see that they were wide and alert. She removed the tape from his mouth and said, "Rob, are you all right?"

"I guess so. Can you get these wires off my wrists and ankles?"

Ben pulled Rob up to a sitting position and carefully unwound the wires. "What happened, Rob?" Dani said.

"Have you got anything to drink? I'm pretty dry."

"We'll stop somewhere. Come on, let's get out of here," Ben said.

Rob blinked in the bright sunlight as the three of them got into the Cougar. "What happened?" Dani asked.

"I was on my motorcycle, and this car came along and forced me off the road."

"Where was this?" Ben asked anxiously.

"Military Road. It's a good place for trail riding. They were waiting for me though, and they knew what they were doing. You know that bluff that leads down to the creek? They forced me off right there. I pulled over to let them by, and when they came alongside, they shoved me over."

"What happened then?"

"I was scratched up, but not seriously hurt. When I started to get up, two guys came scrambling down the bank. They didn't give me a chance to say anything. One of them had a gun, and he told me to keep my mouth shut. He tied me up and put the duct tape over my eyes and mouth."

"Had you ever seen them before?"

"No, and I didn't see them this time, not really. They were both wearing ski masks."

Dani pulled back onto the highway and found a convenience store. Ben went inside and came back with a large bottle of spring water. Rob drank thirstily. "That's good," he sighed with relief. He touched his bruised face; a cut on his neck was bleeding. He murmured, "Can we go get my bike?"

"All right," Dani said. She drove as Rob directed. Rob suddenly reached into his shirt pocket. "I forgot. One of them stuck this in my pocket." He scanned it, then passed it over to Dani, who took her eyes off the road long enough to read it. It said, "Next time he'll be dead, or maybe your kid sister. Maybe your parents too."

"Who are these guys, Dani?"

Dani couldn't answer. A sense of helplessness overcame her.

Those evil men had found her most vulnerable spot. If the threat had been against her personally, she could have taken it more easily.

When they reached the spot where the motorcycle had gone over, Ben got out, saying, "I'll bring the bike home. You two go ahead."

"All right, Ben." Dani waited until he scrambled down the incline, started the bike on the third try, and climbed up the hill. She moved the Cougar out and turned back toward town.

Rob was silent for a moment, then said, "What's going on? Why did those guys do what they did?"

"I'm still trying to help Reverend Flatt, and he has a very powerful enemy."

Rob felt the bruises on his face and said, "It would have been better if they hadn't worn masks, wouldn't it? At least you'd know who to go after."

"Yes," Dani agreed. "I don't know what to do next."

Rob turned toward his sister. He put his arm around her and smiled. "You'll think of something, sis. You always do."

Thirteen

A PROSPEROUS JOURNEY

Dani put down her pen, flexed her fingers, and rubbed her fatigued eyes. From far off she could hear the sound of the church band practicing, though most of it came to her only as a muffled hum. She had left the agency office and had come to the church to go over the books again, although she knew it was a futile exercise. The monthly bills kept coming in, and the contributions were so small that there was no way to even come close to striking a balance.

The strain of working at the agency and trying to fill in for Pastor Flatt had drained Dani of much of her energy. That was partly because after she went to bed at night, she couldn't put the problems of the church aside. She had turned and twisted most of the previous night trying to come to some resolution, but there seemed to be none. Just before finally falling asleep she had prayed, *God, You have told us to cast all of our cares on You because You care for us. So I'm dumping all this on You, Lord. Let me sleep, and let me trust You for all of these needs . . .*

Now Dani's wandering thoughts were interrupted when the door opened and Jacob Gold stepped inside. "Oh, sorry, Miss Dani, I didn't know you were here."

"It's all right, Jacob." Dani smiled, having gained a real affection for the man. She studied him as he stepped inside and noted again the earlocks of a Hasidic Jew. A fine-looking man, though somewhat overweight, he was forty-seven and had iron gray hair. She knew little about him except that whenever he wasn't working in a cloth-

ing store as a salesman, he helped however he could at The Greater
Fire Baptized Church of Jesus Christ. "Sit down and have some coffee, or do you prefer tea?"

"Either one is fine, Miss Ross." Jacob put down the vacuum
cleaner and moved to take a seat in a painted blue chair. He looked
at it for a moment and shook his head. "Sometimes I think we
don't have two chairs that match in the whole church. Isn't that
an awful shade of blue?"

"Oh, I don't know." Dani smiled as she walked across the room
to pour coffee into two mugs. "I think it's a rather nice shade of
azure."

"It looks more like robin's egg blue."

"No . . ." Dani shook her head. "I don't agree. Maybe powder
blue." She smiled at Jacob and said, "Sugar free?"

Jacob shook his head fiercely. "Real men don't take sugar or
cream in their coffee. Only wimps."

Knowing Ben would heartily agree, Dani laughed and sat down.
"It's not very good coffee, but it's hot, and there's lots of it."

The two sat there sipping their coffee, and Jacob spoke eagerly
about the service to be held that night. "Three of my friends are
coming. All Jews. But they're not religious Jews."

"What does that mean, Jacob?"

"It means they're Zionists, I suppose. Their Jewishness is tied
to modern-day Israel, but they don't have a God. Not even the
God of the Old Testament."

"Was it very hard for you to come to Christ, Jacob? I've never
heard your testimony."

Gold sipped his coffee, holding the cup in both hands. For a
time he stared into the depths of the black liquid. Finally he looked
up, and there was sorrow in his dark brown eyes. "You wouldn't
believe it by looking at me now, but I was a pretty rich fellow at
one time."

"Why, of course, I'd believe it if you told me so."

"I had a good business, a wife, a son, and a daughter. I had
everything, or so I thought." Gold looked down into the coffee

cup again, studied it intently, then glanced back at Dani. "The trouble was, I didn't have God. You know how that is. You can have a lot of religion and not have God at all."

"You're right."

"I won't tell you the whole story. It's a little bit like the patriarch Job, I suppose. I began getting hammered. First I lost all my money in a bad business venture. I had to take a job selling suits for a man I had helped put in business. He enjoys having me work for him. It gives him some sort of feeling of power. Anyway, the next thing I knew, my wife left me for a man with a lot more money. I loved her very much. I still do."

Dani said quietly, "I'm sorry, Jacob. That must be very difficult for you."

"Yes, it is. Then my children . . ." A catch came into his voice, and tears rose in his eyes.

Dani got up and walked around the desk, then drew a chair closer and sat down beside him. She reached over and took his hand, and for a while the two were silent. "I'm so sorry," she said quietly.

"Thanks, Miss Dani. I know you are. You see, my son died of AIDS, and my only daughter has lost her way. She's not leading a moral life."

Dani didn't know what to say. She always felt this way when she met someone who had been thrown into a fiery trial. She had led a relatively easy life, and she didn't want to give simplistic answers or pious clichés. She simply held his hand, and the two sat quietly. Jacob looked at her and patted her hand. "Thank you for not unloading a bunch of Scriptures on me about how to bear tribulation."

"I wish I knew what to say."

"It's not words that make the difference," Jacob said quickly. "Just your sitting with me and listening to me helps me feel the strength of the Lord. That's the way it is, Miss Dani. All of us who are believers have the Lord Jesus inside of us, and we're all supposed to communicate what He is and who He is to those who are facing trouble and grief. And that's what you just did for me."

"You're a good man, Jacob. I appreciate so much what you do for the church and for Brother Flatt and his wife. They think the world of you."

Jacob Gold smiled, and despite the sorrow in his dark eyes there was pride and honor in his face. "This church is all I have, Miss Ross. I was the most miserable man in the world until I met Brother Flatt. He spent weeks with me reading the Scriptures, and I knew he loved me. He wasn't just looking for another convert. He really cared about what happened to me."

"Yes, he did, and that's the way we all should be. I'm glad you've found your way, and I pray that God will bless you richly."

Jacob said, "I can't do much. I'm not a talented man. But I can pray. And I can take up the offering. I can move the chairs around and do a little janitorial work. That's not much, but I can do it for Jesus who's done so much for me."

◆ ◆ ◆

"I get really hungry for Chinese food every now and then, Luke, don't you?"

"I get hungry for any kind of food," Luke Sixkiller said. The two had met at Hunan's for lunch, and now they were seated at a table with steaming food piled before them. Dani had chosen egg drop soup, crab legs, and a rather small portion of fried rice. The white china pitcher of steaming tea had been half emptied as the two waited for their meal, and now she poured herself another cup as she looked at Luke's plate. "Well," she said, "it looks like you've come out pretty well." Luke had piled his plate high with noodles, sesame chicken heaped on top of fried rice, several steaming vegetables, fragments of chicken fried and impaled on oversized toothpicks, samples of fried pork and deep fried shrimp, and three egg rolls.

Dani smiled at him. "The trouble with eating a meal like this is that in two or three days you get hungry again."

Luke picked up an egg roll and dipped it into the sweet and sour sauce. Carefully he brought it to his mouth, then bit it off and chewed thoughtfully. "A man has to keep his strength up to be a crime fighter. Even Superman has to eat at a place like this."

The two sat there eating slowly and savoring the food. Dani did most of the talking, telling Luke the trials she was encountering with the church. Somehow he was one of the few she could talk to. Except for her father and Ben, no man she knew listened to her so intently.

"Well, I've bored you to death with all my troubles, Luke. Now tell me yours."

"My main trouble is that a certain woman won't take me seriously."

"Oh? Which woman is that?"

"Oh, she's a good-looking broad who works over on Bourbon Street. She thinks I'm just kidding when I tell her I'm getting serious."

"Are you sure you are?"

Sixkiller picked up a square of egg fu yong, studied it, then put the whole thing in his mouth. He chewed vigorously as he spoke around it. "Of course I'm serious. I've been in love seven times, and I've been serious every time."

Dani laughed. "See there? Who could take you seriously?"

Luke's hand moved to quickly grab her arm. "I *am* serious, Dani."

Dani felt the strength flowing out of the man. He was exceptionally powerful physically, and his eyes held her attention. He had the most intent gaze of any man she had ever met, and his bronze skin seemed very dark against the white of his collar. She waited until he released her and then said rather nervously, "Keep that up and that woman will begin to think about you a little differently."

"Just what I'm hoping for."

The two finished their meal and sat drinking the scalding tea. Luke suddenly picked up his plate, set it aside, and studied the paper that served as the place mat. A red dragon breathing fire with outstretched claws occupied a fourth of the page, while around the edge were sketches of various animals—a rabbit, a tiger, an ox, a rat, and several others. Luke studied it for a moment, then said, "According to this there's a twelve-year cycle. Each year is named after a different animal, and people born in that year get the characteristics of that animal."

"What are you, Luke?"

Luke ran his eyes across the page. Underneath each animal was a list of birth years. "I'm a dragon. It says, 'You are eccentric and your life complex. You have a very passionate nature.'"

"Does it say you will marry a horse?"

"No. It says to marry a monkey or a rat late in life. Avoid the dog."

She laughed aloud. "Marry a monkey! That sounds awful," Dani said. "I don't believe any of this anyway."

"Neither do I," Luke said. "I don't believe in astrology or anything like that. I think it's dumb."

"So do I, but a lot of people run their lives by it."

The time passed quickly, and when Dani finally glanced down at her watch, her eyes opened wide. "We've been here over an hour!"

"My, how time goes by when you're having fun. By the way, Dani, we haven't found out anything yet about the two guys who roughed up Rob."

"I didn't think you would. These guys are professionals, and you had so little to go on."

Sixkiller drummed his fingers on the table. "You've got that right. It's going to be hard to find them since Rob didn't see their faces. What are you going to do about the threat?"

"I'd like to just forget it," Dani said. "But I can't do that."

"Could you ask the preacher to sell out and move to another place?"

"I've already done that, Luke. He says God told him to plant a church right at that spot and he won't do anything else."

"Well, according to you he's going to lose it all."

"I don't think so. God's going to come through somehow."

Luke thought about that for a while, then said, "What do your folks and siblings think about the threat? Are they scared?"

"I think they are, but they all said for me to stay on the case."

"Good people you've got there."

"Luke, thanks for sending the police car to park in front of the house. It's made us all feel better."

"It's all I can do, and I can't even do that for long. But I did come up with some guys who'll help on their own time."

"I've hired a man to watch the house at night too. He's really good."

"Who is it?"

"His name is Jimmy Vance. Do you know him?"

"No. Who is he?"

"Someone my dad knew. I think he was on the wrong side of the law once, but he's doing fine now. He goes out with the shrimp boats, but he stays on shore until it's time to go. He can help us with security." Dani sipped her tea. "I've never seen anybody like him. He can be invisible."

Sixkiller's eyes glinted. "What do you mean invisible?"

"I mean he stays outside the house, but you never see him. I went out for a walk last night looking for him. I looked everywhere. I was out beside the barn where I keep Biscuit, and I declare, Luke, I looked all around and he wasn't there. Then suddenly he spoke. I whirled around and there he stood. It was like magic. He just — *appeared.*"

"How'd he learn to do that?"

"I think he was in the Special Forces for a while. Anybody who tries to get by him is in for trouble."

"Does he pack heat?"

"I've never seen a gun, but I'm sure he carries one."

"He must be pretty expensive."

"Not too much. I insist on paying him something, but he's doing it mostly for Dad. We can handle the situation for a while."

"Oh, by the way, I got something on Hal Borman, that cop you asked me about."

Dani quickly asked, "What about him? Did you find out anything about his ex-marriage?"

"Yes. I got a mixed story about the marriage. He's not too close to anybody, but here's his ex-wife's name and number. You want me to talk to her?"

"No, let me do it, Luke. Thanks."

"That's all right. I haven't done that much." He looked down at the place mat again and said, "Why couldn't I have been something romantic, like a snake? Well, I guess being a dragon is better than being a monkey or a rat!"

◆ ◆ ◆

"I'm glad you came by, Miss Dani. You're just in time to have one of my wife's great delicacies."

Alvin Flatt was sitting in the tiny living room of a small apartment located four blocks from the church. Dani wanted to give him an update on the situation. Myrtle Flatt had met her at the door, ushered her in, and led her to a lumpy easy chair. The furniture was all secondhand and the worse for wear. The walls were covered with pictures of all kinds. Some were religious prints, the largest one an angel guiding two small children over a dangerous bridge. There were pictures clipped out of magazines, and some framed photographs, many of them resembling tintypes. A delicious smell filled the apartment, and Dani sat down saying, "I just had lunch. I can't eat another bite."

"You can eat this. Mama, bring Miss Ross one of them little fried apple pies, and bring me one or two while you're at it."

Myrtle disappeared through a door and came back at once with two plates. "Oh, I couldn't eat that! I'm too full," Dani protested.

"Have you ever eaten one of my wife's fried apple pies?"

"No. I didn't even know you could fry pies. I thought you baked them."

"Oh, it ain't hard," Myrtle said quickly. "You just take dried fruit, make a good crust, wrap it up in it, and fry it in deep fat."

The pie was still hot. Spearing a piece with her fork, Dani put it into her mouth. Her eyes flew open. "Why, this is delicious!"

"Best fried pie cooker in the world!" Flatt said enthusiastically. He didn't bother with a fork but simply picked up the pie and bit off an enormous mouthful.

"Dad, you're going to choke yourself, and you're eatin' too many of them pies!"

"Impossible for a man to eat too much of your good cookin', wife. Now bring us some coffee, and I'll promise to be good."

Dani ate the whole small pie and figured she'd have to fast for the rest of the day or more, knowing the pie probably contained more fat and cholesterol than the entire meal she had had at Hunan's with Luke.

"I heard about the trouble your brother had. I'm right sorry about that," Flatt said as the two drank coffee out of large white mugs.

"Well, that's just part of the whole picture, Dad."

"You may have to back off. I know how it is when your family's threatened."

"I can't do that. God told you to build a church there, and God is telling me to help you. We have to obey God rather than men. Isn't that what the Scripture says?"

"Surely. Me and Mama will have to fast and pray that your family will be all right."

Myrtle smiled at her husband. She was wearing a plain, dark green dress, and her silver hair was done up in a bun. She wore no jewelry except a plain wedding band on her left hand, and there was a warmth in her eyes as she said, "God sent you our way, dearie. We thank God for you every night and ask for His protection over you and your family."

Dani was flustered by the straightforward praise, but suddenly all the worry and the concern left her, chased away by the presence of these two elderly people who knew God so intimately. At an age when most people simply give up, they had thrown themselves into a work for God in the most dangerous part of New

Orleans. Her heart grew warm as she thought about what sort of faith that must have taken, and for a while the three simply sat there talking about the work.

Dani's eyes suddenly lit on an enlarged picture fastened to the wall. It was framed, and she walked over and looked at it. It showed three people, a younger couple and an older man. They were standing in front of what apparently was a restaurant of some kind.

"This isn't you, is it, Dad?"

"No. That's my father." Flatt struggled to his feet, grabbed his crutches, and swung his left leg, bound in a cast, with ease as he crossed the room. He stood beside Dani, and she noted again what a short man he was. She was tall for a woman, and he came barely to her shoulders. Of course she was wearing two-inch heels, and he had on worn house shoes.

"You know that pair standin' beside my dad?"

Dani studied the picture. "They look somehow familiar, but no, I don't know them."

"That's Bonnie and Clyde."

"Bonnie and Clyde! Your father knew Bonnie and Clyde?"

"Oh, he knew them well, Miss Dani. Everybody did down in that part of Louisiana. My dad had this small cafe, and I grew up there. They stopped in there and ate all the time—when they wasn't holdin' up banks, that is."

Dani stared at the picture. Flatt's father had the same features as his son, and the same small size apparently. Clyde Barrow and Bonnie Parker were smiling into the camera. Clyde had his arm around Flatt's shoulders, and his other arm around Bonnie. The faces of both Clyde and Bonnie had expressions of joy, and Dani said, "I can't believe it. Right out of history."

"My dad served them their last meal on this earth."

"Really?"

"Yeah. They came by, took breakfast with him. Dad always told me how happy they were that morning. But they got shot down that same day."

"Weren't they dangerous criminals?"

"I guess if you owned a bank they were, but to a lot of folks in the country they were sort of folk heroes. But you're right, they did tend to get violent sometimes. If they had just known Jesus, it would have been different." Flatt reached into a pocket and pulled out a large pocket watch. It was fastened to a gold chain, which was in turn fastened to one of the buttons on his vest. "Clyde gave this watch to my dad, and my dad left it to me when he passed on."

Dani studied the large watch and shook her head. "That's a museum piece."

"I don't know about that, but it keeps good time."

"Dad, you better sit down over here," Myrtle ordered. "You've stood up long enough."

Guiltily Alvin Flatt turned and made his way back to the rocking chair. He sat down reluctantly. Dani said, "I'd better get going. I'm trying to work out the financial troubles at the church, but it doesn't look good." Flatt listened as she summarized their dilemma.

Alvin Flatt reached over to the table and picked up his worn black Bible. It was tattered, and the cover was fastened on with duct tape. When he handed it to her and she opened it at random, she saw that every page was well worn and that notes were written around the edges.

"This is a very old Bible, isn't it?" Dani inquired.

"That one? Oh no. Only a couple of years old."

Dani marveled at how much the preacher must have used the Bible to put it into such a condition. "Turn to Romans 1:10." He waited until Dani found the place, then said, "Read it."

"'Making request, if by any means now at length I might have a prosperous journey by the will of God to come unto you.'" When Dani finished, she looked up. "Why did you want me to read that?"

"What kind of journey did Paul pray for?"

Dani's eyes fell to the page. "A 'prosperous' journey."

"That's right. Paul asked for a prosperous journey to Rome. I always thought Paul pretty well got what he prayed for, but just think about that journey and how it came about. Within twelve days after entering Jerusalem, Paul ran into all kinds of trouble.

The Jews stirred up all the people and laid hands on him. That's in Acts 21:27. After that the Jews intended to kill him by beating him to death. You find that in the same chapter in verse 31. Then he was bound with chains in verse 33. He was mistaken for an Egyptian who had a band of 4,000 murderers. Roman soldiers bound him with thongs and intended to scourge him with forty lashes, and the Jews banded together and bound themselves under a curse saying they wouldn't eat or drink until they had killed Paul."

Dani listened carefully and marveled again at the old man's mastery of the Bible.

"All that happened in two weeks. And remember, God was answering his prayer for a *prosperous* journey. You remember he finally got on a ship, and the ship sank. Then when he got on shore he got bit by a poisonous snake. And even after he got to Rome he was under arrest and chained to a Roman soldier for two years and kept in one of them bad prisons they had over there."

Dani listened as Flatt continued, and finally when he paused, she said, "And that was Paul's *prosperous* journey?"

"That's right, daughter. Most Christians would have decided somewhere along the way that God had gotten mixed up, that this journey wasn't what they'd asked for. But I think it was. I think Paul knew God was in it, and he was able to comfort himself with that. That's why he said in 2 Corinthians the fourth chapter in the eighth verse, 'We are troubled on every side, yet not distressed; we are perplexed, but not in despair; persecuted, but not forsaken; cast down, but not destroyed.'"

Dani felt a strange emotion rising within her. She had been bowed down with all the troubles, but as she thought about what Reverend Flatt had shown her from the Bible, she said, "I never looked at it like that."

"Most of us don't. When trouble comes, what's the first thing we do?"

Dani thought for only a moment. "We begin praying for it to go away, for God to get us out of it."

"That's exactly what we do. But sometimes the trouble is sent by

God. Why, when Lazarus died, Jesus was only a short distance away. Lazarus was His special friend. He'd stayed at his home along with his sisters Mary and Martha many times. But when they sent word to Jesus, He didn't come. So their brother died. When they met Him, the sisters both said the same thing—'Lord, if you had been here, our brother wouldn't have died.' And Jesus said, 'This sickness is not unto death but for the glory of God.'"

Myrtle Flatt spoke up. "Trouble sometimes comes in order to bring glory to God. We don't understand it, but we have to accept it by faith."

"That's right, Mama. You keep that on your mind, Miss Dani. We're in a heap of trouble right now, and there's no way out. But God makes a way for the righteous to pass through the depths of the sea. We're goin' right through the middle of a sea of tribulation, but God's going to make a path. You see if He don't."

Dani said, "Don't you ever have doubts, Dad?"

"Don't I have doubts!" He laughed and stroked his mustache. "The devil knows my address, daughter. He comes to call every now and then to tell me all kinds of lies. You know what I do? I just tell him, 'You take that to Jesus. He handles all my problems!'"

Fourteen

FAMILY AT RISK

The Studebaker uttered a loud rumble as Savage pulled off Highway 10 onto the narrower state highway. He loved the sound of power that the engine made, just as he loved the heaviness of the antique vehicle. He often said, "They made cars out of steel in those days. Now you can punch through a fender with your finger." He had always longed for a Studebaker Hawk, and when he had found this one he couldn't resist buying it and fixing it up. One dream realized, at least, in a life that had known some broken dreams.

The narrow road that turned off from the state highway led to the Ross house, but Savage stopped the car 300 yards away, pulling it onto the side of the road. He got out, locked the doors, then made his way down the lane. Overhead the moon was a circle of pure light casting its cold, silver rays down on the road as it wound on ahead of him into a sharp turn.

The large live oak trees that lined the road and arched over it met and embraced at times. Large bundles of Spanish moss were silvery in the moonlight.

A hundred yards before he got to the house, Savage turned and made his way through two clumps of second-growth timber. All the big trees that had been here when Jean Lafitte had had a high time in New Orleans were gone. Nevertheless a dense forest flanked the east side of the Ross house. He moved as quietly as he could, which was quiet indeed, then stopped and stood looking at the house. His eyes were accustomed to the night now, and the

November moon overhead drove the dark shadows away. The yard was clear; he did not see any movement. He was concerned about the safety of the Ross family, for they had become very valuable to him since he had begun to work for Dani. Not only her, but her parents and her brother and sister had all made him feel part of their family circle. He had not known anything like that growing up in an orphanage, nor later in his travels with the circus. It had been the first taste of family life he had ever experienced up close, and it somehow made him feel better just to know that there were people like that in the world. He knew that what they had was what he wanted.

He remembered an argument he'd had once with Dani when she asked him what he wanted out of life. He remembered saying, "If I can think of it, it isn't what I want." That had seemed like a profound answer to him at the time, but now he knew it was a lie. He could think of having a family, with children around him and a wife at his side, the kind of life Daniel and Ellen Ross had managed to achieve. Ben knew what he wanted, and it didn't go against any of his dreams.

His attention was suddenly drawn to a slight movement overhead. He glanced up to see a huge barn owl gliding silently through the air. He watched as the owl disappeared and wondered how many mice would meet their Maker tonight.

Savage had the ability to remain perfectly still, something he had learned the hard way. Now he seemed to have become part of the tree that he leaned against, but after a time he headed toward the house. He hadn't gone more than three steps when a voice suddenly broke the silence and caused him to whirl around, his hands held high in a defensive position.

"Hello, Ben. Beautiful night, isn't it?"

Savage dropped his hands and expelled his breath. A dark shape suddenly separated itself from a small group of trees, and Jimmy Vance appeared in front of him.

"You're good at sneaking around, Jimmy."

Vance just grinned at him. He wasn't more than five-ten, but was trim and muscular. He had a square face, a broad mouth, and a pair of light blue eyes. He was wearing a soft cap of some kind and a navy pea jacket. He pulled off the cap, tossed it in the air with one hand, and caught it with the other.

"How you doin', Ben?"

"I'm fine. Dani told me you were like a ghost. Things okay?"

"Nothing's happened."

"The folks really appreciate your guarding the place."

"I owe Dan a big favor. He pulled me out of the fire once."

"He's a good guy. Look, Jimmy, you can take off now. I'll take this shift."

"You sleep any today?"

"I'll sleep in late tomorrow. You go on now."

"All right, Ben. I'll see you later." Vance took two steps backwards, whirled, and disappeared into the underbrush. Ben didn't hear a sound—not the crackling of a leaf or the snapping of a twig. It was as if a shadow had just passed by.

"He would have made a good Indian," Ben murmured under his breath. He went around the house checking all the security devices. He and Vance had installed a wire within a hundred-foot perimeter all around the house. If anyone tripped over it, floodlights would go on, making all the grounds as light as day. Ben had wanted to put in an alarm outside as well, but Daniel Ross had said, "That would scare the neighbors. Just put a small alarm inside."

Ben circled the house, saw nothing, then spent a couple of hours wandering around the grounds. He didn't really expect Valentine to send anybody to the house. But being careful was better than not being careful.

At ten o'clock, noticing that the lights were still on in the lower part of the house, he went to the front door and rang the bell. Almost at once Ellen Ross answered it, saying, "Ben, come on in. We're having a midnight snack."

"Sounds good." Ben entered the house and was again struck by the exceptional beauty of Ellen Anne Ross compared to the rest of the women in the world. At the age of forty-four she still had the beauty that had been hers years before—at least judging by the photos Ben had seen. Her ash-blonde hair was swept back and tied, and she wore a pair of white slacks and a light turquoise top tied at the waist. Taking his arm she walked down the hall with him, smiling and asking him about himself. She had this quality of not just asking, "How are you?" but meaning it. Ellen Ross was more genuinely interested in people than any woman Ben had ever met. He had told Daniel Ross once, "If I had been around when you were courting Ellen, I would have given you a heck of a race."

The two moved into the kitchen, and Daniel looked up from the table with a smile. "Come on in, Ben. Have some of this terrible, heart-healthy cake."

"It's not terrible," Ellen said. "It tastes good, and you know it."

Daniel Ross, at the age of sixty, still had the look of frailty that a heart attack brings to people. His eyes were bright, but his cheeks were sunken, and there was the faint, unmistakable sign of an invalid about him. Still, his spirit had not been affected, and he said, "Sit down, Ben, and I'll tell you all my troubles."

Ben sat down, and Ellen went to the refrigerator. "I made an icebox pie today."

"Good," Daniel said. "Nothing I like better!"

"It's not for you," Ellen said firmly. "You eat your angel food cake."

"Why can't I have devil's food cake or icebox pie instead?"

"Because it's bad for you. I don't want to go to the trouble of breaking in a new husband. You were hard enough."

"Why, you were thrilled to death to catch me. Chased me all over Texas, this woman did. I finally just gave up out of sheer loss of energy."

Ben laughed and busied himself with lemon icebox pie.

"My favorite," he remarked.

"You said apple was your favorite the last time you ate here," Ellen smiled.

"Well, that's true. Lemon icebox and apple—it's a tie."

"And the time before that," Daniel put in, "you said it was pumpkin."

"That's what I mean. Icebox, apple, and pumpkin."

The three sat there without talking about their potential danger. Dan and Ellen knew Ben was giving them some of his own time to be sure they were safe. They had passed the point in their friendship where they had to express their thanks aloud.

Allison came into the room to join them. At fifteen, giving hints of the beauty that would come later, she had the same ash-blonde hair as her mother and the same bone structure—delicate and yet strong. "Ben," she said, "you have to teach me some more moves on the trampoline."

"Leave Ben alone. He's eating," Daniel said playfully.

"I'm all through," Ben said. He grinned and winked at Ellen. "Put the pie where I can find it. I'll wear Allison out, then come back and eat the rest of it."

"Come on, Ben," Allison said. She took his arm and practically dragged him out of the house. She led him to the small barn that had been converted into a fitness center. Weight machines sat along one wall, and in the center of the room was a trampoline that Allison went to at once. She kicked off her shoes and sprang to the center. "Come on, Ben, teach me how to do a double."

"A double's harder than a single."

"I'm sure I can do a double. I almost tried it earlier tonight."

"You promised me you wouldn't, Allison. Don't ever do that. If you lose your bearings, you can get into real trouble. There are people no older than you who can't move from the neck down because they hit the edge of a trampoline. Don't try anything like that unless I'm here. Even circus people are careful about things like that, and they've done it all their lives."

"All right, Ben," Allison said quickly. "I won't. But what I can't figure out is, how do you know when you've finished two somersaults? I lose my bearings with just one."

"It's one of those things," Savage said slowly, "that nobody can teach you. Some people have the ability, some don't. I knew a fellow once who had never done a dive in his life. We were at the pool together, and I did a few things from the board. Then he went out, hit the board, turned a complete back flip, hit the board again, then turned two full somersaults before hitting the water. And that was on a one-meter board. I asked him later if he knew where he was while he was doing the flips, and he looked surprised. 'Why sure,' he said. 'Doesn't everybody?'"

Ben worked with Allison for an hour, enjoying the time. Finally he said, "I guess that's about enough."

Allison took a towel and began to mop her face. "Ben," she said, "I want to ask you something."

"Shoot."

"Are you ever afraid?"

"Of course I'm afraid. You think I'm an idiot? Only an idiot wouldn't be afraid sometimes."

"What are you afraid of?"

"Snakes. Large animals of any kind. Making a fool out of myself." Savage made light of the question, but he knew that this young woman had a reason for her question. Having great affection for her, he asked, "Having troubles, are you, pumpkin?"

"Oh, I just worry sometimes. I don't really believe you're afraid. I think you're just telling me that to make me feel better."

"No. It's the truth. And it comes in funny ways." Savage crossed his arms and leaned back against the wall, thinking hard. "I've been through some pretty tough times when fear didn't bother me. Then later on I'd face something much less dangerous, and I'd find my hands sweating and my knees kind of weak. One minute it's all the bluebird of happiness, and the next minute the monsters come out of the closet and begin to gnaw on your shinbone."

Ben talked for some time about fear, and he noticed that Allison hung on to every word he said. "Come on, let's go in," he said. "You should talk to Dani about this. She has more courage than any woman I've ever seen. Except for your mom. The Ross women have something going for them."

"Thanks, Ben. I needed that."

"Uncle Ben's Counseling Service to Beautiful Fifteen-Year-Old Girls. We never close." He smiled.

After Ben walked her to the house, she whispered, "Good night" before going upstairs. Ben made his way to Daniel's study and was surprised to find him still up. "Little bit late for you, isn't it?"

"Couldn't sleep. Sit down. I'll beat you at chess."

Ben sat down, and the two men began to play. They had become good friends, but at the chess board all friendship went out the window. They were both aggressive and played for blood. The game seesawed back and forth until finally Daniel leaned back and said, "It's hard for me not to worry about what happened to Rob. Talk about stress!"

"Stress is what you're supposed to avoid, isn't it?"

"Yep. Hard to do sometimes though. I have to go to the Lord with it. I can't handle it alone."

Ben nodded. "It's good you have a resource like that."

"You'll have it one day too, Ben."

That was as close as Daniel Ross ever came to passing his Christian viewpoint along to Savage. He knew Savage wasn't the kind of person who could be pushed into anything, and he was content to give him little bits of Christian truth now and then. A thought came to Daniel, and he said, "Are your intentions honorable, Ben?"

Puzzled, Savage lifted his eyes to meet the gaze of the tall, silver-haired man across from him. "About what?"

"About Dani, of course. Are your intentions honorable?"

Silence fell across the room. The small grandmother clock built out of rosewood and walnut by Daniel Ross himself ticked loudly, sending its regular, monotonous rhythm through the air. Ben was taken aback by the question, and finally he shook his head and looked down at the board. "She doesn't need a guy like me."

Daniel Ross didn't answer for a while. He understood his daughter. He had never seen her show the kind of reaction to a man that she showed toward Ben Savage. True, it was a love-hate relationship right now, but Ross believed that no woman who had strong emo-

tions about a man could write it off. He knew there was some chemistry between these two, though he wasn't sure where it would lead.

Finally Daniel said, "I get worried about her, Ben. She doesn't
need to be stuck in a detective agency on Bourbon Street."

"I think she's doing fine. About my intentions—" Ben suddenly
broke off, for a slight noise had caught his attention. It was a door
closing. He was on his feet at once, his automatic in his hand. He
slipped to the door and glanced out, then relaxed. "It's Dani," he said,
easing the automatic back into the shoulder holster. He opened the
door and said, "Hi, boss. I'm just beating your dad at chess."

Dani came in and looked at Ben. "I thought Jimmy was on
duty tonight."

"I gave him a break. I'm not sleepy."

"Well, I'm hungry. You two come along and talk to me while I
eat."

The three went into the kitchen, where Dani fixed herself a
chicken salad sandwich. Ben took out the lemon icebox pie, cut a
monstrous slice, and put it on a plate.

"Why don't you just eat it out of the pie plate?" Dani grinned.
"You're going to eat it all anyway."

"Didn't think of it. How did it go tonight?" Ben asked.

Dani sat down, bowed her head, and prayed a simple prayer to
herself. "This sandwich was already prayed over, but I like to make
sure," she said teasingly. She took a bite and then talked around it.
"It was wonderful. Ben, I wish you could have been there. You, too,
Dad. The place wasn't packed, but I never saw the Spirit of the Lord
move more strongly. Fourteen people came forward to be prayed for."

Ben ate the pie slowly, knowing this was the part of Dani's life
he didn't share. Her serving God intrigued him, though he himself
had never made any kind of commitment like that.

After Dani had finished describing the service, she stretched and
said, "I'm really tired. You don't have to stay here tonight, Ben."

"I'll prowl around for a while."

"You can't work all day and all night too," Daniel protested.

"I'll sleep in late tomorrow. Guess I'll go take a look around." He got up, took the plate and fork over to the sink, ran water over it, then left the room.

Dani went over and hugged her father. "You go to bed now. It's too late for you to be up."

"I feel better with Jimmy and Ben looking out for us."

Dani hugged him again and kissed him on the cheek. "So do I, Dad," she whispered. "So do I."

◆ ◆ ◆

Dani arrived at the office early. It was Angie's late day, and there was no sign of Ben. She knew, however, that Jimmy Vance was keeping an eye on the house, and hopefully Luke Sixkiller was still able to send squad cars by periodically.

She went into the office and worked for half an hour. She was startled when the phone rang. She picked it up and said, "Ross Investigation Agency."

"May I speak with Ben Savage?"

It was a woman's voice, but Dani didn't recognize it. "I'm sorry. He's not here at the moment."

"Can you give me a number where I might reach him?"

"I can't do that, but I will do this," Dani said. "If you'll give me your number, I'll get it to Mr. Savage so he can call you back."

A long silence followed, and finally the woman said, "All right, but it has to be within an hour. My number's 831-4431."

Dani jotted the number down and said, "Can you tell me what this is about?"

"No, I can't." *Click.*

Dani sat there for a moment perplexed. She suspected the woman was Florrie, though she couldn't be sure. She had no idea what Florrie wanted with Ben, but she felt uncomfortable with the situation. She replaced the phone in the cradle, sat there thinking, and after a moment began dialing.

Fifteen

LOST HOPES

A body pressed against Savage, drawing him out of a deep sleep into a twilight zone where he was neither asleep nor awake. But Savage slowly returned to consciousness. Ordinarily he would come awake instantly, but there was something sensual and suggestive about the pressure he felt against his arm. He became aware of other senses as well—the familiar smells of his own place, the faint aroma of coffee that he always kept on the fire even when he was asleep, the crisp feel of the sheets and the weight of the blanket. But more pressing than any of these was the touch that seemed to be drawing him out of sleep.

Suddenly awake, he looked into the beautiful blue eyes staring into his, apparently waiting for him to rejoin the land of the living.

"Hello, Jane." Savage whispered the name quietly, reached out, and drew the form closer to him. "You're up early this morning. It seems like you always want attention at the most inopportune moments."

Jane Eyre purred and lowered her head as she pushed against Ben's hand. Her fur was white and silky and immaculate. She spent hours every day cleaning herself, and now the Persian laid against Ben, her purr sounding like a motor.

"Jane Eyre, you are a worthless female." Savage stroked the long, silky hair. He turned over on his back, and she crawled up on his stomach and stared down into his face. Tentatively she reached out a paw and touched his lips. The claws were retracted, and the paw seemed as soft as feathers to Savage. It was a game they played every night and usually in the morning if there was time. Jane seemed to take special pleasure in lying prone on his chest and touching him with the pads of her right paw.

"You're a pesky female. I'm going to throw you out one of these days."

Jane Eyre did not seem particularly alarmed at this suggestion. The purr increased in volume, and she withdrew her paw and closed her eyes, her head dropping.

Savage watched her with amusement, her face only inches from his. He had found the wet, bedraggled kitten almost dead in an alleyway. Against his better instincts he had brought her home and nursed her back to health. He had never had a pet of any kind, although in the circus he had grown quite friendly with some of the tigers. But this was different. Now when he came home there was a living creature waiting to greet him. He had always heard that cats were aloof and appeared not to notice their owners. One old story said that when a man came home, his parrot would say, "Polly want a cracker," and the dog would go up immediately wagging his tail as if saying, "The god is home," but the cat would look up lazily and say, "Who's *that*?"

But Jane Eyre was always waiting for him, no matter what time he came home. She always met him at the door, demanding attention. And it wasn't just food she wanted but *him*. It gave Savage a particularly pleased feeling to know that some living, breathing entity cared whether he lived or died.

For ten minutes he lay there slowly drifting back into sleep, with the cat prone on his chest, absolutely motionless but still purring. When the phone rang, the sound startled Jane, who dug her claws into Ben's chest and opened her eyes wide.

"Get your claws out of me!" Savage leaned to one side, reached over, and picked up the phone. "Hello?"

"Ben, did I wake you up?"

"No, I'm always awake. We trained detectives never sleep. What's going on?"

After a short silence, Dani said, "I took a call for you. A woman. I think it was Florrie."

Instantly all traces of sleep fled from Savage. He sat straight up and said, "Florrie! What did she say?"

"Nothing really. She wouldn't even give me her name, but I'm pretty sure it was her. I told her I'd give you her number."

"What is it?"

Dani read off the number she'd written on the pad of paper, then said, "She told me you'll have to call her within an hour."

"How did she sound?"

"Scared. Definitely scared."

"All right, Dani. Thanks for calling."

"Let me know if I can do anything."

"Sure. I'll see you later."

Ben put the receiver back in the cradle and swung his feet over the side of the bed. He wrote the number down on a pad resting on the nightstand and immediately punched in the numbers. After only one ring, he heard Florrie's voice, cautious and barely audible. "Yes?"

"This is Ben."

"Ben!" She sounded obviously relieved as she spoke his name.

"What is it, Florrie? Are you in some kind of trouble?"

"I—I need help, Ben. I need to talk to somebody, and you're the only one I could think of."

"Where are you?"

"In the Quarter. I can't be seen with you though. Can you put on some kind of disguise? Wear dark glasses or something?"

"All right."

"I'll be at Louie's on Canal Street. Do you know it?"

"Yeah, sure."

"I'll be in a booth as far at the back as I can get—with Tommy, my baby. I've only got an hour."

"I'm on my way." Ben quickly opened a closet from which he extracted a pair of baggy pants, a worn sweatshirt, and a World War II bomber jacket so worn the leather was flaking off in places.

He pulled a soft cap off the shelf and stopped only long enough to supply Jane Eyre with food and water. "Take care of yourself, Jane. I'll be back."

He left his apartment, running down the stairs instead of waiting for the elevator, then dashed out and unlocked the Studebaker. He got in and noted that it was later than he thought—ten o'clock. All urges for sleep left him now, and as he sped toward the Quarter, he pulled a pair of dark glasses from the glove compartment and put them on. It wasn't much of a disguise, but if he pulled the cap down and turned the collar of the jacket up, it would do.

He watched his speed, going no more than five miles an hour over the limit. The New Orleans police force was always alert for speeders and were not known for negotiating. When he arrived at the Quarter, he parked a block away from Louie's, got out, slammed the door, then forced himself to stroll nonchalantly down the sidewalk. There were few tourists this week, so the streets were not crowded. He walked down Canal until he came to a small café with several tables on the outside. No one was sitting in any of them, for it was a cold November morning. He walked in and looked down the long narrow room. There was a scattering of customers but nothing like during the tourist season, especially Mardi Gras. During that time this place would have been packed with dozens waiting for a table or a booth. Louie's was famous for beignets, and Ben had been here often. He saw Florrie sitting at a booth against the back wall holding a baby, and he strolled toward her. He slid into the seat across from her and didn't take the glasses off. "Hello, Florrie," he said.

"Thanks for coming, Ben," she answered quietly.

A waitress came up, a small, dark-complected, young woman no more than eighteen. She had dark eyes and a smear of egg on the white apron she wore. "What'll it be?"

"A beignet for me."

"The same for me," Florrie said quickly.

"Comin' right up."

"I'll have some black coffee too," Ben added.

"Coffee for me too," Florrie said.

After the waitress left, Florrie sat quietly, studying Ben's face. "You've changed, Ben."

"Everybody changes."

The words seemed to strike Florrie in a way that Ben Savage had not anticipated. She bit her lip, lowered her head, and said nothing for a moment. When she finally lifted her eyes, he saw strain on her face. She had always been beautiful, but he remembered her as a rather immature young girl back when she was still in her late teens—when they were both with the circus. She was still a beautiful woman but more mature. "You're right," she said. "Everybody does change, but not always for the better."

Savage studied Florrie, noting that her usual exuberance was gone. She'd always been happy, laughing, her eyes flashing, but now all that had disappeared. A somber look shaded her face, and there was fear in her eyes. The waitress came back with the beignets and coffee. They said nothing until she had moved away. Ben picked up his coffee, sipped it, and said, "The coffee's never hot enough."

"I'm in trouble, Ben."

"What kind of trouble?" He had a pretty good idea, but he wanted to hear it in Florrie's words.

She hesitated again, then slowly said, "When you came into Lenny's with Miss Ross, I thought I was dreaming for a moment. I never expected to see you again."

"I've thought about you a lot, Florrie. I tried to get in touch with you."

"I know. I was ashamed to write back, Ben."

"Why?"

Florrie looked down at Tommy, sleeping soundly in her arms. She brushed a dark strand of hair back from his forehead and said, "After I left the circus I—well, let's just say I led a hard life. I didn't want you to know."

"You could have told me. I would have understood."

The words softened Florrie's face, and her eyes were luminous as she said, "I didn't think so. I was too ashamed."

"You hated me after Hugo died. You were going to marry him, and it was my fault you didn't. I killed him."

"Don't say that, Ben." Florrie reached across the table and grasped his wrist. "Things like that happen with aerial acts. People fall all the time. It's not anybody's fault."

Ben didn't answer. He enjoyed her touch, and he knew at that moment how much he had missed this woman. He had never been able to put her out of his mind, no matter how hard he tried. Partly because of guilt over what he had done, and partly because of the youthful, first love he'd had for her. He found himself feeling again as he had felt in those early days, but then he came back to the present, and he looked down at the baby. "Is Lenny the father?"

"Yes."

Ben sipped the coffee and ate a bite-sized portion of the pastry. He put it in his mouth and wiped his lips with a cloth. "That's the trouble with eating beignets. You get powdered sugar all over you." He hoped the meaningless remark masked what he was feeling on the inside. He was shocked to discover how his feelings for this girl could still hurt him. "I guess you'd better tell me everything. I can't help you if I don't know it all."

Florrie had released her hold on Ben's wrist. She dropped her eyes and began to speak in a low voice, tonelessly. It was as if she were reciting a lesson she had learned and was not particularly interested in. Or as if she were talking about someone else in whom she had no special interest.

"After you left the circus, Ben, I didn't stay long. There were too many bad memories there; so I just left."

"That must have hurt the folks."

"It *did* hurt them. I've hurt them terribly. Have you seen them lately?"

"Yes. Just last month. They're still keeping the act together. They have two fine young fliers, a young man and a young woman. When I saw them it was as if I were seeing you and me up there, Florrie."

Florrie lifted her eyes, and the sharp corners of her lips grew softer. "I think of those days all the time. They were the only good days I ever had." She blinked and then said, "But those times are gone forever. After I left I went to Hollywood. I was going to be a movie star. What a fool I was!"

Ben had no appetite, but he took another bite of the beignet just to try to settle his emotions. "What happened?"

"I found out that I was no actress. Hollywood was full of young women prettier than me, and most of them with more talent. So I began drinking. Then I met a man I thought I was in love with, then another one, then . . . Things just got worse and worse. I even experimented with drugs. That scared me so much I stopped, though I kept on drinking." She looked into his eyes. "I wish I could go back and make different choices, but nobody can do that."

Ben Savage was suffering inside, but he was determined not to let it show. He had managed to bury his memories of Florrie—or so he had thought; but now they were all coming back. Her sweet loveliness, innocence, and purity had been the surest thing in his life—the North Star around which all else revolved. To think of her leading the kind of life that he knew she'd later gotten into ate away at him. It was like a razor inside his heart, and the memories that had been so good now became bitter.

"I was with a traveling company doing a play that was no good. We came to New Orleans, it folded up, and I was broke. I had no money at all. I got a job as a hostess in a nightclub. Lenny Valentine came in. He asked me out, and I said yes. He asked me out again, and we started seeing each other real regular." Her voice choked with emotion, and Savage saw her left hand clasp into a fist and her fingers grow white. "Trouble was, he was married. He told me his wife was sick and he needed my company. I guess I felt sorry for him, and I was impressed with his money and power, so . . ." She broke off as if she couldn't finish, then looked up and whispered almost inaudibly, "So I started living with him."

The idea of this girl whom he had loved so desperately giving herself to a monster like Lenny Valentine brought almost overwhelming pain to Ben.

"Then," Florrie said, "I got pregnant."

"Valentine's child."

"Yes. He told me he'd pay for an abortion, but I just couldn't do that. So I had the baby."

"He's a fine-looking boy. He looks like you."

Florrie's face brightened for a moment. "Yes, he does. He's like me, Ben, and nothing like Lenny."

"So what's going on now? What's the trouble you mentioned?"

"I want to leave him, Ben, and start over. But he won't let me go."

"Lincoln freed the slaves a long time ago."

"You don't know him! He hides it pretty well now, but he started out as a hit man. He's killed people—I don't know how many. Now he has others do it for him. I don't dare leave."

"Do you love him?"

"Ben, I hate him, and I hate myself for giving in to him. But I love Tommy."

Ben studied the sleeping infant's face. "What do you want me to do?"

"I don't know, Ben. I just had to talk to somebody. Lenny's wife is very sick. She won't live much longer. He wants me to marry him, but I don't want to. I hate what he is, and I hate what he does. But I've given him what he's always wanted—a son. I've tried to get away, but I'm watched all the time. I don't dare even stay here talking to you for very long."

Florrie looked down at her watch, and a startled expression swept across her face. "I have to go!" she said breathlessly. "One of Lenny's men dropped me off at the beauty shop. I told him to go get something to eat and pick me up later."

"How can I help you, Florrie?"

"I don't know. I have to go."

Ben reached into his pocket. "Here's my cell phone number. Memorize it, then tear it up. You can call me anytime."

Florrie took the card, glanced at it, and looked back at him. There was pleading in her eyes and a soft gentleness about her that belied what she had become. "Don't hate me, Ben. Please don't hate me."

"I—I won't do that."

"I didn't think you'd come. Thanks."

"Why didn't you think I'd come?"

Florrie stood up and flung the diaper bag over her left arm, and Ben rose with her. The two paused there, oblivious to the rest of the world.

"I've lost all the good things I had, Ben, and I'm afraid to hope anymore."

Sixteen

SIXKILLER MAKES A CALL

Dani couldn't ignore the fact that something was really bothering Ben. Ever since the morning she had called him and he had evidently talked to Florrie, he had been withdrawn and silent. He'd had none of the flashes of humor she was accustomed to. She had hoped that he would talk to her about that morning, but he had said absolutely nothing. Finally she worked up the courage to ask him, "Did you ever get in touch with Florrie?"

Ben gave her a look she couldn't decipher. When he chose to, Ben Savage could be as inscrutable as the Sphinx! He merely answered, "Yes," then quickly left the room. At first Dani was hurt at his refusal to trust her, but finally she reasoned, *It's his business. If he doesn't want me poking around in whatever's going on with Florrie, that's okay.*

At day's end Dani came home to find Ben sitting outside the house staring blankly into space. He had been keeping watch, and when she came up and sat down beside him, he blinked and reacted as if her presence pulled him out of some other world. He greeted her pleasantly enough, and the two sat there for a time talking about several matters. Finally Ben blurted out, "Florrie's in trouble."

"I thought so."

Ben seemed to be struggling with words, and Dani, knowing better than to interrupt, merely sat there. The air was cold, and the sky overhead had turned gray. The days were short at this time of the year. A neighbor's dog began barking. The wind moved the

FOUR OF A KIND   183

branches of the live oak, and they seemed to have a life of their own as they stirred gently.

"Dani, there's something you ought to know. She had a baby without being married, and Lenny Valentine's the father. She's been living with him."

Assaulted by a jumble of emotions, having no idea how to respond, Dani simply sat and waited. The barking became more insistent, as if the dog had treed something. Ben lifted his head to listen for a moment, then turned toward her. There was pain in his eyes. "She wants to leave him and start over again, but he won't let her."

"What's stopping her?"

"She's afraid. Valentine's a violent man, Dani. She tells me he wants to keep the boy. So when his wife dies, which could be at any time, he's going to force her to marry him."

Dani remembered the only time she'd ever seen Ben weep— when he had first told her of his days with Florrie, his love for her, and the tragedy with Hugo, whose death Ben blamed himself for. She knew a specter from his past had returned to haunt him. She said gently, "We can help her, Ben."

"Valentine is not a man who will listen to reason." His words were cold as ice. "If he hurts her, Dani, our problem with the church may be solved."

Dani felt sudden fear. "What do you mean, Ben?"

"If he hurts Florrie, Valentine won't be around to give Reverend Flatt or anyone else any more trouble."

Aware that Ben Savage had led a violent life and was basically a man of action and reaction, Dani knew what he meant. She had longed for Ben to make a commitment to Jesus, but he had not yet done so. She knew that he was thinking like a soldier, and she knew that if Valentine harmed Florrie, Ben would go after him like a Navy Seal going after a terrorist. She had seen that streak in him several times, and it was always shocking when this side of him suddenly emerged. "You can't see that as a viable option, Ben."

Ben sat there quietly, not saying a word, and finally Dani couldn't help asking, "How do you feel about Florrie now?"

A long silence ensued, and then Ben shook his head. "My feelings are all mixed up. There was a time when I loved her more than I loved life itself. I thought I'd buried all that, but something's still there."

Dani didn't like the jealousy she was undeniably feeling. She had long realized that she couldn't marry Ben as long as he was not a Christian, but now the idea of another woman in his arms brought a sharper reaction in her spirit than she had thought possible. She was so upset that she couldn't continue the conversation. "Good night, Ben," she said as she walked toward the house. She didn't hear his answer if he made one. The thought of his finding happiness with Florrie was like a knife within her. She was ashamed of herself, and as she entered the house and went up to her room, she tried to put the matter out of her mind.

She sat on her bed and stared blankly out the window, seeing nothing, aware only of the memory of Ben's tortured expression as he spoke of Florrie. She finally sat in her chair to read, trying desperately to focus on more constructive thoughts. She picked up a book and read three pages, then realized she hadn't retained one iota of meaning. She might as well have been reading Sanskrit!

♦ ♦ ♦

"Are you Mrs. Mary Robinson?"

"Yes, I am." She was an attractive woman in her late twenties. She had dark auburn hair, an oval face, and gray-green eyes. She wore a simple, maroon wool dress that revealed a trim figure. There was a wariness in her manner.

"My name is Dani Ross, Mrs. Robinson."

"Actually it's *Miss* Robinson." The woman took the card that Dani held out, and her eyes flickered with surprise. "Ross Investigation Agency?"

"Don't be alarmed, Miss Robinson."

"Are you investigating a crime?" the woman asked quickly.

"No. Nothing like that. I just need some information in order to help a friend of mine. Could you spare me a few minutes?"

"Well . . . I guess so. Come on in."

Dani stepped inside. It was an inexpensive apartment but tastefully decorated. The furniture was new and, though not expensive, well chosen. The pictures on the wall had been carefully selected to give the room a homey feeling. The colors were basically green or blue-green, and there was a cool feeling throughout the room. "What a lovely apartment you have."

"Thank you. I just moved in a month ago. Won't you sit down? Would you like some tea, coffee, or a Coke?"

"Oh, don't go to any trouble."

"Hot water's on. I was about to have tea myself."

"That would be very nice. I love tea."

Dani seated herself on an oyster-gray chair that proved to be as comfortable as it was attractive. After Miss Robinson brought the tea and the two went through the ritual of pouring and adding cream and sugar, Dani said, "You were fortunate to find such an attractive apartment."

"Oh, it wasn't attractive. It was nothing but bare walls. I painted the whole place and furnished it and did all the decorating myself."

"You must be an interior decorator."

"I planned to be." Miss Robinson studied Dani, and a light came into her eyes. "I wanted to be a decorator a long time ago, before I married, but I gave up that career. There's not much money in it at first. I had to take a better-paying job."

"Well, I think interior decorating is your real calling. I just might call you when I have a house of my own to decorate."

There was a calmness about the woman that Dani admired, but there was a directness too, and she suddenly asked, "What about your friend?"

"She works for me, and she's been seeing your ex-husband."

"Oh, I see." Her voice was cool as she said, "What is it you'd like to know?"

"To be truthful, I'm afraid my friend's making a big mistake. She's rather vulnerable and hasn't been too successful in her relationships with men. Right now she's thinking of spending a great deal of money to get some cosmetic surgery. I've been trying to talk her out of it, but she seems to think it would help her as a woman."

"I've never liked that idea."

"Well," Dani smiled, "you certainly don't need any such surgery. Perhaps both of us will feel differently as we get older."

"I don't think so." Miss Robinson thought for a moment, sipped her tea, and shook her head. "I think Americans are rather foolish about the effects of aging on our appearance. There's nothing sadder to me than to see a forty-year-old man at a football game still wearing his high school jacket."

"Or a forty-five-year-old woman on the beach wearing a swimming suit that should be worn only by an eighteen-year-old."

"Exactly." Mary looked into her tea, then lifted her eyes. "You want to know about my marriage."

"Anything you could tell me that might be helpful. I don't want to pry, of course, but I'm very worried about my friend."

"You should be."

"Was Hal Borman abusive?"

"Yes. Verbally abusive. Nothing I ever did was right. He never once complimented me on a meal. The clothes I wore were never right for me."

"Was he physically abusive as well?" Dani asked tentatively.

The silence grew long as Mary Robinson tried to decide how she should answer. "Yes. He hurt me many times. He was smart though. He never left bruises on my face. But there are other ways to hurt a woman." Unspoken fear and grief leaped into her eyes. "He's definitely abusive," she said flatly. "If you have any influence with your friend, tell her to stay away from him."

"May I tell her that you said so?"

"Certainly. As a matter of fact, if things get more serious, I'd be glad to talk to her myself."

"It may come to that," Dani said. "I can't tell you how much I appreciate your honesty."

"Hal's always had his way with women. He can put on a good act. He's probably doing that with your friend. But I'm sure it'll end up the same way it did with me. I found out long ago that I wasn't the only woman in his life. He'll bring nothing but trouble into any woman's life whom he manages to meet."

Dani drained the tea, then stood up. She smiled rather sadly and said, "Your apartment's beautiful, and I wish you success in every way."

"Thank you, Miss Ross. That's kind of you."

Dani left, filled with apprehension. From what she had heard about Hal Borman, he was good-looking and knew it, but there was something condescending in his manner toward women. Mary Robinson's comments had confirmed Dani's worst fear. *I have to get Angie away from him*, she thought fiercely. A maternal instinct rose in her, as if Angie were her daughter and not merely her friend.

◆ ◆ ◆

The quarter horse exploded in a start that would have unseated Dani if she hadn't been ready for it. She felt the horse's muscles tense, and exultation raced through her as Biscuit headed straight down the field toward the barrels. All was blur and motion and the sound of drumming hoofs as she leaned over the horse's neck. When they reached the barrels, she simply leaned against the quarter horse, confident he knew which way to go. Biscuit's shoulder brushed against one of the barrels, and Dani had a fleeting glimpse of it as it teetered, but she knew it wouldn't fall over. Without any further command, Biscuit shot like a bullet toward the next barrel. Dani leaned in the other direction and saw earth thrown up in chunks by the horse's churning hooves.

As they headed toward the last barrel, she let out a cry of excitement, and Biscuit's ears lay back, then pricked forward. The animal made its way around the barrel, again brushing it but not upsetting it. He then shot toward the other end of the field, Dani sticking like a burr on his back. She reined the horse to a stop and reached over and patted him lovingly on the shoulder. "We ought to quit all this detecting and start following the rodeos, Biscuit."

Biscuit pumped his head up and down, then skittered around, his eye on the barrels at the far end of the field. "No, that's enough for now," Dani said. "Let's just go for a little ride."

There were still enough woods left in the area around Mandeville for horseback riding. Whenever Dani was home and there was time, one of the greatest pleasures of her life was to ride Biscuit down the trails so strewn with pine needles that the horse's hooves made no sound. Now overhead the large trees laced their branches together, forming a cathedral-like atmosphere. The morning sunlight broke through, making a shattered pattern of yellow light on the ground. Everything was fresh, and New Orleans might have been a million miles away as she made her way along. Even at this time of year, the place abounded with birds and a few flowers whose names she did not know. There were enough evergreens to give life to the scene, and she rejoiced as she made her way down the trail.

She made a complete circle and then headed home. When she came into the pasture she saw her mother wave and heard her call faintly, "Dani! Telephone!"

Dani put Biscuit into a dead run, then brought him to a halt in front of the porch and dropped his reins to the ground. Well trained, Biscuit stood there as Dani headed into the house.

"You're going to break your neck on that horse someday."

"No, I won't," Dani said. Her cheeks were flushed and her eyes were flashing as she entered the house. The exercise always did her good and raised her spirits. Picking up the phone, she said, "Hello?"

"Sis, I have to talk to you."

"What is it, Rob?" Dani said in alarm. Rob was at a motorcycle meet in Pascagoula, Mississippi, not too far down the coast.

"I just remembered something about those guys that mugged me. I couldn't see their faces, but the guy who put the duct tape on me . . . I got a glimpse of his arm. It was cold that day, but his arms were bare. And, sis, I don't know why I never thought of it before, but he had two tattoos."

"Could you make out what they were?"

"One of them was a dragon, and the other one was some kind of emblem."

A sudden thought came into Dani's mind. "Could it have been the Marine Corps emblem?"

"Why do you say that?"

"I think I know who it was. When are you coming back?"

"I could come now."

"No. Let me talk to Luke first. I think you'll have to identify this man by his tattoos, but give me your phone number. By the way, are you having a good time?"

"Yeah, I am, but I'll come back if you need me. I want to nail those guys."

"I'll call you one way or another later today, after I talk to Luke."

"All right. Be careful."

"You be careful. I wish you'd ride something sensible like a horse instead of that awful motorcycle."

Rob laughed, his voice youthful and filled with eternal optimism. "It's all right. Us hyper-Calvinists don't worry about things like that. What is to be will be."

Dani couldn't help but laugh. "All right, all right."

"Good-bye, sis."

Dani's mother said, "Was that Rob?"

"Yes."

"He's not hurt, is he?"

"No. He's fine. He's not coming home for a day or two. I have to go downtown."

Dani ran outside and took Biscuit to the stable, then pulled off his saddle and bridle. She dumped some oats into his trough, slapped him on the rump, and hurried back to the house. She ran upstairs and showered, then slipped into a dark green pair of slacks, a silky cream-colored blouse, a dark green jacket with brown buttons, and a pair of brown low-heeled shoes. She came downstairs and quickly drove away. At police headquarters she asked if Luke was in. The sergeant at the desk grinned at her. "He's in his office, Miss Ross."

"Thanks, Tim."

Going down the hall, which smelled strongly of floor polish, Dani knocked on the door. When Sixkiller said, "Come on in," she stepped inside.

"Dani!" Luke got up. He was, as usual, dressed in the latest fashion. He had on a crisp, black pair of linen slacks, a stark-white shirt with a black, blue, and white abstract silk tie, and a black linen jacket that hung neatly over his massive form. He had on a gleaming pair of Johnston and Murphy shoes. The huge solitary ruby that he wore on his right hand caught the light and flashed as he came around to meet her. He held onto her forearm as if she might run away. "You wouldn't believe how many ugly people come into this office. You ought to come in once a day just to give me something pretty to look at."

Ignoring the flirtatious compliment, Dani responded, "Luke, I just got a call from Rob. He remembered something else about one of the men who ran him off the road and tied him up."

Luke's eyes grew instantly alert. "What did he say?"

"He said the man had two tattoos, one on each forearm. One was a dragon, and the other was the Marine Corps emblem or at least something like it."

Luke shook his head. "That might help, might not. We have a file on offenders with tattoos, but sometimes people get them taken off, and sometimes they get new ones."

"We won't have any trouble with this one."

"Why not?" Luke demanded.

"Because I know who it is."

The burly detective stared at her for a moment, noting the excitement in her eyes. "How so?"

"Remember the first time Ben and I went to church and two men were hassling the people there?"

"Yeah, you told me about that. Ben roughed them up, didn't he?"

"I even remember their names—Sonny Riggs and Chino Smith."

"Hmm, they're petty thugs. You sure it was them?"

"Chino Smith had those tattoos on his arms, and I saw them clearly. Do you think that'll be enough?"

"It'll be enough for me to pick them up—Smith at least. I don't think we can nail Riggs, but if I can squeeze Chino hard enough, we might be able to get him to turn state's evidence."

"Do you think you'll have enough to convict them?"

"Can't be sure. We can catch a guy with a smoking gun, and when we go into court some do-gooding tree hugger turns him loose. Remember that old movie *Boy's Town*? That priest said there's no such thing as a bad boy." A look of disgust swept across Sixkiller's face. "He evidently was never in the New Orleans projects. Lots of bad boys down there."

"When will you pick him up?"

"Right now."

"Let me know how it comes out."

"I'll do better than that. I'll come over to your office. We can go out tonight, and I'll give you a full report."

"Luke, don't you ever get tired of asking me out?"

"Nope."

"Dinner it is then, before my church service. You're a good guy, Luke."

"My strength is as the strength of ten because my heart is pure." He winked at her and then turned back toward his desk. He picked up the phone and began talking.

◆ ◆ ◆

When the phone rang, Lenny snatched it up. "What is it? Yeah, this is Mr. Valentine." He listened intently, then said, "Okay, I'll be right down." He put the receiver back in the cradle and walked out of the study. He found Lex shooting pool by himself in the rec room. "That was the hospital. They say Marie's worse."

"That's too bad."

"I got to go down to the hospital. I want you to keep an eye on Florrie and the kid."

"Sure."

As the two were speaking, Luke Sixkiller was pulling up in front of the heavy wrought-iron gates that barred the way to the interior of Lenny Valentine's castle. The officer got out of the car and saw two men sitting under a tree. They were seated at a table and were playing poker despite the cold temperatures. "Hey, open this gate!" Sixkiller demanded.

Riggs cursed and lurched to his feet. His face was red; he had obviously been drinking. "Who do you think you are?" he said.

He came to within a foot of the bars, his piggish eyes glaring. He cursed again as Sixkiller's arm shot between the bars. The police detective's fingers closed on the lapel of the pea jacket Riggs was wearing, and he jerked the thug's whole body backwards and bent his arm. Riggs's face smashed against the bars, breaking his nose; blood stained the front of his jacket. His eyes were dazed, and he reached up to his face. Riggs had taken many beatings in the ring, so a little blood didn't frighten him. He started to reach inside his pocket, but Sixkiller suddenly pulled him back three times in rapid succession, striking his face again and again.

"Hey, slimeball, open the gate!" he ordered the other thug.

"Let him go!" he yelled.

Sixkiller pulled out his Colt Python and aimed it directly at Chino. "Stop right there. You're under arrest. You have a right to remain silent."

As Smith reached inside his coat and pulled out a gun, Sixkiller lowered the muzzle of his weapon and shot the man through the upper part of the thigh. The sound was thunderous, and Chino dropped his weapon and went down screaming in a high-pitched voice, "You shot me! You shot me!"

At that moment Lex Noon and Lenny Valentine came barreling out the front door. Lenny said, "Get him, Lex!"

Lex Noon reached for his gun, but before it cleared the shoulder holster, he saw the Colt Python in Luke's hand. He recognized the police officer instantly and said, "What do you want, Sixkiller?"

"I'm taking in Chino. He's under arrest for kidnapping. You can go with me if you want, Lex, or even suffer something worse. Just go ahead and take a shot with that gun. You've already had a pretty full life, I guess."

Lenny said, "You can't get away with this!"

"Open the gate or I'll take this place apart!"

Lenny's face was filled with fury, but he had no choice. "Open the gate, Lex, and put that gun away."

Lex went over and pulled the switch. The gate opened, and Luke released his grip on Sonny Riggs. He stepped inside and pulled out his cell phone. He punched in a number and said, "This is Sixkiller. I'm at Valentine's place. Send backup and an ambulance."

Lenny glared at him, then pulled his phone out. He dialed a number and said, "Steen, get out here. We got some trouble."

"Is that old Ambulance Al Steen? He's stopped chasing ambulances, but he's still a lowlife."

Sixkiller walked over and stood beside Chino Smith, who was pale and holding on to his bleeding leg. "You're not dying. But we do have enough on you to put you away for a long time."

"What's the charge?" Lenny demanded.

"You're not listening, Valentine. Besides what he's done today, we've got an eyewitness who can finger Chino for kidnapping Dani Ross's brother. Quite a coincidence, Lenny, your thugs hitting the brother of the woman who's standing in your way of buying that church property."

There was murder in Valentine's eyes as he stared at Sixkiller, and the detective knew Lex Noon was a killer. He stood watching the two, waiting for them to make a move. Instead Valentine whirled and walked away. "Come on, Lex. Are you arresting Riggs too?"

"Nope. Not this time anyway. I figure Chino will pull him in though."

Valentine just glared at Riggs, and the three men went inside.

As soon as they were in the house, Noon whispered to his boss, "I told you not to send those two on a job."

"This won't come to anything. The kid can't identify him. They wore masks."

"Sixkiller's got something. He don't play around, Lenny. And that idiot Chino is liable to say somethin' that will bring you into it."

"Sixkiller's got nothin' or he would have arrested me. Steen will get Chino out on bail. And as soon as he does, I'll get him and Riggs out of town. Come on, I've got to get to the hospital."

"A MAN CAN CHANGE"

Dani Ross sat across from Reverend Alvin Flatt, as always feeling somewhat awed by the preacher's command of the Scriptures. She had come to give him a report on the activities at the church, but it had turned into a Bible study, as it usually did. She had simply mentioned that she had been troubled and unable to sleep the night before, and immediately Flatt began going through the Bible with her. He had taken her from Genesis to Revelation, and now his eyes sparkled as he said, "I used to spend a lot of time worrying about what was going to happen, but finally one day the Lord showed me that was a waste of time. You see, daughter, God already *knows* what's going to happen. You're worried about making the mortgage payment on the church, but in God's mind that's already taken care of. We've prayed about it, and God has promised that if two of us will agree, why, it will be done."

Dani smiled and shook her head ruefully. "I know that's true, Dad, but I just can't help thinking that next Wednesday if I'm not there at the bank with the money for the payment in my hand, then according to the contract the property goes back to the bank, and then Lenny Valentine can buy the church building and the land it sits on."

Flatt leaned back and shifted his leg with the cast to a more comfortable position. He muttered, "I never knew how important two legs were until I got in this mess, but I'm not complaining. God knew this was going to happen before the world began, and

He knows I'll get this cast cut off pretty soon and everything will be normal."

"It must be wonderful to have faith like that," Dani said almost wistfully. "Why is it that I know more than I put into practice?"

"What do you mean by that, daughter?"

"Well, I've read many books on prayer, but my prayer life isn't what it ought to be. I've read books on soul-winning, but I still don't feel I'm achieving much in that area." A thought came to her, and she gave a rueful half laugh. "My favorite book was *A Coward's Guide to Witnessing*. I thought I'd finally found the answer, but that didn't work either. In other words, I know what to do, but I'm not doing it very well."

"Well, God ain't through with you yet," Flatt said. "You're making progress. Jesus Christ is being formed in you, Sister Dani, and when you stand before Him, you'll be complete."

Dani leaned back and glanced down at the Bible he had given her to read along with him. It was almost unreadable, for he had made notes all over every page with a fine-point pen. She knew that he went through a Bible like this once every year or two, for she had seen a stack of them beside his chair. Now she ran her hand over the pages that looked almost like hieroglyphics and said, "I guess I need more faith."

"Well, turn to Psalm 3. If you want to know about faith, there it is."

Dani turned to that psalm, and Flatt said, "Read it."

Dani began reading the psalm aloud:

Lord, how are they increased that trouble me! Many are they that rise up against me. Many there be which say of my soul, There is no help for him in God. Selah. But thou, O LORD, art a shield for me; my glory, and the lifter up of mine head. I cried unto the LORD with my voice, and he heard me out of his holy hill. Selah.

"Now right there in verse 4 the Psalm could have ended. You see? David said, 'I cried to the Lord, and he heard me.' Well, that set-

tles it! If God heard him, then everything's going to be all right. Now
I want you to look at verse 5. What did David do?"

Dani read aloud, "'I laid me down and slept: I awaked; for the
Lord sustained me.'" She looked up and smiled. "That's what you're
trying to tell me, isn't it? That if I have faith, I'll sleep instead of
taking my problems to bed with me."

Flatt slapped his hands together. "That's right! That's faith!
Don't you worry about that mortgage payment. God's going to
open the windows of Heaven! I don't know how He'll do it. He
may send a millionaire in to write a check and pay for the whole
dadgum building. Or it may come another way. That's not our business. Ours is simply to believe that God is in control and to wait
for Him to show His mighty hand."

◆ ◆ ◆

Florrie was sitting beside the heated swimming pool drying her hair.
Tommy was in the baby pen industriously gnawing on one of the
plastic toys, this time a large yellow fish. It was quiet except for the
sound of the heated air being pumped in through vents. She had
swum enough laps to make herself tired. Now she sat back and
picked up the dryer. As she switched it on and waited for it to heat
up, she tried to put the future out of her mind. She had slept very
poorly the night before, thinking about her situation and striving to
find some way out.

She began to dry her hair and at the same time kept an eye on
Tommy. He was a beautiful baby, and her whole life was tied up
with him. She had never been especially interested in children.
Her hopes had been in other directions. She remembered a family from her circus days, Derrick King and his wife Martha, who
had a child. They had a trained tiger act and handled the big
cats as though they were no more than house cats. The baby had
blonde hair and blue eyes, and Florrie had fallen in love with
the child. Whenever she wasn't practicing the act, she took care
of her.

I never thought about having a baby of my own, and now I have Tommy. And I've got to take care of him. I've got to!

She finished drying her hair and was just sitting there when Noon walked in through the door. Florrie stiffened and pulled her robe closer together. Noon had a quiet way of getting from place to place. He stopped and looked down at Tommy, an odd expression on the man's smooth face. He watched the boy as he played, and when Tommy looked up and stared at him, grinning toothlessly, Noon turned to Florrie. "He seems okay."

"Yes, he's fine."

Florrie saw that something was on Noon's mind. "What is it, Lex?"

"It's Marie. She's in intensive care." He hesitated for a moment, then shrugged his shoulders. "She's not going to make it. It would probably be better if she'd go now. She's had so much pain."

It was the first expression of sympathy Florrie had ever heard Noon express. Hope came to her, and she said, "Lex, please let me go."

"We've been over that, Florrie. I can't do it."

"Yes, you can." Florrie walked over to where Noon stood. Since he was a tall man and she was a small woman, she was forced to look up at him. She was wearing a white terry cloth robe and had on blue sandals. "Lex, you don't know what it's like. Or maybe you do. I can't let Tommy grow up thinking this is the right kind of life. It's not! I know it's not."

Noon listened as the woman pleaded, but the look on his face didn't change. Finally he said, "Florrie, you'd better make the best of it. Some people have it a lot harder. I know some women who would give anything to change places with you."

Florrie didn't argue. She searched his face for some hint of compassion, some sign that he might possibly help her, but saw none. She turned wearily, picked up Tommy, and left the swimming pool.

Noon stared after her and chewed on his lower lip for a moment. Finally he shook his head and muttered, "That's just the way it is sometimes."

"Lieutenant Sixkiller is here."

"Send him in, Angie." Dani rose and went around the desk to meet Luke as he came into her office. "Hello, Luke," she said, managing a smile. "Sit down. Would you like some coffee?"

"All right. Just black."

"I know—real men don't use cream, or so I keep hearing."

Luke smiled at her, but a preoccupied expression was on his face. He accepted the large white mug from Dani, took a swallow, and then said, "Chino Smith is out of jail."

Dani said quickly, "You expected that, didn't you?"

"Yeah, but not this quick. Ambulance Al was there immediately, and he made bail for Chino."

"He'll have to be tried, won't he?"

"Sure, if he lives long enough."

Startled by Luke's words, Dani said, "What do you mean?"

"I mean there's only one link tying Rob's kidnapping to Valentine. Only two men can testify. One of them is Riggs, and the other is Chino. So it would be to Valentine's advantage if Chino vanished, you know? Of course if Lenny is afraid to risk doing something so drastic, Chino's still not off the hook. He's on the hot spot because he knows he's got a good chance of doing time because Rob can identify his tattoos. He's a two-time loser, and he could get up to twenty years, maybe even life."

"You think he'll be convicted?"

Sixkiller took another sip of coffee and shook his head. "I think the prosecutor will cut a deal. He'll offer to give Chino a ten-year sentence if he'll tell who hired him, and I think Chino would go for it."

"And that'll be good, won't it?"

"It'll never get that far, Dani," Luke said. The cup looked very small in his large hand, and he stared down into its contents, swirled the coffee, watched it for a moment, then lifted his head.

"I don't think he's long for this world. Lenny can't afford to let him live."

"You think Valentine will have him killed?"

"He's done it before."

"Luke, we have to keep him alive!"

"Not much I can do. He's already out, and I suspect Valentine told Riggs to take him out of New Orleans. I think we can say good-bye to Chino Smith."

There was a knock, and the door opened and Ben stepped in.

"Come in, Ben," Dani said. "You want coffee?"

"No thanks. Hello, Luke."

"Chino Smith's out."

"Ambulance Al strikes again, I take it."

"You're right. I was just telling Dani that if Chino had a lick of sense, he'd stay in jail. He's a lot safer there than he is outside."

The three stood there talking about what could be done, and finally Ben said abruptly, "I have things to do" and left the room.

"Something's eatin' Ben. I've never seen him like this," Sixkiller said.

Dani didn't answer for a moment, preoccupied with her own thoughts about Savage. Finally she murmured, "Yes, I'm worried about him."

After drinking the rest of his coffee, Sixkiller walked over and put the cup down, then came to stand before her. "It's the Contino woman, isn't it?"

Dani didn't want to admit it. "Luke, I don't know what's wrong with him."

"Sure, you do. It's her. He acts like he's been hit in the brain by a bullet. That's not like Ben. Well, love does funny things to a guy."

"He's not in love with Florrie Contino!"

Luke blinked at the vehemence in Dani's tone. His eyes narrowed, and he said thoughtfully, "Methinks the lady doth protest too much."

"Don't quote Shakespeare at me, Luke Sixkiller!"

"What are you so sore about? So Ben's in love with Florrie Contino. Does that bother you?"

"It wouldn't be good for him."

"Or for you either, I guess."

"Oh, Luke, don't be silly!"

Sixkiller had long known there was some sort of chemistry between Dani and Ben. He saw that they were drawn to each other, though in some strange way also mutually repelled. "What makes you think he can't be in love with her?"

"Oh, Luke, he knew her a long time ago. They were practically teenagers, I think. It was just puppy love."

"And you think puppy love never turns into anything else?"

"I don't have time to talk about all that, Luke." She walked over and put her own cup down, then sat down at the desk and looked at him with a sudden intensity. "Maybe he *was* in love with her. He says he was. But they were very young, and she's a different woman now."

"Nice theory, but it doesn't always work out that way, Dani." He studied her for a moment, then without another word turned and left the office. Though he wouldn't admit it, he was troubled over the same thing that had Dani agitated. He and Ben had become friends, and he knew Florrie Contino was bad news. If she was Valentine's mistress, that said enough. Even if she cared for Ben, Valentine would never allow anyone to take his woman away. As Luke walked out of the office and turned down the stairs, he thought, *Life is sure a tangled mess.*

In her office Dani rose from her desk abruptly and paced the floor. She glanced up at the portrait of her ancestor, Colonel Daniel Monroe Ross, in his ash-gray, Confederate uniform. His eyes seemed to bore into her, and Dani studied the stern face for a moment, then shook her head. "I wonder what you would have done."

The door opened, and Angie came in with a sheaf of papers in her hand. "You need to look these over, Dani," she said, putting them on the desk, then turning to leave.

"Wait a minute, Angie." Dani knew she had to say something.

"I talked to Hal Borman's ex-wife. She's a nice woman. I think you ought to have a talk with her before you go any further with this man."

"You had no right to do that, Dani! That's my private life."

"I know it is, and if I didn't care what happened to you, I would have just let things take their course. He's no good for you, Angie. His ex-wife said he abused her verbally and physically."

"A man can change!"

"How many times have I heard that?" Dani groaned. "You must have heard it too, Angie. Remember back in high school when so many nice, young girls fell in love with the wrong kind of guy? The girls were usually churchgoers and very sweet, and they always said the same thing. 'Sure, Johnny is rough, but I can change him after we're married.'"

"This is different."

"No, it's not, Angie. If a woman can't change a man before she marries him, she certainly can't change him afterwards."

Angie cast a tormented look at Dani, then turned and walked out of the office, her head held high.

As the door slammed, Dani spread her hands out. "Nicely done, Ross. You managed to drive her right into the arms of that thug!"

FATHER RANIER'S PROBLEM

The overhead light made a myriad of colors in the reflections of the contents of the jewelry box. The rich sapphire necklace glowed with a frozen flame; the opal earrings had a polar look about them. Florrie's favorite had been the emerald stones on a gold chain. There was a coolness about the green that was like nothing she had ever seen. It reminded her of the sea at certain times of the day when the ocean was still and the sun was almost gone; the greenish glow had always pleased her.

Florrie shook her head angrily as she stared down at the jewelry box. It was made of some sort of expensive wood, and the inside was divided into compartments, each made of a light beige, soft velvet that set off the color of the jewels. As she stared at the jewelry, she could remember how excited she had been at first that Lenny was showering her with pieces of jewelry she had only dreamed about before. Now there was a bitter taste in her mouth as she realized these were really not her jewels. As a matter of fact, she had discovered that many of them had belonged to the women who had preceded her as Lenny Valentine's mistress. She could not bear the thought of wearing them any longer, and although Lenny frequently asked her why, she never gave him a direct answer. A sense of distaste rose in her as she stared at the flashy gems.

Angrily she slammed the box shut, walked across the room, and put it into the safe behind the painting. The jewels were all that were kept in this particular safe. Lenny, she knew, had other hidey-holes where he kept money, jewels, and other valuables. This was the only one she had access to.

Turning quickly, she said aloud, "He'll take them back the minute he gets tired of me. Just like he did with those other women."

The restlessness that had begun growing within her months ago had now become almost unendurable. She slept very little at night, and her days were miserable. Sometimes she would catch naps, but always upon waking her first thought was a cruel reminder of her condition. Florrie was angry at herself for becoming engaged in things that once would have repulsed her. *How did I get here? What possessed me to let myself become what I am? I'm no better than a prostitute.* She brushed her palms against her temples in a vain attempt to drive the troubling thoughts from her mind.

A slight tinkling noise caught her attention, and she quickly walked over to Tommy's crib. He was slapping at the bells that dangled over him, and he kicked with ecstasy as the sound grew louder. He was such a happy baby! Everything seemed to please him. He had never been any trouble at all, and now she yearned more than anything else in the world to take him out of the bed and flee. Where she would go didn't matter; anything would be better than what she was enduring now.

The door rattled, and she turned, knowing it must be Lenny. Everyone else knocked, but he simply came in. Moving over, she unlocked the door, and when she stepped back, he pushed his way in. "Why do you have the door locked?" he demanded.

"I don't know . . ."

"Well, don't do it again."

"All right, all right."

Lenny moved past her and went to stand over Tommy. He reached down and touched the baby's cheek with a forefinger. Although his back was to Florrie, she knew there was a smile on Lenny's face. Crossing her arms, she stood there, knowing he had not come up just to see Tommy. When he turned, something in his square face frightened her, although she struggled to hide her fear. He was not a handsome man, and all of his expensive barbering and manicures didn't help; neither did the trainer who came daily to the exercise room filled with weight machines. Lenny was still squat and fat, going through the motions of exercise but eating rich foods. His eyes had always frightened her a little bit, and even more as she learned what all he had done. She had read a book once that spoke of "men without chests," men with no heart or emotions. Lenny seemed to be a man with something missing. Perhaps he'd had a gentleness or love or affection for someone when he was a child, but that was long gone now, except perhaps for Tommy, and Florrie waited with apprehension until he spoke.

"Marie is dead."

Just like him, Florrie thought, *to announce the death of his wife much as if he were announcing that he's bought a new house or made a good business deal.* There was no elation, but neither was there the slightest trace of grief. His eyes seemed to have no depth in them. As he waited for her reaction, she could only say, "She had suffered so much. I'm sorry."

Lenny didn't respond, and Florrie knew he had closed the page on Marie's book. "We can get married now," he announced casually.

This had been coming for a while, but now that it was here, Florrie couldn't seem to think clearly. She wanted to scream, "No, I will never marry you!" but said nothing. As she stood under the merciless scrutiny of his eyes, she couldn't utter a single sound.

"You hear me? We're going to get married."

"I heard you." With every ounce of strength that Florrie could summon, she said in a voice that was really no more than a whisper, "I won't do it, Lenny. I won't marry you."

If he heard her, he gave no sign of it for a moment, simply staring at her. Finally he nodded. "Yeah, you will. I'll apply for the marriage license today. It takes three days, I think."

"I won't marry you."

He grabbed Florrie by the forearm, and the strength of his fingers seemed to crush her arm. She opened her mouth but then closed it, determined not to cry aloud. "You'll do it one way or another. You know I mean it, Florrie." He released her arm, and when she stepped back he stared at her. "Things are going to change. I'm going legit. I'm getting out of all the drugs and the gambling. I've been waiting for this a long time. It'll be different now."

Florrie knew he might indeed do what he said, although she doubted it. He loved money and power, and his illegal operations and the criminal elements that he submerged himself in had always furnished this.

"I have enough dough to do it, and when we get that new mall built I'll be rolling in it. So from now on we're legit. We're gettin' married, and we're movin' in different circles. I've got to have a family. I've got Tommy, but I want more kids. A lot of them. I know you don't care about me. Maybe you never have. But we'll make a good couple. They'll take pictures of us that will be in magazines. I'm gonna build a bigger house than this. We'll be invited to the governor's ball. The governor is a pal of mine. He'll come over, and the photo hounds will love us."

Florrie listened as he kept talking, and she saw that he had his mind made up, though she doubted he could actually bring it off. Finally he cocked his head to one side and said, "You can have anything you want, Florrie—jewelry, cars, clothes. And you can build any house you want. I'll pay for it. But you're staying, and so is Tommy. Make it easy on yourself. If you don't—" He didn't finish, but he didn't need to. Florrie knew there was no choice for her, and when he turned and left the room, she stood still as a statue, unable to move. The tears flowed down her cheeks in rivulets.

◆ ◆ ◆

Sweat ran down the hairy body of Lenny Valentine, and his eyes were almost closed from the physical effort. He lifted the bar, and the trainer, a young man in perfect condition with clear eyes, said, "One more time. You can do it, Mr. Valentine."

Valentine simply said, "That's enough for today."

The trainer, James Taylor, knew better than to argue. He said, "All right. How about thirty minutes on the treadmill?"

"I'll do it tomorrow."

Taylor stood there rather helplessly. He was paid a fabulous salary, far more than he made with any of his other clients, but he knew he was getting nowhere. Lenny Valentine could not be pushed, but a man doesn't lose fifty pounds and get his heart in condition by doing things tomorrow. The trainer thought for a moment, then said, "Maybe a little on the bicycle?"

"All right, I'll do the bicycle." Lenny climbed on the stationary bike, and Taylor leaned over and set the resistance. Lenny shoved him away, and Taylor went reeling backwards. "That's too high!" Lenny snarled.

"All right, Mr. Valentine. Whatever you say."

Lenny set the resistance at the lowest possible level and began pumping. It required little effort, which was what he intended.

Ten minutes later Lex Noon entered and said, "We have a visitor."

"I don't want to see anybody."

"You'd better see this one. It's Sixkiller."

Instantly Lenny stopped peddling and turned to face Noon. "What does he want?"

"He won't tell *me*, Lenny. You know that."

"Tell him I'm busy."

"I already told him that. He says you can talk to him here or he'll talk to you downtown in the interrogation room."

Valentine cursed and glanced at the trainer. "Get out of here. Come back tomorrow."

"Yes, Mr. Valentine."

As soon as Taylor made his exit, Lenny said, "He can't have anything on me. He ain't got no warrant."

"He didn't say anything about having one, but you might as well talk to him. You know what he's like."

"Someday—" Valentine closed his mouth and picked up a towel. "All right, let him in." He got off the bicycle, picked up another towel, and dried his body. As Sixkiller entered accompanied by Noon, Lenny forced himself to be amiable. "Hello, lieutenant. What can I do for you?"

Sixkiller didn't come any closer. He was aware that Lex Noon had stationed himself to the right, and he wanted to keep the man in his line of vision. He looked at Valentine and said, "This won't take long, Lenny."

Something about Sixkiller got Lenny's attention. He had dealt with dangerous men for many years, and he knew Sixkiller's reputation. "What's the problem?"

"Chino Smith."

"Chino? He's out on bail. You'll have a chance to nail him when he goes to trial."

"You know better than that, Lenny. Chino's off the board."

Surprise flashed across Valentine's brutal face. "What are you talking about?"

"I got the report from the Baton Rouge Police Department. According to your men he killed himself. Shot himself in a rented room."

"Hey, that's too bad," Lenny said flatly. "Chino was a good man."

Sixkiller simply stared at Valentine and let the silence in the room grow. He was aware that Noon was standing ready for action.

"All three of us know Chino didn't kill himself. He was the only tie to you about what happened to the Ross boy. Now he's gone, and you're off easy."

"Hey, I don't have to take that kind of talk!"

"Shut up!"

Perhaps no one had told Valentine to shut up in years. He straightened up and opened his mouth, but something in Sixkiller's eyes cut his words off while they were still in his throat. The underworld figure simply stared, glancing nervously at Noon. Noon stood motionless, watching Sixkiller the same way he would watch a dangerous animal. "Be careful, boss," he said quietly.

"That's good advice. I'd take it if I were you," Sixkiller said, his voice low but with a menace that was unmistakable. "I'm just going to say this once, Lenny—you're standing on a ledge. One little push, and you won't have any more problems. I won't say this again, so listen good—and you'd better listen too, Lex. If anything happens," Sixkiller said slowly and precisely, "to Dani Ross or to her brother, sister, father, or mother or anyone else even remotely connected to Miss Ross, I'll bring your life to an abrupt end."

The silence grew almost palpable. Lenny had never taken such talk, although he'd been threatened many times before. Something in the obsidian eyes of the detective made him understand that this was no idle threat.

Sixkiller relaxed then and turned to leave. He walked to the door, then said, "Here's the way I'd do it. I'd arrest you, but you'd get shot trying to escape. I'd be carrying a throw-down; so when the rest of the force gets there, they'd find the gun on you that you tried to shoot me with. I've never done that before, although I know guys who have. But I'd do it to you, no doubt about it. No trial, no lawyers, no judge. I expect I'd have to do you in too, Lex. You're stupid enough to be loyal to this toad, so I'd probably take you out first."

Lex Noon didn't move. He had turned his body to face Sixkiller but said absolutely nothing. Sixkiller gave Lenny one glance, then left, shutting the door quietly.

Lenny Valentine found that his knees were weak, and his hands were trembling. To cover this he began to curse and slap his fist into his hand. He cursed Sixkiller in every way he could think of, and Noon listened. When Valentine finally grew quiet, Noon said, "I think you'd better take his words seriously."

"Nobody can talk to me like that!"

"Lenny, you've been around a lot of bad guys, but I'm tellin' you, Sixkiller is the worst guy walking around. He's smart, he's tough, he's careful, and he means exactly what he says. If you're smart, you'll lay off Dani Ross or anybody near her. You'd better forget about that woman."

Lenny Valentine seemed to slump down in dejection. When

he looked up, for the first time since Noon had known him, there was fear in his eyes.

"All right," Lenny snarled. "Who cares anyway? Chino's dead. They ain't got nothin' on us. Let the woman go. We'll get that church some other way."

♦ ♦ ♦

Father Francis Ranier found his greatest pleasure in his greenhouse. So much of his time was taken up with his pastoral duties and the struggle to keep his parishioners on the path to Heaven. That was his life. But as he often said, even angels must have some recreation, and his recreation was working with flowers. For some time now he had been developing a new strain of petunias. This humble flower fascinated him—so delicate, yet so tough that it would prosper when other plants dried up and shriveled from heat and disease and insects. The dream of his life was to produce a strain of ruby crimson that had never been seen. Not the dull maroon or the bright fire engine red but a rich crimson that would give delight to himself and to millions of others who loved the plant.

He had been in the greenhouse for thirty minutes, and sweat was dripping off him, for he believed in plenty of heat. As he delicately began transplanting one of his petunias, the beeper he wore on his belt suddenly vibrated. He was somewhat hard of hearing, but he could never mistake that vibration. It was an unpleasant sensation, and most of the time the beeper led him to the phone, which would produce more unpleasant things. People rarely called on the phone to give good news. With a sigh he plucked the beeper from his belt, then stared at the number. It was vaguely familiar, but he couldn't place it. He knew he had called the number more than once, but then he used many numbers, and at his age the numbers seemed to merge in his mind. With a sigh he picked up the cell phone he kept with him and punched in the number. When a voice said "Hello," he didn't recognize it. "Hello. This is Father Francis Ranier. I'm returning your call."

"Oh, hello, Father. This is Lenny Valentine."

Instantly Father Ranier's face went pale. Valentine was one of his parishioners, true enough, but he had seen the man only three times since he had come to this particular church. Each time he had been impressed that here was a man totally impervious to goodness. He knew, of course, Valentine's reputation as a criminal, albeit one who was clever enough to stay out of the clutches of the law. He waited for Valentine to speak. Then something passed through the priest's mind, and he remembered the funeral for Marie Valentine held only two days earlier. Ordinarily he would have conducted the funeral, but somehow Valentine had enough influence with the hierarchy so that the bishop himself did the honors. Ranier had played a small part, but when he had gone by to express his sorrow, Valentine had merely nodded. "I have been intending to come by and make a call, Mr. Valentine," Father Ranier now said carefully. "Perhaps I can be of some help during your time of sorrow."

"Are you free tomorrow morning at ten o'clock?"

"That would be an excellent time for me. I will—"

"I'll send my car by at 9:30. My driver will bring you here, and he will take you home after you're finished."

"Well, thank you very much. I know this is a difficult time. Perhaps you'd like me to hear your confession."

He had never heard Valentine laugh, but he heard a deep-throated chuckle. "No, not a confession. I want you to perform a wedding."

"A wedding?"

"That's right—a wedding. You *can* marry people, can't you?"

"Well, certainly, Mr. Valentine. Of course there are legal requirements—"

"That's all taken care of. My driver will be there at 9:30. I'll see you tomorrow."

"Well, just a minute please!" Ranier said as quickly as he could. "I need to know a little more. Usually when my parishioners get married I spend some time counseling them."

"I don't need any of that. I just need you to perform the ceremony."

"Well, who is the couple? Are they relatives of yours, or perhaps friends?"

Again the throated chuckle. "No. I'm getting married myself."

Alarms went off in Father Ranier's mind. He thought, *I must have misunderstood him. His wife was buried only two days ago.* "I'm sorry . . My hearing is bad. I thought you said *you* wanted to get married."

"You heard correctly. I'm marrying Miss Florrie Contino. We'll have the license and all the papers. You just come and do your stuff. The driver will be there at 9:30. I'll see you tomorrow, Father. Good-bye."

For a long moment Father Francis Ranier stood there stricken dumb. He was in the middle of some beautiful flowers, and he could smell the perfume of them. This was a place of beauty. But Ranier knew that evil can extend its presence anywhere, and it had just come to him. He stared at the phone as if it were a deadly snake, then shook his head. He pushed the *off* button and suddenly felt that he had to talk to someone. He turned to leave, but then he knew that it would do no good. The bishop would not be sympathetic if he attempted to persuade him to look further into this marriage. Ranier knew he could refuse, but if he did, someone else would go. "God help me," he murmured, and he left the place of beauty for the world outside.

◆ ◆ ◆

Ben picked up the phone and answered it after the first ring. "Savage here," he said.

"Ben—it's Florrie."

Just those few words and Savage knew that something was wrong. "What's the matter?" he snapped quickly.

"It's Lenny. He's going to make me marry him."

"He *can't* make you marry him."

"Yes, he can. Ben, you don't know him. The priest is coming in the morning. I don't know what to do."

Ben listened as Florrie began to weep, his mind racing. Finally he came to a decision. He leaned back against the seat of the Studebaker Hawk and held the phone so tightly, his fingers grew white. "Listen, Florrie—tell me everything you know about the security system of the house. Tell me about what's inside, all the rooms. Where does Lenny stay? I want to know everything."

For the next thirty minutes Savage pumped Florrie for every detail. Finally he said, "All right, listen—at three o'clock in the morning you be ready and have Tommy ready. I'll be there, and I'll get you out."

"Ben, you can't. He'll kill you. His goons are vicious, and the dogs are back now too."

"I'll take care of the dogs and the guards. Trust me, Florrie." She was weeping so hard, he wasn't sure she understood. "Florrie, remember when we were flying and I would catch you sometimes? You'd turn loose of the bar, and there'd be nothing but air, but then my hands would be there."

"I—I remember."

"I'll be there in the morning at three o'clock."

"All right, Ben, if you say so. But be careful."

"I will."

"Ben, you're my only hope."

"Good-bye, Florrie. I'll see you in the morning."

He turned the phone off as his thoughts raced ahead, listing the things he had to do. One thought came to him out of nowhere— at three o'clock the next morning he might very well be dead.

Nineteen

BREAK-IN

The soft tap on Ben's door got his attention quickly. His hand went to the nine-millimeter in the shoulder holster, and for a moment he stood absolutely frozen. Then he heard a voice calling, "Ben . . . Ben?" Stepping to the door, he threw the latch, unlocked it, and demanded, "What are you doing here, Dani?"

"Let me in!" Dani shoved her way past him, and as he shut the door she asked him, "Where have you been? I've been trying to find you all day."

"I've been busy."

"You shouldn't just drop out of sight like that." Dani stared at him and saw the tension in his face. "What's going on, Ben?" she demanded.

For an instant Savage hesitated, then he shrugged. "It's Florrie. She's in trouble." He told her all about the phone call, and when he had finished he said curtly, "I have things to do, Dani."

Taking a deep breath, Dani braced herself for further talk or action. She was wearing a charcoal pants suit; a single strand of pearls circled her throat. Her shoes had low heels, and she teetered back and forth for a moment as if thinking, then said defiantly, "I'm going to help you get her away from that awful man."

"No, you're not!"

"Yes, I am! I've made up my mind, and you won't talk me out of it."

"It'll be too dangerous. There are some things you can do and some things you can't."

Dani's eyes flashed, and she shook her head stubbornly. "You always say that, but I can be just as stubborn as you are."

Ben argued for what seemed like a considerable time, but Dani simply stood there, her lips drawn tightly together, her chin lifted slightly. Savage well knew what that look meant, and finally he threw his hands up. "All right, all right! But if you get yourself killed, don't come complaining to me."

Dani laughed. "If I'm killed, I promise I won't say a thing about it. Now, how are we going to get her out?"

"It won't be easy." Savage went over to a table and pointed down to a large sheet of paper. "Look at this. " The paper contained a sketch of both floors of Valentine's house and also the walls that protected the place. "It's built like a fortress," he said. "I pumped Florrie about all she knew about the security system, but it'll be a hard nut to crack. This wall, for instance . . ." He touched the drawing with his forefinger and shook his head. "It's going to be tough."

"We can climb it, can't we?"

"That won't do any good. There's an electric eye that runs all around the wall, and I don't know how high above the wall it goes. Probably at least a foot or two."

"So how are we going to do it?"

"*We're* not. *I* am. You can't possibly get over that wall." He ignored her protests and said, "You can come, but you're going to have to obey orders. All right?"

Dani swallowed hard, then nodded. "All right, Ben—but I *am* going."

"Okay. I'm glad we've got the chain of command settled." Moving over to another table, he picked up two odd-looking weapons. "I spent all day chasing these down. Two trained Dobermans roam the yard at night."

"Can't you throw some meat over with dope in it? I read that once in a mystery novel."

"It wouldn't work in real life. These dogs will only take food from their trainer, so we'll have to eliminate them another way. I got these drug guns from a friend. He uses them to bring animals down so they can be tagged or treated. It doesn't kill them, just knocks them out." He held out one of the guns, and Dani took it. She studied it intently for a moment, then looked up to say, "These darts have enough dope in them to put the dogs down?"

"Yep. The trick is to stun them before they attack you."

"What happens after you get past the dogs?"

"I have to find a way into the house without breaking a circuit. Then I'll go to the control center and shut it down."

"And once you do that you can let me in."

Savage smiled. "You're a piece of work, Dani Ross!" he exclaimed. "Why can't you be like other women and stay home, get married, and have babies?"

"That's for later. This is for now."

"All right." Ben took the gun from her and placed it on the table. "Are you hungry?"

"I'm starved."

"Good. We'd better eat something, then take a nap if we can. We're not going in until three o'clock."

"You want me to make something?"

"I'll do it."

Dani went over and sat down on the couch, watching as Ben moved about the kitchen. Ben went over to the refrigerator and began removing six eggs, a carton of milk, a green pepper, a small onion, a small block of cheddar cheese, and four small mushrooms. Taking these ingredients to the counter he expertly prepared two delicious-smelling omelettes, serving them with buttered toast on small plates. A sudden movement caught Dani's eyes, and she turned to see Ben's cat march out of the bedroom.

"Hello, Jane Eyre," she said.

Jane Eyre paused, gave her a cool look of pure arrogance, then walked right by her to a bowl of water on the floor. "She doesn't like me," Dani remarked.

"She doesn't like anyone but me. I guess that's what I like about her."

"You would like a cat that didn't like anybody else, Ben."

Dani again tried to entice Jane Eyre, but the cat simply stared at her with eyes as cool as polar ice. "All right," Dani said, "be like that then."

◆ ◆ ◆

"Dani, it's 2:30. Let's go."

She helped Ben carry the equipment to the car, and when they got outside, he said, "We'd better take yours. Mine's too conspicuous."

"Definitely."

Dani helped as they loaded the trunk, and then she picked up an aluminum rod of some sort. "What's this?"

"That's what gets me inside."

The two got into the car, and Ben said, "You can drive. Do you have your gun with you?"

"Yes."

"Is it loaded?"

"Of course!"

"Good. I hope you don't have to use it, but you might."

Dani started the Cougar and drove through the silent streets. There was very little traffic, and it was a dark night. Only a few stars sparkled faintly overhead. When they were almost to Valentine's place, she swallowed and said, "Ben . . . ?"

"What is it?"

"I'm scared."

"So am I."

"You are not. You're never afraid."

"That's what you think. I made a career out of being afraid when I was with the circus. I never got used to it."

"You sure don't show let it show."

"Fear's okay, Dani, as long as you control it. It's when fear controls you that trouble starts. You think you can do this?"

"Yes. I know I can."

"All right." He said nothing for a moment, then turned to face her. He reached over, put his hand on the back of her neck, and squeezed it. "I'm glad you're here, boss."

His words made Dani feel good even though the fear still lurked nearby, waiting to come flooding in. "This reminds me of some other tight spots we've been in," she murmured.

"We'll get out of this one too. Park over there. I don't want to drive right up to the house."

Dani parked the car, and the two got out. As they unloaded the equipment, Ben said tightly, "I took a run around here, and there's a streetlight right in front of the house. To avoid it, we'll take a shortcut through these yards. I hope none of the neighbors have Dobermans too."

Dani followed as Ben led the way. He seemed to have eyes like a cat, and once she stumbled against him. "Sorry," she murmured.

Ben didn't answer, but finally he halted and in a whisper said, "There's the wall. I'm glad it's not lit up here. Now get this, Dani. I'm going over the wall. Then I'm going to try to get into the house and disconnect the security system. If I do that, I can come and let you in through that gate. If something goes wrong, no Dani Ross rescues. Call Luke."

"Whoops. I left my cell phone in the car."

"If you hear any ruckus inside or shots or anything like that, get back to the car and make the call. Don't try to come in. Promise me that, Dani."

"All right, I promise."

The two approached the tall wall, and Dani watched as Ben lengthened the pole he was carrying. "What is that thing?" she whispered.

"They use it in the circus. I borrowed it from a friend of mine. It's strong but light." He finished extending the shiny metal to its full length, then leaned it against the wall. "I'm going up this thing, but it's going to be tricky. I want you to hold it; don't let it fall to one side or backwards. You think you can do it?"

"Yes."

"Good girl." Savage put a bag of tools around his neck, then suddenly turned to her. Without warning he leaned forward and kissed her on the lips. "Well, the old man's got to go to work. Try to have a pot roast when I get home tonight, sweetie."

"Ben . . . be careful!"

"Careful's my middle name." Ben grinned at her. She could barely see him in the darkness as he began to ascend. It looked so easy, but she knew she could never do it. He reached the top of the wall, and the pole began to sway to the left. Quickly she pushed against it and heard an approving grunt. "Here I go." Craning her neck backwards she saw him climb past the level of the wall, and then he did what she could never do. Somehow he managed to shove himself upward like a pole vaulter, then arch his body. The pole jerked violently as he shoved against it. Dani held it with all her might, and suddenly there was no pressure. She heard him land on the other side and whispered, "Are you all right?"

"Yes."

As soon as Savage hit the ground, he yanked the bag from around his shoulder. He zipped it open and pulled out the two dart guns. He had loaded them with an extra supply of dope and remembered what Charlie Jolly had told him: "This will knock down any dog you're liable to hit. It'll put 'em out all day. Just don't shoot yourself with it!"

As Savage yanked the second dart gun from the bag, a movement caught his eye. There was just enough light for him to see the two shadowy forms as they came toward him. Savage didn't hesitate. He was a good shot, but he wasn't sure about the range of the gun. One of the dogs moved forward quickly. He centered the dart gun, pulled the trigger, and heard a high-pitched yelp. Instantly he transferred the other gun from his left hand to his right and was able to get off the second dart. The second dog had charged past the first, who was snapping at the dart in his chest. The second Doberman took the dart in his throat, but his momentum carried him into Ben, knocking him backwards. Ben managed to get his hands on the dog's throat. Its white fangs were snapping inches from his face, and the dog was stronger than he'd thought. The two rolled around for a few seconds, and Ben knew the animal would tear his throat out if he got free. For a moment he felt overwhelmed with fear. Then without warning the dog made an odd sound and collapsed.

With relief Ben got up and wiped his brow with an unsteady hand. He quickly gathered his tools and, slinging the bag over his shoulder, moved toward the house. His mind raced rapidly. He knew every window would be wired, and every door too; so he couldn't go in through any of those. He circled the house, looking upward, then glanced to the lower part of the house, searching for some other entrance, perhaps a dog door. But there was none. He saw that one of the rooms on the lower floor extended past the main structure of the house. He stood staring upward, and a faint bit of the moon emerged from behind a cloud, casting minimal light on the upper part of the house.

"Got it!" he whispered. He climbed quickly and silently to the roof of the lower room, then reached up to an aluminum grill. A motor purred behind it, and he knew it was the exhaust for an attic fan. He disengaged the grill, making more noise than he would have liked. He stopped all movement when he thought he heard a noise below. For a long moment he stood there, finally expelling his breath and continuing to remove the grill. When he was finished, he lay it on the peak of the roof, making sure it wouldn't slide down. It was a small opening, but as an acrobat he had no trouble shoving his body through the hole headfirst. He held on until he got his legs through, then lowered himself into the total darkness of the attic.

His feet suddenly encountered something very soft. He was wearing only thin canvas shoes, and he moved his feet around until they struck something firm. He knew that the soft material was the insulation in the attic, and the hard surface was the ceiling joists. Hanging by one arm, he reached into his pocket and pulled out a tiny penlight, throwing a narrow beam into the darkness. As he had thought, there was nothing here but insulation and wiring.

Lowering himself until he balanced on the thin side of a beam, he glanced across the room. His view was blocked by air conditioning ducts, but he immediately started moving across the attic. He had often envied wire walkers, and now he wished he had paid more attention to their act. He had nothing to hold onto, and if he fell he would no doubt knock the plasterboard loose from the ceiling and awaken everyone in the house.

Fortunately, that didn't happen, and he walked from beam to beam until he came to a door. He turned the light off and slowly and silently turned the doorknob. It moved under his hand, and the door opened with a faint creaking. He paused again, and when he was confident no one had heard him, he stepped into a hallway of some sort. He shut the door and moved down the hall to the stairs that went down to the other two stories. The top floor was evidently used for storage, for boxes were stacked everywhere.

Moving down the stairway, he crept past the second floor and on down to the first, then turned to the room where Florrie had told him he would find the security controls. The door was locked, but pulling a small leather pouch from his pocket he opened it and withdrew a pick. The first one didn't work, but the second was successful. The door made a tiny click that sounded like a roll of thunder to Savage. He opened the door, moved inside, and shut it after him.

He was fairly familiar with alarms and security systems, and he studied all the circuits carefully. Then he took out a pair of needle-nosed pliers and selected a green wire. He hesitated for a minute, wishing he could be 100 percent sure this was the right wire. *If Dani were here, she'd pray over this. A heathen like me will just have to take a chance.* He cut the wire in two, hoping the alarm wouldn't sound. There was nothing but total silence. He waited for a moment, his heart pounding in his chest, then glanced at his watch. *Five minutes to 3.* Stepping outside the room, he drew his gun, but the house was silent as a tomb. He moved through the darkness, exited the house, and went at once to the iron gate where he had told Dani to wait. "Are you there?" he whispered.

"Yes."

Ben threw the switch, and the lock released. He swung the doors back, saying, "Come on—and don't make any more noise than you have to."

The two moved inside, Dani staying close to Ben. He pointed upward, and she nodded. The two climbed the stairs, and when they reached Florrie's room, he tapped with his fingernails. Instantly a voice replied. "Ben, is it you?"

"Yes." Ben pushed on the door, and Florrie stepped back. Florrie was wearing slacks and a coat. Her eyes went to Dani, and she was about to ask a question, but then she simply turned and went to the baby's bed. As she picked up Tommy she said, "I gave him something so he wouldn't wake up when I move him."

"That's good thinking. Let's go."

"Can you carry the diaper bag, Ben?"

"I'll do it," Dani said. She hooked the diaper bag over her shoulder. Her heart was beating like a trip-hammer, and she froze when she heard a man's loud call. "What's that?"

"They found the dogs," Ben said thinly. "We have to get moving. Get your gun out, Dani."

Dani reached behind her back and under her coat and pulled out the Lady Detective. It felt cold to her grasp, and she hated possibly having to use it.

"We'll have to go out through the front gate. You two can't climb that wall."

Ben went first, his automatic in his hand. As they stepped outside, a shot rang out.

Ben fired a shot at the flash and cried, "Come on! Florrie, do you have a key to any of the cars?"

"Yes—to the Mercedes." The three jumped back into the house and ran down the hall. They heard more shouts now, and Ben wondered if the mission had been a mistake. If he had been alone, he knew he would've gotten away. But with two women and a helpless baby against Lex Noon and whoever was with him—the odds were not good.

When they reached the garage, Ben jerked open the door of the Mercedes. "Get in the back," he said.

As the two women scrambled in, he threw himself into the driver's seat and started the engine. "How do you open the garage door?"

"There's a remote button right beside the cigarette lighter."

Ben punched the button and called out, "Stay low! They'll be shooting at us." He crouched over the wheel, yanked the car into gear, and jammed his foot down on the accelerator. A shadowy form appeared just as the Mercedes raced out into the night. Ben flinched as shots broke out. A hole appeared in the passenger-side window. "Stay down!" he yelled as he ran into someone and saw them fall.

He steered the Mercedes straight for the gates and was glad they were unlocked. He knew they'd have to smash through them and hoped that wouldn't disable the car.

A steady fuselage of shots began to ring out, nearly all of them striking the Mercedes, but Ben kept driving. Just as he hit the gates he heard Florrie cry out. He didn't dare stop the car, but as soon as he cleared the gates and turned right, he asked, "What is it, Florrie?"

"She's been shot," Dani said.

Ben shook his head but could only say, "Is it bad?"

Florrie's voice came quickly. "I—I don't think so, Ben. Just get us out of here."

"Is there a phone in this car?"

"No, and I didn't bring one," Florrie said weakly.

"We can't stop now. We'll check you out once we're safely away. Noon will come after us without delay, you can be sure of that."

In minutes he saw a pair of headlights in his rearview mirror. He knew it was Noon—and he knew Noon wasn't coming after them alone. He'd probably have other goons try to head them off too. Gritting his teeth, Savage sent the Mercedes screaming through the quietness of the street between the silent houses.

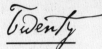

CORNERED

As the Mercedes hurdled through the darkness, Ben glanced into the mirror and noted that the lights were gaining on him. "What other kind of cars were in that garage, Florrie?"

Florrie's voice was faint and tinged with pain. "There's quite a few of them. Most of the time they use the Viper or a Lincoln Town Car."

"That must be the Town Car. It's too large for a Viper. I don't think we can outrun them though. Dani, roll your window down. When they get close, try to shoot out a tire."

Dani swallowed hard. She knew she might hit someone inside the pursuing vehicle too, and that made her uneasy; but there was no other choice. She rolled the window down, and the wind whipped through the car. She leaned out and fired the .38. There was no response. Steadying her hand, she fired again. "I hit him!" she cried. "One of the headlights went out."

"Try to get the other light too. They've backed off a bit."

Savage's thoughts were racing. If he were alone, he would simply stop the car and shoot it out with Noon and the other thugs. But he could find no way to balance the odds, so he kept going until they left the residential section. He turned onto a side road, hoping their pursuers would miss the turn. They didn't.

"Where does this road go?" Dani asked.

"It winds up at Houma, and then there's a gravel road that goes through Dubach."

Noon's car pulled up close. Shots rang out, and Ben heard two slugs strike the Mercedes.

"He's going to get us sooner or later. I'm going to try something more drastic. Get down on the floor."

Hearing the baby awaken and begin to whimper, Dani said, "Florrie, let me hold Tommy."

"No. I will."

"You're hurt. Let me do it."

Dani took the child despite Florrie's protests, and Tommy settled down and fell asleep again. "Are you hurt bad, Florrie?" she said.

"No. It hurts, but I don't think it's serious."

Ben knew this part of the outskirts of New Orleans very well. He often went down this same road to an isolated spot to practice shooting or simply to get away from it all. The road wound up at a swamp, and he liked the sight of the huge trees as they stood like sentinels over the still waters. Knowing it was also filled with snakes and gators, he raced down the street, then swerved onto a gravel road. Since Noon was right behind him, he pulled the Mercedes behind a clump of trees beside a large drainage ditch, then quickly spun the car around so it was pointing out at the road. *I have to time this just right.* Aloud he said, "I'm going to hit the other car and try to knock it into the ditch. Then we'll get out of here."

Savage waited for the Town Car with its one eye to come along. As it shot down the gravel road sliding sideways, Ben gunned the Mercedes, timing it perfectly. The heavy car shot forward and caught the left rear fender of the Town Car. There was a wrenching sound of tearing metal, and the force of the blow knocked the Town Car into the ditch. Ben slammed on the brakes and headed down the dark gravel road. He knew Noon wouldn't be able to get out of the ditch for a while. "That gives us a little time, but I'm sure they have a phone. They'll have other cars or even a copter after us in no time, and a dented Mercedes will be easy to spot. It'll be light soon too."

Dani sat up and said, "Turn the overhead light on, Ben." When he did, she said, "Where are you hit, Florrie?"

"In my side."

Dani leaned forward, still holding the baby, who cried a bit, then was quiet. Florrie's garment was soaked with blood under her left arm. Dani checked the wound more closely and then reported, "It's a nasty gash, and it's bleeding badly."

"Can you stop it?"

"I don't have any bandages."

Florrie whispered, "Use one of the disposable diapers."

As the car raced along, Dani jerked a diaper out and stripped away the plastic covering. She winced at the sight of the ugly, raw wound and knew it must be terribly painful. "We don't have any tape, so you'll have to hold your arm tight against it, Florrie."

Florrie didn't answer, and Dani thought, *She's going to faint.*

Florrie, however, simply said, "Let me hold Tommy."

Reluctantly Dani surrendered the baby, then leaned forward and said, "Ben, we have to get her some help."

"There's another road out of here. I think we can—" He stopped speaking because the car had begun shaking violently.

"What's wrong?" Dani asked anxiously.

"They must've hit the radiator—the car's overheating. I'm not sure how long I can keep it running."

"Long enough get us to a hospital?"

"No," Ben grunted just as the car gave off a loud thumping sound. He shook his head. "They must have hit the engine too. We're losing power fast."

The engine shuddered, and Ben surveyed the side of the road. He couldn't see much, but he knew this road quite well. It was covered with small saplings and high grass. He turned the wheel and drove the Mercedes into what appeared to be a grove of half-grown saplings. He went thirty feet, then slammed on the brakes, just short of a live oak. "We'll have to walk out of here."

Ben got out of the car, and Dani took the baby. "Can you walk, Florrie?" she said.

"I—I think so."

Ben checked his automatic. "I still have a full clip," he said grimly. "What about you, Dani?"

"Only four shots left, I think."

Ben shook his head. "There are no houses down this road for at least a couple of miles."

"You think they'll be here before then?"

"Yeah. If only . . ."

Suddenly Ben straightened up. "Dani, do you remember how you ran away after we put Lady Victoria in jail?"

Dani remembered the case. She had been responsible, mostly, for putting one of the finest women she had ever known in the penitentiary. The case had put Dani into a deep depression, and she had fled to a shack that belonged to a friend of her father's. Suddenly she said, "Is this the same road, Ben?" With all the excitement and danger, she had lost her bearings and hadn't recognized where they were.

"Yes. It turns off no more than a mile further down. If we can get off the main road and get into a boat, I think we can make it to that shack."

"There's usually a boat of some kind moored there."

Ben made his decision instantly. "If we can make it, I think we'll be all right. We can get you patched up, Florrie, get the bleeding stopped, and then I can walk out and find a house where I can call for help."

The three of them walked along with Dani carrying Tommy, who was now awake but quiet, curiously looking at their new surroundings. Ben walked beside Florrie. "Are you all right? Can you keep walking?"

"Yes. My wound isn't that bad, and the bleeding is almost stopped," she said quietly. "Ben, thanks for coming for me."

"It didn't work out exactly like I'd planned."

"We'll be all right," Florrie said. "I know we will."

They walked along for nearly a mile, and Dani said with relief, "There's the road that goes down to the swamp."

"I hope there's a boat we can use." Ben looked up, listened, and shook his head. "There's a serious flaw to our plan. They'll find our car, and then they'll know we came this way. We'd better keep moving as fast as we can."

Ten minutes later they reached the edge of the swamp. The dark waters lapped onto the shore, and Ben said, "Stay here. I'll see if I can find a boat." He hadn't gone more than twenty yards when he yelled, " Come here. I found a johnboat."

The women walked carefully over the uneven ground. When Dani got to the boat, Ben helped her in. He put Florrie in the front, and he got in the back. "There's only one paddle, but if we can get to that shack, I'll feel better about our chances. Since we're using the only boat here, they shouldn't be able to find us in the swamp."

Ben handed a flashlight to Dani and said, "You probably remember there were rags tied on trees to mark the way. They'll be hard to see at night, so I need you to find them with the flashlight."

Dani wanted to remark that the gators came out at night too, but they had enough trouble without that. She held the flashlight up and held on to Tommy tightly as Ben shoved the boat out into the swamp, then began paddling. "Tell me whether to go right or left," he said.

The johnboat slid almost noiselessly over the surface of the water. They passed within five feet of a fifteen-foot alligator but didn't know it. The gator's cold eyes watched them, but he didn't move. If it had been summer, it might have been a different story.

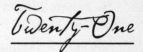

SANCTUARY

There's another flag," Dani said, her voice breaking the intense silence of the bayou. "A little bit to the right, Ben."

The johnboat moved to the right as Ben applied pressure on the paddle, and in a few moments Dani said, "There's the cabin—straight ahead." She kept the flashlight trained on the shore, and soon the prow of the johnboat hit the bank. After handing the baby to Florrie, Dani quickly jumped out, grabbed the rope, and pulled the boat up as far as she could. She took the squirming baby back from Florrie and watched as Ben grabbed the diaper bag and reached down to help Florrie disembark. The two made their way to the bank, and Florrie looked around in confusion. It was almost impossible to see anything except tall cypress trees reaching out like dead men's fingers in a ghost story.

"Let's go to the cabin," Dani urged. "We need to treat your wound, Florrie." She turned and walked to the cabin, thirty feet from the bank. It stood on stilts, and a pair of rickety steps led up to the deck on the outside. When she reached the top, she waited for the other two, Florrie moving slowly, helped by Ben. Dani shoved the door open. Swinging the light around, she laid Tommy on a couch, where he fell asleep again, then moved over to light a kerosene lamp. "We'll have to get the generator started, Ben."

Ben helped Florrie sit in one of the kitchen chairs. Dani walked outside and tentatively touched the starter button on the generator. She was afraid the battery was low, but it started at once. The lights flickered on in the cabin, and she walked back inside.

"Is Tommy all right, Dani?" Florrie said. Her face was pale and twisted with pain.

"He's fine," she answered quickly.

"Dani had better have a look at that wound," Ben said. "We don't want it to get infected."

With Dani's help, Florrie painfully removed her blouse, and Dani pulled the blood-soaked diaper away.

"Is there a first aid kit here?" Ben asked.

"Yes. I don't know what's in it right now, but my dad's friend always kept it well stocked." She moved into the other room, a large bedroom, and found the first aid kit in a cabinet. Returning, she saw that Ben had heated some water. Dani began carefully bathing the long, ugly tear in Florrie's side. "We'll have to get some antiseptic on this. It'll hurt, Florrie."

"Go ahead," Florrie said.

Dani took the antiseptic bottle, soaked a cloth with it, and began to apply it to the wound. Florrie took a deep breath as the sting hit her, and Dani said, "Sorry, but this has to be done."

Ben looked over at Tommy. He was still sleeping. He watched as Dani cleaned the wound, then put a thick bandage on it. "You were fortunate, Florrie." There was relief in Ben's voice. "If the bullet had hit a little more to the right, it might have hit a lung."

Florrie reached out for her blouse. Dani said quickly, "That has blood all over it. I think there are some clothes in the closet you can use." She went into the bedroom, returning with a long-sleeved, denim shirt. "This will be too big, but it's quite cold in here, and this will help keep you warm."

Ben said, "I'll get the heat going too."

As Dani helped Florrie put on the shirt and found a sweater for her as well, Ben started the small heater. It used up a great deal of the electricity being produced by the generator, but the cabin was cold, and Florrie needed to stay warm.

"I'll fix something to eat," Dani said. She wasn't hungry, but she needed something to do. Going into the kitchen area she opened the cabinet and found that the stores were rather low, though there were some canned beans, potted meat, canned fruit, a few cans of soup and vegetables, and a large tin of saltine crackers. Knowing they might need the meats, soup, and vegetables for later meals, Dani grabbed a can of baked beans, a can of fruit cocktail, and some saltine crackers. She opened the cans and heated the beans on one of the burners of the small two-burner gas stove. She heated water on the other, and soon the fragrance of coffee filled the cabin.

"Come and get it, such as it is," she said.

All three of them gathered at the table, and before they ate Dani said, "I think we should give thanks for the food and for our escape."

Florrie gave Dani an odd look but bowed her head, and Ben did likewise.

"Lord, we thank You for this food. We thank You so much for letting us get away safely. And now, Lord, we are in Your hands. We know there are dangerous times ahead, but You said that when the enemy comes in like a flood You will raise up a standard against them. And I ask You, Lord, to raise that standard now. Amen."

None of them were particularly hungry, but Dani said, "We need to eat something. We're going to need our strength."

Ben ate silently for a while, but his mind seemed to be roving here and there. "We can't stay here long."

"They'd never find us out here," Dani protested, staring at him.

"I think they will. They'll find the car, and they'll know we couldn't have walked far, so they'll spread out. They'll guess we couldn't have walked to the next town with two women and a baby. So we won't be safe here for very long."

"Well," Dani said, "Florrie can't travel far. One of us will have to go for help."

"You're right. Florrie, I want you to go into the bedroom and get some rest."

"I'll take Tommy with me."

"Just leave him where he is," Ben said. "He's all right. We can take care of him."

Florrie was too weak to protest. She followed Dani into the room and watched as Dani stripped the covers back on the single bed. "What about you and Ben?"

"I doubt we'll be able to sleep. Just make yourself comfortable. You need to stay warm and rest up."

"All right. I will." Moving awkwardly, Florrie slipped out of her slacks and lay down on the bed. Her face twisted with pain as Dani covered her, and Dani said, "We should have given you something for the pain. I think we at least have aspirin. I'll go get some." She left the room and came back with a glass of water. "Take two of these. You need to rest."

Obediently Florrie took the water, swallowed the pills, and lay back down. She looked up as Dani covered her and whispered, "Thanks, Dani."

"Don't mention it. We girls have to stick together."

"Take care of Tommy. If he gets hungry, wake me up."

"You're breast-feeding him?"

"Yes."

"Well, that's one less complication. I'll wake you if we need you."

◆ ◆ ◆

Florrie had slept for four hours, and the sun was climbing in the sky. Ben had gone outside to look around, but now he came back and at once went over to Tommy, who was beginning to toss and turn.

Dani watched as Ben stared down at the baby and wondered what was going on inside Savage's mind. He had a way of revealing little, especially when he was worried. She sat quietly sipping a cup of hot, strong coffee and finally said, "Come and sit down, Ben. Have some coffee."

"Sounds good." As he poured a cup of black coffee into a white mug and sat down, Dani noticed again how strong his hands were. His arms were powerful and thickly muscled. He was a very strong man, she knew, not only physically but in other ways. She had learned to trust him and depend on him, and now they began to speak of practical things, primarily food and escape.

Tommy suddenly began to kick. Alarmed, Ben went over and looked down at the child. Dani followed him.

"What's wrong, buddy?" Ben asked, a worried frown on his face.

Tommy began to scream, and Ben said, "What's the matter with him? Do you think he's sick?"

"No. I think his diaper needs changing," Dani said with a smile. She went over to get the diaper bag, and a mischievous thought suddenly came to her. "Do you want to do it?"

Ben turned to her, his eyes wide open. "Me?"

"Yes."

Ben knew she was teasing him, but, determined to get the best of her, he grabbed the bag. "Sure, I'll do it!" he snapped.

Dani went over to get a basin, laughed, and said, "You just won't admit there are some things you're not good at, will you?"

Ben glared at her as he removed Tommy's clothes. "Wow, he sure did make a mess!" he said. He stared at the baby helplessly, and Dani gently moved him to one side. "Here, let me do it." She cleaned the baby and changed his diaper swiftly as Ben watched.

"You're good at that, Dani."

"It's not hard, and you'll have to admit that women are better at taking care of babies than men."

"I don't know about that," Ben protested. "Given a little practice I could do that. It's not really much fun though, is it?"

Grinning, Dani put Tommy's pajamas on him and saw that he was smiling up at her.

"He's a good-looking kid," Ben said.

"Yes. He looks a lot like Florrie."

Both of them were thinking the same thing—it was fortunate Tommy hadn't taken after his father. They were also hoping Tommy had the same temperament as Florrie. Ben said, "He has a good mother, but bad blood from his father's side. Do you think that matters?"

"I think he has enough good stuff from Florrie to make it— with a little help from his friends. Especially if he comes to believe in Jesus as his Savior. We all need that."

Ben reached out and picked up the baby. Tommy grinned at him toothlessly, gurgling. Ben awkwardly touched his cheek. "Kind of scary to think how many bad things are lurking ahead for this youngster."

"That's true for all babies," Dani nodded. "That's why they need all the help they can get."

Ben moved over and sat at the table holding Tommy. He began to play with the boy, and as Dani cleaned up the room, she noticed how fascinated Savage was. *He hasn't had much to do with babies*, she thought. *But it's good to see that he's interested in them.* Uncomfortable with that thought, she teasingly rebuked herself for her growing interest in Ben Savage.

Shortly afterwards Tommy began getting restless, and suddenly he began to cry, his face turning red. Alarmed, Ben said, "What's wrong with him now?"

"I think he's hungry."

"Well, what does he eat?"

"Florrie's nursing him. She said to wake her up if he got hungry."

"Oh!" Ben blinked his eyes and handed Tommy to Dani. "You'd better take him in. I'm going to look around outside. I don't think anybody will be coming this soon, but you never know." He quickly left the room, pulling the automatic from the holster and checking the safety.

Dani moved into the bedroom and sat down on the bed. "Florrie," she said quietly, "I'm sorry I need to wake you . . ."

Florrie came awake at once. "Oh! What's wrong?"

"I think Tommy's hungry."

Florrie sat up in bed and began to unbutton her shirt. "Here," she said. "Give him to me."

Dani remained in the room as Tommy nursed, and neither spoke until Florrie asked, "Where's Ben?"

"He's outside keeping watch."

"I wish we were a million miles from here!"

"So do I, but we're not. Not many women nurse their babies. Why did you decide to do it?"

"I don't know, Dani. I just wanted to." She held the baby tightly, then lowered her head and kissed the top of Tommy's head. "I wanted to be as close to him as I could, and this is just one way. You'll never know, Dani, how many sleepless nights I've spent worrying about what's going to happen to him." She looked up, and her eyes were filled with torment. "I couldn't stand it if he became a man like Lenny."

"He won't."

"He will if Lenny gets his hands on him."

"We won't let that happen," Dani reassured her.

The two women sat there until the baby finished nursing. Then Florrie buttoned her shirt and put Tommy down beside her on the bed. He kicked and cooed for a while, and finally the two women began talking. Florrie wanted to know more about Dani, and the detective found herself telling almost her entire life story. She didn't usually tell so much about herself to people she didn't know very well; but Florrie was lonely, and she obviously didn't want to talk about herself. Florrie listened carefully, her eyes going from the baby to Dani from time to time. Finally she said, "So how long has Ben been working for you?"

"Not for very long."

Florrie was silent for a time. She was obviously thinking about Savage, and finally she said, "He's a good man, Dani." After another long silence she whispered, "I wish *he* were Tommy's father."

Dani didn't know what to say to that, so she just sat there. Finally Florrie said, "If I get out of this, I don't know what I'll do.

I've made such a mess out of my life. I've done awful things. I'm so ashamed."

"We've all done things we were ashamed of later."

Impatience showed on Florrie's face. "You don't understand, Dani. You've always led a good life. I've scraped the bottom. I've done things that I—that I wouldn't want you to know about, or anybody else for that matter."

Dani knew the moment had come for which she had been praying. Slowly but with warmth, she said, "You need God in your life, Florrie. You think you're a worse sinner than others, but you're not. We're all sinners, all equally guilty before God. There was a man in the Bible who said a prayer that I pray every day."

"What is it?" Florrie asked, her eyes alive with interest.

"He prayed, 'God be merciful to me, a sinner.'"

"But you're a Christian."

"I know. I'm saved, and I know Jesus as my Savior. But every day is another day that I have to remember how strong the world is. If I didn't go to God every day and tell Him I am weak and helpless and that I am basically a sinner and that only His grace keeps me going—why, I would fall in a minute, Florrie!"

Florrie took that in with narrowed eyes. "I never heard anything like that before. I thought you just lived, and when you died God added up the good things and the bad things, and if the good things outweighed the bad things, He'd let you into Heaven."

"It's not like that, Florrie. Nobody would ever be saved if it were. The Scripture says it's not by works of righteousness that we have done, but according to His mercy that He saves us."

"I don't understand that."

"It simply means that no matter how good we try to be, we're still flawed, and we still need Jesus Christ."

"But how do we get Him into our lives?" Florrie asked simply.

"It's not hard to become a Christian, Florrie, once you understand what that means. It's much harder to be the Christian you become. It's like becoming a wife. You become a wife in a few seconds during the marriage ceremony, but it takes the rest of your life to become the kind of wife you should be."

"I never heard that before."

"The Gospel of Jesus is not what the world wants to hear. The world wants to hear that if I don't do anything very bad, and if I do some good things, I'm all right. But the Bible declares that all people sin and come short of the glory of God. And it says the wages of that sin is death. That's why God sent Jesus—to bear our sins."

For twenty minutes Dani spoke earnestly and with love in her heart for this woman. She had been jealous of her, but now she saw only a hurt, wounded, fragile soul in a great deal of trouble. Finally she said, "And that's why you need Jesus, Florrie."

Florrie shook her head. "I'm too far gone for that."

"Nobody's ever too far gone. The thief on the cross might have thought the same thing. There he was, a criminal, dying, but right next to him was Jesus. Of course Jesus didn't look like the Son of God right then. He was in as bad shape as the thief. He had been whipped. He was bloody and stripped naked and nailed on that cross. And yet the thief saw something more in Him. That's why he said, 'Remember me when you come into your kingdom.' And Jesus said, 'This day you shall be with Me in paradise.' All it takes is a willing heart and a cry to Jesus."

Florrie turned her face away. After a while Dani leaned over and touched her shoulder. "You rest if you can." She left the room, wondering if her words had meant anything to Florrie. She walked outside and went down the stairs to find Ben staring out over the bayou.

"Everything all right?" he asked.

"Yes. Have you seen anything?"

"No. Not yet. But they'll come. One of us," he said suddenly, "will have to leave here and go get help."

"I think I'd better go, Ben."

"It's dangerous. You might meet up with Noon or even Valentine himself."

"But as you yourself said, we can't stay here, Ben. Florrie's doing okay for now, but she still needs medical attention. We have got to get out of here."

Ben turned to her and studied her carefully. "I know you trust God in spots like this."

"Yes, I do."

There was a sadness in Ben's voice as he turned and gazed at the swamp. "All I've ever had to depend on," he said quietly, "was myself. And right now that's not enough."

Twenty-Two

"I LOVED HER ONCE"

Lex Noon stood beside the road, staring to the west. When he saw a dark car approaching, his eyes narrowed. The Cadillac slowed down and pulled onto the shoulder. The door opened, and two men got out—Legs McCoy and Olin Swenson. McCoy was a tall man with a dark complexion, and Olin Swenson had the Swedish look— chunky and square and blond. "We came as quick as we could, Lex," Legs said. He glanced down at the car and shook his head. "They got away, huh? What's going on?"

"Just like I said, Legs, a guy broke in and kidnapped Lenny's woman and the kid."

Swenson stared at Noon in disbelief. "How'd he get through all that security? I didn't think a gnat could get through."

"There's always somebody who can get through," Lex said. He was angry at himself, for he had installed the security system. He shook his head and said bitterly, "There never was a system that couldn't be beat."

"Never was a horse couldn't be rode," Legs said. He had been a rodeo rider once, and his speech was filled with the terms of the circuit. "What do we do now?"

At that moment the phone in the newly arrived car made a buzzing noise.

"That's probably Lenny," Legs said as he grabbed the phone. He punched the button and said, "This is Legs."

"Let me talk to Lex."

Noon took the telephone and said, "It's okay, Lenny, I'm on it."

"You're on it!" Lenny screamed. "You were *on it* when you designed that system!" He cursed violently and shouted over the phone, but Noon just stood there quietly. He was accustomed to Lenny's fits of rage, though usually they were addressed to someone else. Gradually his face grew pale, and he finally said, "Wait a minute, I told you all the time that no system's perfect. If a guy's determined to get in, he will."

"Find 'em! Do you hear me?"

"We'll get 'em. They couldn't have gone far, and I called ahead. I got Noonan and Jerry closing in from the other direction, and they brought in some more guys. I think I hit the car too. Maybe I damaged somethin'. Anyway, we're closing in on 'em."

"One more thing, and make sure you keep this to yourself."

"Sure. What is it?"

"When you find 'em, I want you to ace Savage, and the Ross woman too if she's there. I've got a feelin' she's in on this. They've been in my hair long enough. Their lives are over, understand?"

"That's no good, Lenny. It's not smart."

"Don't tell me what's good and what's not! I'm telling you I want 'em put down!"

A hard light glittered in Lex Noon's eyes. "Is that all?"

"No, that's not all! If Florrie gives you any trouble, give her the same thing you're gonna give Savage and Ross."

"I wouldn't want to do that. She's not a bad kid. She's been good to you overall, you know? And she's the mother of your son, Lenny."

"True, true. All right, just bring her back. But she can't ever leave me again. Keep in touch, you hear? I want to know as soon as you find anything."

"All right. They can't be far."

"I think I need to come out there," Lenny said abruptly. "I'll have Benny drive me. Keep that phone with you at all times."

"All right, Lenny."

Noon pushed the button, and the red light faded out. He looked at the two men who were watching him and said as briskly as he could, "Okay. We've got backup coming from the other direction. Now, they might have pulled off anywhere, so we gotta drive slow." He got into the front seat behind the wheel, and the other two men followed him into the car. Noon started the engine and tried to quiet the anger that was rising within him. He didn't care about Dani Ross or Ben Savage, but the compassion he'd felt earlier for Florrie hadn't faded. *Maybe Ross and Savage will have to go—but not Florrie. She doesn't deserve that. Of course, she doesn't deserve to be stuck with a guy like Valentine either.*

◆ ◆ ◆

Ben had turned the radio on, and the sound of big band music rose in the cabin. He stood beside the window watching Dani as she walked slowly along the edge of the bayou, her eyes alert for any movement. He hummed along with Frank Sinatra as he sang "Down Mexico Way." Finally he glanced toward the door of the bedroom, and an impulse came over him. Crossing to the door, he tapped on it, and when Florrie said, "Come in," he stepped inside. She was sitting on the side of the bed, and Tommy was beside her on his stomach, gazing intently at a box of Mennen Baby Powder. He was drooling, and Florrie said, "He loves that baby powder box for some reason or other."

Ben paid no attention to her words. He knew she was striving to keep back the tears, and he could see that she had already been crying. He hesitated for one moment and then walked over and sat down on the bed. He put his arm around her and said, "It's all right. We'll get out of this."

"Oh, Ben, I wish I was dead!"

"Now that's foolishness."

"No, it's not. There's nothing good ahead for me."

Ben tightened his grip. "Don't talk like that. It's dark right now, but you're young. Things will get brighter."

"You sound like those old songs you always liked so much from the forties and fifties. Like 'Let's Pretend.'"

"You still remember that?"

"Yes, I remember. Nat King Cole sang it, and he said no matter how bad things are, let's just pretend they're all right." She turned her face toward him and said, "I can't pretend anymore, Ben. I've been pretending too long."

Ben was aware of the warmth of her body as she pressed against him. Clearing his throat, he said, "Dani says there's no mess too big for God to straighten out."

"Do you believe that, Ben?"

"I believe it's worked for her."

"What about you? Do you believe in God?"

Ben hesitated. "Yes, I do, but I'm not sure He believes in me anymore. I've given Him too hard a time."

"Me too, I guess." Tears formed in Florrie's eyes, and she reached for him. She put her arms around him and whispered, "I'm scared, Ben."

Savage held her, and as the sobs racked her body, a great compassion rose within him. She suddenly pulled his head down and kissed him, then pulled away and stared at him for a long moment. He didn't know what she was thinking, and finally she moved away so that she was no longer touching him. But her eyes were still fixed on him, and she whispered, "I think we might have had something once, Ben, you and me—but it's passed us by."

◆ ◆ ◆

Dani watched as a blue heron lowered his long legs toward the shore. Spreading his wings, he came to a perfect two-point landing. He stared at her with his cold, pale eyes, then stalked down the bank. Finally his bill darted down to grab a small fish. He tossed it in the air, caught it head-first, and swallowed it.

Dani watched as the lump went down his long throat, and then she turned, hearing footsteps. She waited until Ben got there and then, studying his face, said, "What's wrong?"

"Florrie's facing a dangerous dilemma. I have to see her through it."

"I know."

Something moved in the distance, and Dani and Ben both turned instantly. Ben reached under his coat, grasping the handle of the nine-millimeter, but he didn't draw it. They both relaxed when a raccoon came out, stared at them, then turned and disappeared.

"Guess I'm getting a little nervous," Ben said.

"So am I."

Ben's mind was still on Florrie, and he said, "We have to help her get free from Lenny Valentine."

"We do, and we will." Dani knew she had to ask the question she hadn't dared ask before. She had hidden from it herself, but now she wanted to know. Turning to face him, she looked him in the eyes and said clearly, "Do you still love her, Ben?"

He didn't answer for a moment. "I did once," he said slowly. He thought about the scene he'd just had with her and shook his head. "I loved her once, and we still care about each other, but it's different now."

Dani felt a rush of relief, and she put her hand on his arm. "We'll get her out of this, and we'll help her. Both of us."

"We can't wait here any longer. Somebody has to go."

"It should be me. If they find this place, it would be better if you were the one here with Florrie and Tommy."

Savage had already come to the same conclusion, but a worried look swept across his face. "It'll be dangerous for you. Even if they aren't already in the area, they'll surely be waiting for somebody along the way by now."

"I'll be careful."

"You'd better go soon."

"I'll go now." She looked at the johnboat and said, "I'll be leaving you here without any chance to get away."

"That's right, boss. I'll be depending on you."

Dani moved to the boat and tossed the rope inside, then turned to him. "Be careful, Ben."

"You too."

She took her seat in the stern and picked up the paddle. Ben shoved the boat into the bayou. She had used boats for most of her life, and now as she drove the paddle into the water, the small johnboat shot forward. She sent the boat straight out of the small cove, and just before she disappeared around the giant cypress trees that almost masked the house, she turned. Ben lifted his hand and waved, and she smiled and called, "God will help us, Ben." She waved at him, then turned and drove the johnboat through the still, black water.

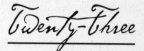

NOON'S CHOICE

The red Dodge Viper pulled up with a screech of brakes, and at once the door opened. Lex Noon moved forward to meet Lenny, who had trouble getting out of the low-slung sports car. As Lex expected, Valentine was explosively angry and cursing like a sailor. Noon stood there listening to the stubby man's obscenities, and then he said in a steely voice, his eyes half closed, "We've had some luck."

Valentine stared at him. "What do you mean *luck*?"

"We found the car. I disabled it with some of my gunshots, so they had to start walking."

"Walking where?" Valentine looked around. "There's no town around here, is there?"

"No. As I say, we've had some good luck. We ran across a kid running a trotline, and we asked him if he'd seen any people walking along. He said he had. I gave him ten bucks, and he said three people—two women and a man, and one of the women carrying a baby—got into a boat that stays docked at the little landing off the highway. "

"Boat? What kind of a boat?"

"Just a johnboat. According to the kid, it really isn't built to haul that many people, but they used it anyway. They're somewhere in that bayou."

Lenny Valentine said, "Show me." He followed Noon, and by the time they reached the landing, the shorter man was puffing for breath. He stood staring at the water as Noon said, "It was tied up right here."

Valentine looked out into the huge cypress trees draped with Spanish moss. He shifted his shoulders uneasily. "We'd never find them in there."

"Actually, I think we will. The kid is pretty sharp. He says there's a cabin up there—and only one. That's where they've got to be headed."

"All right! Let's go get them then."

"Well, we need a boat first. I sent the guys back to the kid's house. He says his old man's got a boat he'll rent to us. It's even got a motor."

"So we've got 'em penned in!"

"Looks like it. The kid says there's no way out on the other side. Everybody who goes to that cabin comes out this way."

"The kid's actually seen the cabin?"

"Yeah. He's a Cajun. Talks funny. I gave him ten bucks, and I think he gave us the truth."

"But I don't see how we're gonna find a cabin in there. We could get lost and never find our way out."

"No problem. The way's marked with pieces of cloth. See that one over there tied onto that bush?"

Training his eyes, Lenny made out a faded white cloth. "They lead all the way in?"

"Yeah. That's what the kid said."

"All right. We'll get them then."

Noon had seen this in Lenny before. His boss was a killer, a destroyer. By the glitter in the round man's eyes Noon knew that he was past reasoning. But, hoping to save Florrie and her son, Noon decided to try anyway. "Look, let me and the boys go up and take care of this."

"I'm takin' care of it myself."

"No sense takin' the risk, Lenny."

"Shut up, Lex! I told you what we're gonna do."

Lex fell silent and said no more but simply stood there. He

watched Lenny puff furiously on a cigar, his eyes half-closed, no mercy in his expression.

Fifteen minutes went by, and then Lenny said, "I hear somethin' comin'."

A battered old Ford appeared, driven by a dark-skinned man. Trailing behind was the Cadillac driven by Legs. There was no trailer, but a small boat was tied down on the trunk.

"This thing's not big enough for all four of us!" Noon said in disgust. "We'll have to get a bigger boat."

"It's big enough for me and you. Put it in the water," Lenny commanded. He turned to the man. "I'll pay you a hundred bucks." He reached into his pocket, peeled off a bill, and handed it to the man.

"All right, but be careful in that swamp. She's bad."

"What's bad?"

"Swamp. She's done killed lots of men."

Lenny glared at him and said, "Get out of here! We'll leave the boat here on the bank when we're done." He turned to see Legs and Swenson putting the boat in the water; there were two short paddles.

"Lenny, let me and Legs go. That's all there's room for in the boat—two men."

"You two guys wait here!" Lenny snapped. "Come on, Lex. We'll take 'em ourselves. We've done harder jobs."

Knowing any further argument was useless, Noon shrugged. There was a fatalistic air about Valentine. "You two stay here until we get back."

"Sure, Lex." Legs nodded. "You want us to find another boat and follow ya?"

"No. You heard Lenny."

Legs and Swenson watched as the two men got awkwardly into the boat. Neither of them were experts, and the short johnboat, no more than ten feet long, sank low in the water. Swenson waited until they were out of hearing distance and shook his head. "I never saw the boss like that before."

"He's got murder on his mind all right," Legs said thoughtfully. "And he wants to do it in person. I guess he figures on payin'
off the guy that stole his woman."

"Well, I'm glad they're goin' and not me. I don't like anything
about that swamp, and I don't like boats."

They watched until the boat disappeared, and then Legs said,
"You wait here. I'm going to a store and get us some beer."

"Make sure it's cold," Swenson said. "And get plenty of it. This
may take a while."

♦ ♦ ♦

Dani maneuvered the boat down the passageway. She had been here
many times but still needed the white flags. The entire swamp,
except for the tiny bits of rag, looked just the same. There was no
clear channel, no variation from one section to another. She simply steered the boat between the cypress tress, following the
markers.

"I'm glad it's not summer," she said. "The snakes would be
everywhere. The gators too." She said this half aloud, and the sound
of her own voice startled her, for the only other sound was that of
the paddle dipping into the water. Overhead, beyond the trees, she
could see birds every now and then, but there was no sound of life
in the swamp.

She had covered approximately half of the distance and was
feeling better about getting help when suddenly she heard a voice—
faint but definite. Instantly she wheeled the boat to her right and
headed toward a huge tree, maneuvering until the johnboat was
completely behind it. She cautiously peered over the top through
foliage growing on the ancient trunk. She remained absolutely
motionless until she saw the boat. She started to crouch down, but
not too far because she wanted to see who was coming. As the boat
drew nearer, she saw Lenny Valentine in the front and Lex Noon
in the back, each wielding a paddle. They were almost opposite

her when Valentine said, "There's another flag, Lex—over there by
that big cypress. Let's go for it."

"We'd better be careful. We don't know when we're going to
come across the cabin. And that Savage is dangerous."

For an instant Dani was tempted to pull her gun and open fire
on the two. But she knew she was a rather poor shot. Besides, she
had no doubt the two were both heavily armed. So she waited until
they had completely disappeared down the channel, then sent the
boat forward through the water with all of her strength.

As she covered the rest of the distance, she began to feel des-
perate. *I know those two probably didn't come alone. And whoever came
with them is still at the dock. Somehow I'll have to land without them
seeing me.*

She decided to get through the swamp as quickly as she could
and try to get ashore, but not at the landing where she would be easily intercepted. The going grew very hard, and her arms became so
weary she could barely lift the paddle. Several times the boat was
caught by branches of undergrowth. The large trees were no trouble,
but the many smaller trees seemed to reach out and grab at the boat.
One slapped her in the eye, making her bite her lip to keep from crying out.

Finally she had gotten as far as she could. The boat was resting
on a mat of moss, twisted vines, and weeds. She peered as hard as
she could through the undergrowth but could see little. "It's got to
be just ahead," she whispered. "I'll have to wade in."

Dani was terrified by snakes, and although she knew the snakes
were hibernating, the fear was still there. She also knew that gators
were not always completely asleep, and the exceptionally warm
winter might have caused them to revive. Still, she had no choice.
She took a deep breath and prayed, "Lord, get me out of this," then
eased herself over the side. She sank down to her waist, and her
feet pushed through the branches and moss to mud that gave way
under her feet. She started forward, fighting her way and losing
one of her shoes. She considered stopping and fishing for it, but it
was already under several inches of soft mud. Gritting her teeth, she

forged ahead. It was a fight to make any progress at all. She knew that if it had been summer, the flies and mosquitoes would be eating her alive. After a long struggle her strength was almost gone, and she lost her other shoe. Once she stepped on something sharp, and she gave a stifled cry. But she had no choice except to keep going forward.

Her breath was coming in short gasps, and she stopped to rest. But not too long because she knew time was precious. Ben was an able man, but the two men approaching the cabin were killers, and she didn't know how much ammunition Ben had.

Finally the water began to recede and soon came only to her knees. Then it was only ankle deep, though the mud still tried to pull her down. An ugly sucking noise accompanied each movement, but ultimately she stepped on something almost like dry land, and five minutes later she found herself clear of the water and standing on firm ground. *I think the road's right over there.* She staggered forward. Her feet were so tender that they couldn't stand much more.

Five minutes later she reached a road of some sort, and looking up she saw smoke marking the sky with a clear spiral. "It must be a house," she muttered. She made her way down the dirt road, moving as fast as she could.

As she followed the turn in the road, she saw a cabin. Quickly she ran toward it, and as she did, she saw someone come out. He was a short man with a slouch hat on, and he had a rifle in his hand. Dani was too exhausted to do more than make her way forward. The man had direct, brown eyes. He hadn't shaved in several days and appeared to be in his mid-fifties. He didn't point the rifle but watched her steadily. "Please help me," Dani said. "We need the police."

"What for?"

"My friends are trapped—a man and a woman and a six-month-old baby. Some killers are going after them. My name's Dani Ross. Do you have a phone?"

"No."

"Can you take me to a phone? It's a matter of life and death."

The small man studied her. He spat out a stream of amber juice and nodded. "Reckon I can. Come on. Get in the truck."

Relief washed through Dani, and she limped over to the ancient pickup and crawled in. Just doing that took almost all her strength.

"Your feet look pretty bad."

"They're all right. Please hurry! We have to get the police."

◆ ◆ ◆

"Wait a minute," Lex whispered. "There's somethin' up ahead."

From the prow of the boat Lenny took his paddle out of the water and stared through the undergrowth. "I don't see nothin'."

"I do. There's an opening up there. I think we might be coming to the cabin."

"Let's go then."

"Wait a minute. They'll be looking for us from this angle."

Lenny thought for a moment. "You may be right. But what else can we do?"

"Let's ease closer a little bit at a time. If we see the house, we'll try to find a place to land. We'll come up on 'em from the back."

"All right, we'll try it."

Both men kept their eyes forward, and finally Lenny whispered, "You're right. I see a little of the cabin."

"Let's go between those two cypresses there."

The two men rather awkwardly moved through the swamp for a hundred yards or so, and then Lex said, "Okay, let's see if we can find a place to get out."

They wound their way between the trees and undergrowth, and finally Lenny said, "I think there's land right ahead." The two paddled hard, and finally the bow of the boat made a crunching sound as it struck against the earth. Lenny got out and waited until Lex had followed suit. Noon pulled the boat up and tied it to a sapling, then pulled his gun out of his pocket. It was a nine-millimeter, and he was an expert shot with it. Lenny pulled a .45 out, and Lex shook his head with disgust. The gun was powerful enough, but it had no accuracy.

"Let's see what's up there," Noon said.

"All right, but I'm gonna take them out personally."

"This is not a good idea. There's been too much going on, and that Ross woman's well connected. Remember, she's in tight with Sixkiller, and if we kill her he'll never stop looking. And sooner or later he'll turn somethin' up."

"Shut up, Lex!"

The words were sharp and final, and there was something like insanity in Lenny Valentine's eyes. Lex had seen him like this before, and he knew that when Valentine was in this mood, nothing could convince him to change his mind.

The two carefully moved forward until finally Valentine said, "There's the cabin."

Noon stood very still beside him. "I don't think we can do it. They're on the second floor. We'd have to cross that open space and climb the stairs. They'd hear us."

"We're gonna take em, Lex."

"You'd better be smart about this, Lenny."

"What do *you* want to do?" Valentine challenged.

"There are windows in that place in the front and on the side, but the back of it is pretty much up in the bushes. Let's move around and get under the house. When somebody comes down the stairs we can take 'em easy."

"All right, all right, we'll try it."

It took the two men thirty minutes to sneak into place, but finally they were underneath the house. There was a walled-off section in which parts of outboard motors and other rusty equipment were piled. They had a good view through the slats beneath the steps. The sound of a radio came from upstairs, and Lenny pointed the gun upward and whispered, "I'd like to just start shooting."

"If you miss, Savage won't give us a second chance. I'm tellin' you, that guy's bad news!"

"You know anything about him?"

"I know enough to know he's nobody to fool with."

Grudgingly Valentine nodded. "All right," he muttered, "we wait."

The wait wasn't long, for fifteen minutes later Noon stiffened, then touched Lenny's shoulder and pointed upward. Lenny nodded. He had heard the door close, and now the sound of footsteps came down the steps. The two men waited with their eyes fastened through the open space between the latticework.

Lenny moved then, and Noon knew there was no more waiting. Lenny stepped out and shouted, "Hold it right there, Savage!"

Ben had come down to scan the swamp again, but he wasn't expecting anyone close at hand. When he saw Lex Noon and Lenny Valentine each aiming a weapon at him, he feared that all was lost. He had a wild impulse to go for the nine-millimeter, but Noon must have read that in his eyes. The automatic in his hand was steady as he quietly said, "Don't try it, Savage." He waited to see if the detective would make a move, then stepped forward. "Take that weapon out with two fingers." He knew better than to get close and to put himself between Savage and Lenny, for he figured that the smaller man was lightning swift. He and Lenny watched with their fingers on the triggers as Ben Savage pulled the automatic out.

"Lay it on the ground."

Ben obeyed. "Kick it over here," Noon demanded.

Ben did as he was commanded. Without taking his eyes off Savage, Noon stooped and picked up the weapon. He stuck it in his pocket and turned to Lenny.

"Where's Florrie and the kid?" Valentine demanded.

"In the cabin."

"They have a gun?"

"No," Savage said. He had been in tight spots before, but not quite like this. Both these men were killers; both were unafraid to shoot. He saw death in Lenny's eyes, and he knew the man would do what he had come to do regardless of the cost.

"Get up those stairs! I'll blow your head off if you try anything."
Ben turned and mounted the steps.

"Put your hands behind your head. Lock your fingers together."
Lenny's voice cracked with strain.

Ben obeyed, frantically trying to come up with a solution to
the dangerous dilemma. The stairway was narrow, and the only
thing he could think of to do was to reach the top, then throw
himself backwards into the two men. It was a risky move, but nothing else occurred to him.

"Don't try it, Savage," Noon's voice said. He had anticipated
Savage's thoughts and said, "No sense committing suicide."

Ben stopped at the top of the stairs, and Noon said, "Take just
one hand down. Open the door and go on in. And remember, we're
right behind you."

Ben opened the door and stepped inside, the two men close
behind. Lenny stepped forward with a look of pleasure in his murky
eyes. He turned to see Florrie come out of the bedroom. She stopped
dead still, terror flaring in her eyes.

"You didn't think I'd let you get away, did you, Florrie?"

Florrie couldn't move. She stood watching Lenny, who was
enjoying this moment. "Is the Ross woman in there?" Noon asked.

"No. She's not here."

"Don't lie to me. You had two women with you."

"She's not here," Ben insisted desperately. The one chance was
that Dani could get away and call the police. But that would take
time, and he doubted there was enough of that.

"Check the room, Lex," Lenny grunted. He kept the .45 on
Savage as Noon stepped into the other room. He looked around
quickly, then called back, "She's not here. The baby's lying on the
bed."

"She *was* here though, wasn't she?" Lenny walked over and
took Florrie by the arm. He began to curse her and was working himself into a rage.

"We have to get out of here, Lenny," Noon said suddenly. "Yeah,
that woman was here, but she's not here now, and there's no boat

out front. That means she's gone for help. We don't know how soon the cops will show up."

"All right. You're going back with me, Florrie. You're staying here, Savage." He pointed the gun at the detective and grinned evilly. "You know what a .45 slug will do at this range? It'll knock a hole in you that I could shove my fist through! You're finished!"

"No! Don't shoot him!" Florrie moved over and put herself in front of Ben and said defiantly, "You can't kill him!"

"Get out of the way, Florrie."

"I won't do it. You'll have to kill me too."

Florrie stared right into the muzzle of the .45. She felt Ben's hands on her, and he pushed her aside. "Don't do it, Florrie. He'll kill you."

Florrie was frantic with fear, but she had passed this bridge already. "You either let Ben live or I'll never go back with you!"

"You'll go back with me all right! You'll do what I say!"

Florrie shook her head. "You're a poor excuse for a man—a pig!"

If there was ever an instance of a man losing his sanity in a single moment, this was it. Noon was standing to Lenny's right, and he saw the insane look in Valentine's eyes. He had seen it once before—and that time Lenny had killed two men in cold blood. He saw Lenny's fingers tighten on the gun, and he yelled, "Don't do it, Lenny! I won't let you!"

But Lenny Valentine was out of control. He heard Noon shout, and his lips drew back in an insane grin. "Don't tell me what to do, Lex!"

"I mean it, Lenny! Don't shoot that woman or I'll let you have it!"

Without warning Lenny Valentine swiveled and squeezed the trigger. The slug hit Noon in the left arm and turned him completely around. He fell to the floor with a crash, lifted the automatic, and pulled the trigger one time. A small black hole appeared over Lenny Valentine's right eye. His head was driven back by the blow, but he didn't fall. He stood there absolutely still, and then Noon saw his eyes grow dim as if a curtain had been drawn over them. His knees doubled over, and he collapsed. The .45 clattered onto the floor.

Noon's shoulder was drenched in blood, and he looked down at it without saying a word.

Ben stepped over at once and said, "We have to stop that bleeding, Lex."

The man looked up and studied Ben. "All right," he said quietly.

Ben helped him sit on a kitchen chair. He stripped off his coat, cut the shirt away with scissors, and looked at the wound, now bleeding freely. "He missed the bone," Ben said. Quickly he got the first aid kit, and within five minutes he had disinfected the wound and tied a tight bandage around it.

Lex said nothing the whole time. He seemed to have lost his ability to speak. Finally he looked at the slumped form on the floor and shook his head. "He was crazy," he whispered.

"I think he was." Ben nodded in agreement. He looked over at Florrie, who had brought Tommy out of the bedroom and was watching the scene intently. Florrie's face was pale, and she couldn't bring herself to look at the body on the floor. She finally broke the silence by saying, "Lex . . . thanks."

"Yes, thanks. You saved our lives. He would have killed both of us," Ben said.

Lex Noon studied the two of them but said nothing. His eyes went back to the motionless form, and he formed a long thought; his lips drew together in a tight line, and he didn't answer.

◆ ◆ ◆

"Ben, thank God, you're all right!"

Hearing a motor, Ben had come down to the bayou. He saw Dani in the prow of a large boat with Luke Sixkiller and three other police officers sitting behind her. They were all carrying riot guns, and one of them had a high-powered rifle.

Dani jumped off the boat and fell against Ben. "I was so afraid!"

Ben held her for a moment, then said, "Well, it's nice to be appreciated."

Sixkiller stepped off and said, "We caught two of Valentine's guys at the dock. With a little persuasion they told us about Noon and him comin' up here. They didn't make it this far?"

"They're upstairs."

Luke stared at him. "You took 'em both?"

"No, I didn't. They took me. Come on."

"You men wait here," Luke said crisply. He and Dani followed Ben upstairs. When they stepped inside, Luke, with his gun in hand, saw Valentine's crumpled body. Then his eyes went over to Lex Noon, who was sitting with a bandage around his arm and a shirt draped around his shoulders. "What happened, Ben?" he demanded.

Ben looked at Lex and said slowly, "They came up here to kill us. Noon tried to talk Lenny out of it, and Lenny turned and shot him. Then Lex shot back in self-defense."

Luke stared at him. "That's the worst story I ever heard in my life."

"It's the truth, lieutenant," Florrie said. She was holding Tommy, and her eyes were warm as she nodded toward Lex. "He saved our lives—and he almost got killed doing it."

Both Dani and Sixkiller felt that something was wrong with this story, but Luke also knew that with two witnesses insisting that Noon had saved their lives, there was little he could do.

Sixkiller's eyes went back to Lex, who was watching him. The policeman kept his silence for a time, and finally his lips curled up in a smile. "Well, I never thought I'd say this, but we all owe you a vote of thanks, Lex."

Noon for the first time showed surprise. They all understood that he expected to be arrested and hauled off to jail. His eyes went at once to Savage, and something he saw there made him speak up. "I suppose I'll get a medal out of this."

"You deserve one, Noon," Ben said. "Anything I can ever do for you, just let me know."

The simplicity of Ben's reply seemed to shake the gunman. He didn't speak again, and then Dani said, "We'd better get you to a hospital. You too, Florrie."

Luke asked, "She took a bullet?"

"Just a crease, but I'd rather a doctor looked at it."

"All right. We'll all go."

Sixkiller collected the two guns but said, "It looks like you win this time, Lex. I'd remember that if I were you."

Noon didn't say a word, but on the boat going back, Ben sat down beside him. Neither man spoke for a long time, and finally Ben reached over and touched Lex on the shoulder. "I meant what I said in there. I owe you one."

Noon shook his head. "I must be gettin' senile," he said.

"Actually, I think you're getting smart."

◆ ◆ ◆

Dani was sitting beside Florrie. She had been there the whole time the doctor checked the bullet wound. Ben had gone with Noon, and in the interim Dani had been talking to her new friend about the Lord.

Florrie had said little, but when Ben entered, her eyes lit up. "Ben, is Lex all right?"

"He's fine. And he's free as a bird. He saved our bacon, Florrie. I was a dead man when I went up those stairs."

"God was good to you," Florrie said.

Her statement pleased Dani, and she explained, "I've been talking to Florrie about the Lord."

"I thought it was too late, but Dani's helped me understand that it's not. Maybe there's something to this religion."

"I think there is," Ben said.

"Will you be my friend too, Ben?" Florrie asked quietly. "Tommy needs friends, and I do too."

Something changed in Ben Savage's face, and both women saw it. He smiled and came over and kissed Florrie on the cheek. "You betcha!" he said firmly. "Why don't you look on me as a brother, and Tommy can call me Uncle Ben."

Dani looked over at Florrie, and she saw disappointment in the woman's face. But somehow Florrie managed to smile. Ben said, "I'll go down and get the car, Dani."

As soon as he left, Florrie took a deep breath. "Well, you win the brass ring, Dani."

"What do you mean by that?"

Florrie looked at her, and the smile was gone. "He's a good guy. Take care of him."

Dani blinked and looked flustered. "We're just good friends," she said.

"Yeah, right!" Florrie managed a grin, and then she stood up and kissed Dani on the cheek. "I'll go to church with you Sunday, but what about Tommy?"

"We'll put him in the nursery."

Dani embraced the woman, went over and kissed Tommy, then left the room. Florrie Contino watched her go, then took a deep breath and seemed to settle something within herself. She went and picked Tommy up and whispered, "Good-bye, Ben Savage. I wish . . . !"

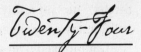

GOD'S MYSTERIOUS WAYS

Reverend Alvin Flatt sat in a straightback chair, looking with satisfaction over the congregation. He had just begun his sermon when Dani Ross interrupted him. It had been two weeks since the funeral of Lenny Valentine, and during that time Dani had been working on the reverend to come back and preach. Flatt had insisted at first, "It ain't normal for a man to preach sittin' down, and I can't stand up that long."

Dani had persuaded him that he could preach better from a chair with his leg up on a box than she could preach standing up. So at last he had agreed.

The service had begun, and Dani had given Reverend Flatt a great introduction. As she spoke she looked down to see Florrie sitting on the front row holding Tommy, with Ben on one side of her and Luke on the other. Dani's own parents were seated to Ben's right, and a feeling of joy had gone through her as the building filled to capacity.

The song service had stirred her, and just as Flatt began preaching, with his wife Myrtle beside him holding her Bible, Dani interrupted his Scripture reading by saying, "I never thought I'd do this, Brother Flatt, but I have an important announcement."

Flatt blinked with surprise, then grinned. "Why, daughter, I reckon you can say anything you like. Some of these folks out here tell me you're a better preacher than I am anyway."

Laughter went through the congregation, and Dani joined

them. "That was kind of them, but that's all it was—just kindness. We're all glad to see you back, aren't we?"

A standing ovation took place then. It lasted for five full minutes. Alvin Flatt was truly a humble man, and his face was red when the applause was finally brought to an end by Dani, who lifted her hands.

"I know you don't like to have a fuss made over you, Dad, but we couldn't miss this. Besides, we have a gift for you."

"Why, that's right nice of you, daughter." Flatt smiled. "I can always use a new necktie. Is that what it is?"

"Not really." Dani's face was glowing, and her family and friends knew something was up, though they didn't know what.

Ben leaned over and said, "Do you know anything about this, Luke?"

"Me? No. I thought maybe you did."

"What about you, Florrie?" Ben whispered.

"She never said a word to me. But look at her face. I've never seen her look so happy."

"Neither have I," Ben said quietly.

Dani had been standing behind the pulpit, and now she walked over to where the old minister was sitting. "On behalf of myself and all the good people of this church, we make this gift to you."

Flatt took the large manila envelope, then glanced up at Dani. "What is it?"

"Open it and see," Dani said with a smile.

"Go on, Dad, open it up," Myrtle whispered.

Flatt's fingers seemed to grow clumsy, but he managed to open the large envelope. He took out what appeared to be several papers and stared at them. "What is this, daughter? I can't read this lawyer stuff."

"It's the mortgage."

"The mortgage on the church?"

"Yes. And look what's stamped on the front."

Flatt glanced down at the paper, and for a moment he didn't

move. When he looked up, everyone saw the shocked look on his face and the tears in his eyes. "It says, 'Paid In Full,'" he whispered.

"That's right. The building is paid in full, Reverend Flatt."

"Glory to God and the Lamb forever!" he shouted. He got up out of his chair and grabbed his walker. He tried to do a dance with Myrtle on one side and Dani on the other.

Dani had never known such joy as that which shone from the Flatts' faces. Finally Myrtle said, "Now you sit down, Dad, before you break that leg again!"

"All right, Mama, I'll do it. Miss Dani," he said in a voice that quivered with emotion, "I know this was your doin'."

"No, it wasn't. I give you my word, I didn't pay off that mortgage."

"Can you tell me who it was?"

"No, I can't."

"Well, I can't fault you there. But I want us to have a prayer right now for whoever done this thing."

Everyone bowed their heads, and Alvin Flatt prayed a fervent prayer for the giver. When he was finished he said, "Now you all sit still. I aim to preach at you. Tonight you're going to hear my famous sermon, 'Turn or Burn . . .'"

◆ ◆ ◆

"Why are you stopping here, Ben?"

Savage was driving Dani home. The two had spent most of the day at the church. They had waited for the evening service, and to Dani's astonishment Ben had attended that as well. Afterward there had been a long altar call, and the two had sat and watched as the Reverend Flatt and his wife prayed for many who came forward.

They had started home late, and Ben had suddenly pulled off onto a side road. He didn't answer Dani but brought the car to a halt on a road that paralleled Lake Pontchartrain. He shut the engine off and sat there without speaking.

Dani looked at him, wondering what was going on.

Suddenly he turned to her and said, "Did you pay off that mortgage?"

"Didn't you hear me tell Dad I didn't have anything to do with it?"

"Who was it?"

"I can't tell."

"You can tell me. I won't let it go any further."

"That's the way gossip gets started." She smiled.

"I mean it, Dani. I can't believe this. I know there was a lot of money involved."

Dani hesitated, then said, "It was J. T. Denver."

Ben turned to her, twisting his body around. "You went to Denver for the money?"

"Yes. He's the only rich client I ever had, and he's doing a great work. He's spending all his money now on the Gospel. He's down in South America drilling wells with his bride and that newfound son of his. They're having a wonderful time. When I talked to him, I told him about this, and he said, 'We'll get an electronic transfer. You can have the money tomorrow.' And that's what we did. But he insisted on keeping it a secret."

"He's a good man."

"Yes, he is."

Ben said thoughtfully, "Was it you who uncovered the governor's involvement with Lenny Valentine?"

"Well, Florrie asked me to help her look into Valentine's financial affairs, and it didn't take me long to find out that Governor Madden was in with him."

"And he's being indicted right now. His connections with gamblers have finally caught up with him."

"Actually, he didn't do anything illegal. He just used Valentine to get the property. But Madden's going down on other charges."

Ben moved restlessly. "Come on, let's walk along the shore."

Wondering at Savage's actions, Dani got out and joined him. The air was cold and crisp, and a three-quarter moon threw its silver beams down onto the waters of Lake Pontchartrain.

The two walked along for a hundred yards, and Savage didn't say a word. Finally he turned to her and said without preamble, "A lot has happened. I was glad to see Florrie there with Tommy."

"She's going to be converted soon. She's hungry for God."

Ben studied her. She was a beautiful woman, robust and filled with life. She was humble and gentle and had an inner fire he didn't understand. He watched her face, trying to find a name for whatever it was that meant so much to him. She was tall and shapely, and her eyes mirrored some kind of wisdom as she looked at him. He wasn't sure what it all meant, but it pulled at him like a mystery.

"Why are you looking at me like that, Ben?"

"I don't know," he said briefly.

She studied his face, so tough and yet sometimes so vulnerable. He was an intriguing man, hard when he had to be, though there was a latent gentleness in him that she had learned to uncover. "Ben, I know I already asked you this, but . . . well, how do you feel about Florrie?"

He lifted one eyebrow and said, "At one time our relationship might have meant more to me than a friendship, but too much has happened."

From far off came a distant cry of a dog howling somewhere, and then it died away. Ben seemed to be searching for words, and finally he said, "We both need to be friends to Florrie and to Tommy, but that's all the relationship is to me now." An impish light leaped into his eyes. "Besides, I have to take care of you. You're always getting into trouble."

"You're the one who's always in hot water!"

"Well," Ben said quietly, "we'll just have to take care of each other, boss." He pulled her forward and kissed her. When he released her, she said, "All right, Ben. I guess we both need somebody to take care of us."

DANI ROSS MYSTERIES

Danielle Ross is a bright, attractive young woman whose future plans have been put on hold. Returning home to run her ailing father's detective agency, she immediately finds herself in a world she never imagined. From one challenging case to the next, Dani and her partner, Ben Savage, unravel each tangled web to identify the sinister minds behind the scenes, even as her faith—and her heart—are challenged.

BOOK 1: *One by One*   BOOK 2: *And Then There Were Two*
BOOK 3: *The End of Act Three*

THE CHRONICLES OF THE GOLDEN FRONTIER

Jennifer DeSpain's life used to be quiet and dull, but that was before a whirlwind romance and marriage—and a tragedy that left her a widow with only a defunct newspaper to her name. With hopes of a fresh start, Jennifer boldly moves her family to Nevada, where she will have to resolve the challenges of poverty, newspaper publishing, a reversal of fortune, parenting—and matters of the heart—all with the help of some colorful friends and the Lord above.

ALL THAT GLITTERS

Standing alone in her mother's empty apartment, Afton Burns is startled by the ringing phone—and the voice of her father on the other end, inviting her to join him on the set of the movie he's directing. Still suffering from the loss of her mother, Afton knows she needs to be near him and reestablish a relationship that was broken long ago. But that tinseled, movie-star world is an alien place that turns even stranger when it becomes clear that someone doesn't want this film to be completed. There is only one person Afton can trust with her heart and her life—and it's the last person anyone would expect.